SHADOW OF THE
MOUNTAIN

SHADOW OF THE MOUNTAIN

— EXODUS —

CLIFF GRAHAM

BETHANYHOUSE

a division of Baker Publishing Group
Minneapolis, Minnesota

© 2015 by Cliff Graham

Published by Bethany House Publishers
11400 Hampshire Avenue South
Bloomington, Minnesota 55438
www.bethanyhouse.com

Bethany House Publishers is a division of
Baker Publishing Group, Grand Rapids, Michigan

Printed in the United States of America

Library of Congress Cataloging-in-Publication Data
Graham, Cliff.
    Shadow of the mountain : Exodus / Cliff Graham.
      pages ; cm. — (Shadow of the mountain ; 1)
     ISBN 978-0-7642-1475-2 (softcover)
     1. Caleb (Biblical figure)—Fiction. 2. Joshua (Biblical figure)—Fiction.
  3. Bible. Old Testament—History of Biblical events—Fiction. I. Title.
    PS3607.R337S53 2015
    813'.6—dc23   2014045828

This is a work of historical reconstruction; the appearances of certain historical figures are therefore inevitable. All other characters, however, are products of the author's imagination, and any resemblance to actual persons, living or dead, is coincidental.

Cover design by Global Virtual Studio / Felipe Zamora and Matthew Finley

Author is represented by Alive Communications Literary Agency

15 16 17 18 19 20 21   7 6 5 4 3 2 1

For Cassandra, L.O.T.T.M.

And for all the older men who
still threaten the Enemy

Note to the Reader

It will quickly become apparent that I have taken a considerable amount of license with the life story of Caleb in the Scriptures. He is only briefly mentioned, and therefore much imagination is required to fill in the blanks where the Bible is silent.

Units of measurement and distance are modernized. Words like *canvas* for tent material and *minutes* for time measurement are used for description, instead of ancient terms that would be too cumbersome for a reader to have to keep track of. Anachronisms are a necessary component of historical fiction; otherwise books like this one would be dry history textbooks.

My goal is to create a plausible scenario for what happened in between the events the Bible explicitly narrates. The books of Exodus through Joshua say very little about Caleb until much later in his life, so I have taken the liberty of creating a backstory for him that will provide the reader with a front-row seat to the events of the Exodus, the wanderings in the wilderness, and the conquest.

Readers of my work will know that I do not hold back on graphic depictions of the realities of ancient warfare and ancient cultures and customs. The intent is not to offend but to portray the realities of a brutal culture like the Egypt of the pharaohs. This is a work of fiction. Please treat it as such.

Glossary of Terms

Military Terms (modernized):

Team: 3 men.

Squad: 6–10 men.

Platoon: 30–50 men.

Company: 200–300 men.

Battalion: 900–1,200 men.

Division: 8,000–10,000 men.

Squadron: 10–50 chariots.

Egyptian Gods, Concepts, and Misc. Terms:

Ammit: Known as the "Devourer," the personification of divine retribution and justice. The evil have their souls eaten by this hybrid demon of a lion, a hippo, and a crocodile.

Anubis: The god of death and dying, a major figure of the underworld.

Ba: The birdlike form that a person's soul takes.

Hapi: A form of the river goddess, usually associated with a hippo.

Horus: The falcon-headed god of warriors, occasionally desert wind and storms, symbolizing power and authority.

Isis: The goddess of fertility and magic.

Khamsin: A massive dust storm that rolls across deserts and can last for days.

Nekhbet: Vulture god, a scavenger and poorly esteemed.

Osiris: Lord of the underworld.

Ra (Amon Re): The sun god, also known as the Chief of the Gods. His name changed variously through the ages when the Egyptian religion shifted, based on which line of pharaohs ruled.

Seth: The god of war, but negatively associated as such. Barbarism, chaos, and destruction. Frequently viewed as the chief antagonist of the other gods and of mankind.

Sobek: Crocodile god.

The Duat: The River of Night, where the sun god Ra takes his nightly journey, and where the dead journey.

Wadi: A creek or small streambed.

PART I

The LORD is a warrior; the LORD is his name.

Exodus 15:3

1

Morning

The mornings were the hardest.

Every bone ached, every old scar throbbed. His wrist no longer bent back fully, and on nights when he slept on his side without realizing it, he was unable to move that side without pain for most of the day.

Caleb greeted this morning like any other, with a casual assessment of these pains. Nothing seemed to be abnormal. Some pains were injuries needing to be tended; others were just the advance of age.

When it was cold, as now, he took longer getting dressed. The approach of spring led the young troops to switch to summer tunics, but he would be wearing the thick wool winter cloak all summer long. Even the desert heat was no longer enough to thaw his bones.

But I can still move, he thought as he rubbed his feet. He squeezed his leg with his sword hand, the fingers pressing hard into flesh. He still had his battle grip. When that softened he would be done, but it was still nearly as strong as when he was in the fiery power of youth.

Now he rolled onto his knees and paused, giving the joints time to loosen before he stood. He would be fine once he was up and his blood flowed through his veins. It was just the wake-up, he told himself.

Just the wake-up.

He exhaled slowly, then held his breath for the effort to stand. With a grunt he forced his back to straighten and pushed off the ground. The muscles relaxed and he was up. As he stretched, he remembered the first time he had been roused by a training master many years before. Shouting, kicking, he had three counts before he was supposed to be fully dressed with weapon in hand. Now it felt like it was three counts just to open his eyes.

"Enough," he said aloud to himself in the dark.

The wind battered the tent, and he heard the thumping sound of heavy raindrops. He scowled. It would be another day of delays. Delays meant lost advantage. Delays favored the enemy.

He tried to be hopeful that it was only a passing storm and would give way to bright sunlight, but as soon as he looked out of his tent and blinked at the sky, he saw nothing but heavy darkness overhead and, as though mocking him, the rain clouds opened up and poured down onto the camp. Puddles formed in the mud nearby. Men who had ventured out into the open scurried to find shelter.

A figure appeared in front of him.

"Permission to enter, lord."

"No," Caleb said.

Silence outside. Caleb smiled to himself. Decided to have mercy.

"Speak quickly," he said.

"We need your instructions, lord."

"Send the others in so we can study the assault. They can spend the day teaching it to the men again and again until it is too firm in their minds to forget. Perhaps the weather will lift tomorrow."

The commander disappeared. Caleb made out other men running from tree to tree and overhang to overhang. The men would be grumbling about the weather, about the lack of information, about how each other smelled. They would complain about everything, including him. Whoever was commanding was complained about. He used to complain, too, when he was a simple foot soldier.

Oh, how he missed it.

He withdrew into his tent. He struck flint and lit a torch, then slid it into the mount on the center pole. He watched the smoke billow heavily at first as the fresh oil caught before wafting out of the slits in the goatskin overhead.

A scratching sound at the tent flap.

"Come in."

A stream of men entered the tent. They shook their cloaks off and shivered, stamping their feet and continuing conversations begun outside. Caleb waited for them to settle, and they all took their seats on rugs.

"Men," he said, trying not to sound tired, "we do not have reinforcements yet. Joshua cannot spare them. But the weather has provided us an opportunity to wait another day or so before attacking. Perhaps they will arrive by then."

He reached out with a short pointing stick, ornately carved by his own hand to resemble a spear, and drew the outline of a city in the dirt. The commanders huddled close to see it.

"Did everyone get a glimpse of the city before night fell?"

Nods and affirmations all around.

"You saw the main gate?"

"Yes, lord," one of the younger ones said. "And the stones we can climb near it."

Caleb nodded. "Your mission?"

"To get over the wall and open the gate using three men."

"These men have been selected?"

"Yes, lord. My best."

Caleb was satisfied. He nodded to the young leader. "Well done, Othniel. Make sure your men rehearse it."

"Yes, lord."

Caleb searched the faces until he spotted a middle-aged man with missing teeth and a nose heavily distorted from multiple breaks.

"Adino, show me what you will be doing."

Adino took the pointing stick from him and traced a route beginning from the outside of the city. "My lead force will follow me through the water drainage to the city's sewer ditch. We will climb through the well shafts until we reach the streets, then attack west along the wall until we have cleared that quarter of soldiers. We meet up with you at the gate if something goes wrong."

"Second mission?"

"Support the capture of the house of Anak in the north of the city if it has not been taken yet."

"Why?"

"The giants control the city. Anakites have been a nemesis to peace for generations."

Caleb reached over for the pointing stick and handed it to the other commanders one by one. They walked him through the plan he himself had created.

It was complicated, more complicated than he was comfortable with. He believed the simpler a plan, the better.

But this city, and these people, had proven to be worthy foes. The Hebrews would have to attack in unexpected ways. Even so, he had simplified it as much as possible. One primary and one secondary mission per unit and therefore per soldier. A soldier could forget a lot of things and be forgiven so long as he knew his mission.

Caleb knew his men were green. They had been tested a bit in battles on the plains and in skirmishes in the foothills, but now they were in the mountains and staring at a fortified city filled with giants. He had no way of knowing how they would respond. They had been trained in how to fight this specific enemy, yet that meant nothing before the first combat. Would they learn? Would they adapt? Would they maintain their ferocity in the face of plans falling apart and suffering losses?

When the last man had finished, Caleb sat staring at the map quietly. The others remained silent, knowing better than to speak when their general was not ready to listen. The wind picked up outside the tent. The rain grew heavier.

"Adino, you are certain they do not know that we know about the waste ditch access into the city?"

"I killed the man we bribed myself. They do not know it. They will never believe that we would be willing to crawl through excrement to kill them. I cannot believe it myself, to be sure."

The others laughed. Caleb nodded. Every approach and main street had been sketched by their spies. But a map was never the battlefield. What buildings were left out? What archery positions? Would the citizens all fight themselves or leave that to the soldiers and surrender easily? Was there enough food inside to provide for his troops once they had it? Was every enemy escape route covered?

He rubbed his forehead. Impossible to know. Trust those in your command to do their duty.

"Go back to your men and let them rotate through the tents to get warm and dry throughout the day. Make sure the perimeter watch stays alert. I will be checking myself to ensure it. If the chiefs of the Anakites hear we are already encamped this close, and they believe our perimeter is weak, then nothing would stop them from sending a surprise attack to frighten us off, even in the storm."

He reclined on his rug, and this was the signal for them to leave. They all stood and began talking again. Caleb stretched his back out flat on the ground, listening to them. He was about to close his eyes when he saw that Othniel had remained behind. The young leader, twenty years old, was staring hard at the map and scratching his short beard in thought.

"It is possible to be too prepared," Caleb said.

"How do you know the difference between being too prepared and not prepared enough?"

Caleb thought about it a moment. "Not prepared is when you stay up all night terrified that you have no idea what you are doing. Too prepared is staying up all night terrified that you have no idea what you are doing."

Othniel smiled. "You tell that to all the young ones like me, don't you?"

"You are prepared."

"I hope so. Do you believe the men are?"

"As prepared as we can make them. They should have enough motivation with their women and children nearby."

"Was that your plan all along?"

"Where else would we put them?" Caleb asked. "This is our inheritance. We have nowhere else to go. We live where we conquer."

Othniel gazed at the map a moment longer, then said, "When did you see your first major battle?"

Caleb laid his head back and looked at the ceiling of the tent. The torch was dimming.

"Could you replace that?" he asked, gesturing to the torch. Othniel picked up a candle lantern and hung it on the pole, using the dying torch to light it. It was a duller light than the torch, but it would last longer.

"Egypt. Many years ago," Caleb finally answered.

"Why haven't you told your story to the men? They would benefit from hearing it."

"What story?"

"The time you were in Egypt. We know the account of Moses and Joshua. Our fathers composed songs and inscribed records. But we have never heard from you on it."

"Why does it matter?"

"It is our history. It would be good for the men."

"What do they say about me?"

"That you were formed out of the mud by Yahweh and have no mother."

"Good," Caleb said. "That's what they need to know."

"Uncle, we have time. There is nothing to do. This storm is not going to calm down before nightfall. Tell me of the old days."

"The weather could clear."

"You know it will not."

The rain fell harder even as he listened to it. Blowing in from the Great Sea, these storms stayed trapped in the highlands and did not move on until the western deserts sent their own dry winds to push it back. He knew he may have to resign himself to the truth that it was one of those storms that lasts for days, possibly weeks, but he bitterly hated the idea and therefore preferred to deny it.

"I do not like reliving the old days," Caleb said dismissively.

"Many young men would learn from it. We would be able to grow in wisdom, unlike our fathers' generation."

Caleb sighed. Othniel knew right where to press him.

"They can read the scrolls of the scribes," Caleb said.

"Those have few details."

"They have all they need to know. They were written by the hand of Moses himself, many of them."

"True. But there is always more to learn. When you go to your grave, you do not want us to squander what we may have learned from you, do you?"

"You are using my own words against me."

"Whatever it takes, Uncle."

Caleb was quiet. No part of him wished to say anything about Egypt. But his nephew was right. If there was a chance that even a single young man could learn from his experience and choose the path of Yahweh over idolatry . . .

"You will check on your men later," he said, resigned.

"I will," Othniel said. Impatient, he added, "They said you were in the armies of Pharaoh. That you were a great hero for him."

"I learned the warrior arts from the Egyptians, as did Moses," Caleb conceded.

Othniel leaned forward. "Please. Tell me of it."

"Where do you want me to begin?" Caleb asked, settling into the cushions that were his only yield to comfort in his old age.

"How you got to Egypt. How you met Joshua. Yahweh parting the seas. Everything." He sat forward, as though unable to believe he had actually convinced the old man to talk.

Caleb saw himself in Othniel's expression. Long ago, when there were not cities filled with giants to attack, or aching bones that hurt even worse during storms.

"I will tell you, on the promise that you will ensure the other young men will read of what the Lord God did."

"I will tell them. I promise." Othniel pulled out a set of charcoal writing sticks and some sheets of parchment.

Caleb eyed him. "You came prepared."

"I expected to win you over eventually. Perhaps a bribe if it came to it."

Caleb smiled. He let his eyes relax behind their closed lids and grew very still. Took several deep breaths. The rain continued to pelt the tent, and he concentrated on the sound. The memories were deep and hidden. They would emerge only if Yahweh allowed them to, and only to accomplish his purposes.

Darkness. Rain. The musty, damp smell of the wet tent.

His senses grew sharp.

From deep within him, an image emerged. An image long lost, but one that grew bolder and clearer until he saw golden sand and piercing blue skies, and mountains made by man.

— 2 —

To the Land of Gold

You will hear it said that I fight to live in peace. Nonsense. I fight so that our women and children can live in peace. You will always find me where there is battle.

Battle is what we are here for. It is all we should know as men while we have breath. Give the enemy battle all of your life, and when you die, chase him into the afterlife and give him battle there. Perhaps then the Lord will give us peace. But don't expect it.

I will go to my grave with honor. It will be written that my woman loved me, my children admired me, and the enemy feared me.

And yet I was not always a warrior.

You must remember that it has been fifty or sixty years since much of this happened. My memory has faded. I will miss some details.

But I remember a few things very vividly. The brotherhood I found as I trained in Pharaoh's armies. The rattle of chariot riggings as teams pulled hundreds of us in a broad hawk formation, striking the purest terror into the hearts of our enemies.

Then there were the ten times that Yahweh smote the Egyptians with his outstretched arm. A river of blood. Swarms of lice gnats and flies. Darkness. Always darkness. Endless, oppressive darkness. Death. The seas parting before us. The pillar of smoke and flame that led us by night. The taste of the manna and quail that we ate. The hot stench of blood and the metal of weapons glinting under the sun as we killed Amalekites. The endless fire of the deserts. All of those things are as fresh to me as you sitting before me.

In the beginning, I remember the day that I left my village.

I carved stone and wood and I was skilled. My hammer and chisel could draw out the form of any animal from the rock; my knife could bring life to any log.

The other children would gather around me as I made small rocks turn into birds and whittled serpents out of branches. My father Jephunneh encouraged it as a hobby, believing it made my fingers strong and my mind sharp, but only when my chores were done, late at night.

I was good enough to draw the attention of a man passing through my village on his way to Damascus, who said they hired men like me in Egypt to create the palaces and idols of worship.

I had heard talk like this before. Living on the frontier of the Negev in those days meant you had to be near the trade roads. But when I told my father what they said, he would have none of it. The Egyptians were our enemy. But I never forgot those words.

My birth clan was the Kenaz. Our lands were in the hills between the Negev and here. We were not concerned with many things other than our goats and how to stay warm in winter.

My father was an elder. He was a just man. He would let me sit on the branch of a sycamore above the meetings of the elders and listen as they passed judgment on the members of the tribe brought before them. He was always careful to let the accused defend themselves, and widows were always met with mercy.

I've thought about him over the years. I wonder if his home as a child affected how he judged. As I remember him, my grandfather was a hard man who treated my father harshly. My father never said as much, but I think it was a relief when the old man lost his powers of speech. When my grandfather finally died, my father wept for hours. I do not think they were tears of grief.

Thereafter, my father loved me and cherished me. I never felt alone. He brought me into the village meetings even when it was protested by other men. He took me into the hills and taught me the flight of arrows and the sweat of a good day's work.

We trained for hours with the dagger, for there were no swords to go around in those days. He knew I must be able to protect my home from bandits one day and ensured that I was prepared.

When I was old enough, he released me. I think it grieved him that I wanted to go to Egypt, but he could no longer forbid it.

"They are wicked people," he told me as we walked down the road outside of town.

"I will return," I answered, "with enough gold to buy cattle for a hundred years."

Father only shook his head and said, "Egypt draws many. She devours many as well."

I did not understand at the time, of course. I was young. To my thinking, Egypt was the land of exotic mystery, and the only place that traveling merchants failed to adequately describe because its wonders were so vast.

I knew I could carve well and draw with charcoal sticks, and I was strong. Those would get me by.

We embraced once more. I felt his hug last longer than it ever had. When we pulled away, there were tears on the rims of his eyes.

My last sight of my father was when I turned back before the road fell away again. He sat, alone, on a boulder near the road, the early morning sun making the land glow around him. I looked at the hills of my youth one more time. I felt nothing for them. But I knew I would miss my father.

A caravan was crossing the Negev to Egypt only hours away from us, and I had to hurry to catch it. The day was terribly hot; they would be encamped at midday to wait for the heat to pass and do most of the travel by night. I would need to convince them to take me before evening, when they would set out again.

I had enough to pay them for the trip if they were willing to negotiate. I even brought a few sticks of wood to carve toys for their children. This always worked at home whenever I needed to get out of trouble.

I arrived in early afternoon. They were camped near a well that had been won by an alliance of clans in the last war, before I was born. It was now fiercely defended by a warlord named Bochba, who expected tribute when passersby filled their pouches and watered their camels.

Bochba.

Yes, he will enter my story again. Many years later, when our people had finally left Egypt, Bochba was there waiting for us. But that is for another day.

I saw several of Bochba's warriors, marked by their colors, reclining under the shade of a tent a short distance from the camp. The merchants must have been wealthy and paid quickly, since I had never seen Bochba's men relaxing like this.

It was disheartening at first. A man stood a better chance of convincing caravans to take him if they were in need of money. I would probably have to use my carving.

My time to barter would be short when it came. I did not want to disturb their rest now, but I also had to barter with them before their camp was packed that evening.

I picked up a piece of wood and stared at it, waiting for inspiration. A bird cawed overhead. It would have been easy to fashion a bird. I had done many. But I needed to deeply impress them with this carving.

Before leaving I had sold my remaining carvings for the journey. Even my lion, the best work I had ever done. It did not fetch as much as I was hoping, but I thought I had enough to travel until I found work.

I pulled out a larger piece of wood. After an hour, I had fashioned a hawk's head cane, hoping there was an aging or lame merchant in the caravan. I gazed at it, pleased and hoping it would be enough.

It turned out that it was more than enough.

Mathea was his name, an old Assyrian who was impressed with my skill.

"Your work is astounding," he said to me as he looked over my shoulder. I had positioned myself near the well where I could not be missed. "They would pay fortunes to employ you in Egypt."

"That is my ambition," I answered.

"I'll give you passage in exchange for your first month's take."

I had no idea if that was a fair wage or not.

"How would I pay for my lodging and food? I only have enough to pay the tribute to Bochba."

"I know a man who will put you up. I will go to him when we arrive and make arrangements when we depart in a few nights."

"A few nights? We are not leaving this very night?"

Mathea smiled at me. "Bochba wishes to pay a visit to the larger caravans in person. His men inform us that it will be a few days before he arrives. It is not wise to refuse him."

That night I lay down on my own at the perimeter. The other fires were spoken for, and there wasn't room enough for me to lie beside them to ward off the nighttime chill. I did not relish the idea of being on my own when surrounded by strangers, but I managed to make a nice fire where I could put my feet near the flames.

I scraped out a divot for my shoulder because I like to sleep on my side. Then I draped my cloak over my legs and lay down. The cloak was a gift from my father. I would never have been able to afford it otherwise. Its wool was new and thick, its brown dye still fresh, and it would mark me for theft so I knew I had to be careful.

The flames warmed me, and I can still remember both the fear and satisfaction I felt before drifting off to sleep that night, my first on my own. I am a man now, I thought. I had bartered like a man, and now I would travel like a man. I stared at the endless stars overhead, the ones I had become so familiar with every night sleeping on our roof, wondering if I would still see them in Egypt.

My eyes became heavy, but right before sleep they caught movement on the edge of the firelight.

This was my first taste of battle, but it was also my first taste of treachery, for the well guards of Bochba I had paid off earlier that evening descended on me with terrifying speed, probably thinking I was wealthier than I had let on.

I reacted just in time, their swords striking the sand where my chest had been. I managed to grab my bag as I rolled and threw it up at one of my attackers.

I could not tell how many there were, only that they were attacking again, swords everywhere. My fingers found the dagger in my belt, and I scrambled to my side.

A foot clamped down on my back, pinning me. I winced, expecting the killing blow, but reacting in pure instinct I plunged the dagger blindly behind me, hoping to hit flesh.

I did, and the man screamed.

I curled up, my feet under me, and leaped forward to gain distance. I landed and leaped again. My attackers were right behind me.

After a third leap, feeling like a toad being chased by a jackal, I was able to turn around and face them at last. Four of them. I did not have time to speak before one of them threw a javelin at me.

I ducked and rolled to my side, the dagger out. Hit and move, my father had taught me, hit and move.

I lashed out with the tip after sidestepping a club. The dagger penetrated the first man's face. Not pausing, not waiting to see what happened, I jabbed again and found a leg. As soon as I could jerk it free I leaped out of the way, then sprinted as fast as my legs could take me into the darkness, away from the firelight.

The howls of both wounded men echoed across the camp. I had been terrified, reacting like an animal, but now I was furious. The darkness was my ally. I could strike from the night and kill all of them.

Battle lust came over me, the first time for that as well. That unknowable power in a man's soul that bursts out of him, and all he can think of is spilling more blood and avenging himself.

It made me sharp. My ears were alert to every sound, every skittering of a viper across the sand, every dung beetle crawling near the camels. I smelled the livestock, the sweat of men, saw with perfect clarity the merchants and their bodyguards rushing up from the camp, one of the two remaining well guards leaning over his comrades.

One of two?

I heard the other one approaching from the side, but I was ready this time. He swiped a long blade toward me. I sprinted away, leaving the wounded guards and drawing him out into the desert. Even at this point, long before I would be trained by the Egyptians or alongside Joshua, son of Nun, I knew that if you were unsure of the strength of your opponent, you avoided him, making him chase you, avoiding all of his strikes until you could seize the advantage.

I climbed a dune, my feet digging into the soft sand. The guard was behind me and gaining ground fast. When I reached the top I turned, bent down for a handful of sand, and then leaped from above over his shoulder, watching his sword slice the night air toward me. I slapped him in the face with the sand just before he could finish the strike.

He coughed and staggered. I landed, remembered my knife, and reacted again. I took two strides to reach him and shove the dagger into his gut. I pulled it out and struck him on top of his shoulder. When he uncoiled and exposed his neck, I sliced it open.

He slumped down. I was panting, desperate for air, exhilarated, all of those feelings you get after a fight. But my fury had not abated, and I charged down the dune and back toward the camp.

I saw the group of about twenty merchants and their guards

standing near the watch fire, listening as the uninjured Amalekite waved his arms about and told them some black lie.

I slowed to a steady walk, approaching unnoticed from behind them. I proceeded past the merchants and directly to the unwounded well guard. A merchant spotted me and held up his hands. "We demand to know what has happened. He says you attacked his men——."

Before anyone could react, I raced forward and stabbed my blade into the eye of one of the wounded guards, then pulled it out and did the same to the other. I was so very fast in those days, not like you see me now. By the time they could even raise their hands to stop me I had kicked the remaining guard's torso, bending him over with agony, and then stabbed my blade into the back of his neck. He fell facedown without another noise.

I whirled on the group, dagger up.

"These men attacked me while I slept, like cowards. Who wants to question it? Who?"

I glared at them, too full of hate to take heed that I was outnumbered by armed bodyguards ten to one.

There was a long silence, then Mathea, the old merchant whom I'd bargained with, chuckled.

"We don't question it. Those men charged us twice the rate they normally do to use this well. Although I fear you have created an eternal enemy of Bochba."

My breathing slowed. He was right. It could never get out that I had done this thing to Bochba's men or my town would be razed to the ground.

Mathea shrugged. "I suppose we should be on our way early, then."

I tried to pay him more to compensate him for his trouble, but he refused. We set out at a fast pace as soon as the camels were ready. He off-loaded some of his wares to make room for me. I have dealt with many Assyrians, and they are mostly treacherous dogs, but I shall forever be grateful for Mathea.

Egypt appeared after many days. I learned that the merchants were correct. It cannot be described. There is nothing similar you have seen in your lifetime.

At my first sight of Raamses and Pithom, I would not be able to speak for many hours. The buildings of dynasty were everywhere. Their temples were lush with gardens and columns, street after street and block after block. Throngs of people, thousands upon thousands, teemed along the Nile in their daily affairs.

Barges crowded the great river. The ships of Pharaoh's navy with their painted hulls and gleaming white sails rehearsed their battle drills. Fishermen picked their way into the marshes in narrow boats, watching one another like spies. When one boat would make a catch, the others would move in and make several while the finder struggled to empty his nets.

Idols occupied every street. It disgusts me to think of it now. They worshiped false gods with the heads of animals and the bodies of men. An abomination.

Abominations were everywhere! But oh, Othniel, how the world does not know the wonders of Egypt. If man worships himself, as the Egyptians worship their god-king, this is what he is capable of. Monuments to wickedness that dazzle the eyes. I could not comprehend the meaning of what I was seeing.

Near Thebes were their great pyramids, burial tombs built by men that are mountains reaching almost to the stars. They were ancient even when our father Abraham was there.

It became my prison, of course, though I would not know

it for many years. Those same wonders were also the evil relics of a Yahweh-hating people. I shudder at the visions to this day and leave them to the realm of my nightmares. May the Lord be gracious enough to cleanse my thoughts of them forever when I am done with my tale.

But I was astounded nonetheless. And when I finally arrived in the markets of Memphis and parted ways with my caravan, I realized how profoundly alone I was in this golden land.

— 3 —

Keeping Watch

Caleb sat up, stretching his arms over his head. He gestured for the water pouch, and Othniel jumped up to grab it. Caleb took several long drinks. His throat was dry from so much talking.

"I will continue in a while," he said, wiping his mouth. "I have not had my morning meal."

"I will go get it for you," Othniel said. "But first . . . I did not know that you are not . . ."

"Not what? Speak up."

"You say you were from Kenaz."

"Yes."

"Which of the tribes . . . ?"

"It is obvious, is it not? Just say it."

Othniel hesitated. "You are . . . not a Hebrew."

"I was not born of the tribal bloodlines. But I am a Hebrew."

"But how is that possible?"

Caleb smiled. "How I became a Hebrew is part of my story. Do you wish to hear it or not?"

"Of course, Uncle. But you have not even mentioned my father yet."

"Your father will come into the story. Be patient."

Caleb waited for what he knew was the next question. The young man's eyes squinted, then cleared.

"If you are not a Hebrew by birth, and my father was your brother—"

Caleb interrupted him. "A man's bloodline does not matter. Only his heart. Yahweh gives his own bloodline to those who worship him."

Othniel nodded. But he was stunned.

Caleb chuckled. "Do not worry about solving it now. Just go find my food."

Othniel walked out of the tent. Caleb could hear him calling out to the cooks.

"Cooks," Caleb grunted to himself. "No cooks in the army in those days. A man made his own meal in the field."

He was thinking about complaining some more when he remembered he was talking only to himself. The rain fell steadily on, and he grew steadily colder. The other old generals had young women lie in their blankets to warm them. Nothing offensive to Yahweh happened between them, but a woman in your bed was a woman in your bed. Always a good thing. He nodded to himself. That was surely one benefit of old age.

He listened to the rain for a while. Steady and heavy. Crops would come from it. Cisterns would fill. Ever since his days in the desert, he never took the rain for granted.

He could not help himself and stood up, making his way to the flap. Stepping outside, Caleb rejoiced in the cold splatters on his face, the streams flowing into his beard. Cold, merciless, beautiful rain.

He walked through the camp, keeping his cloak pulled low over his face to disguise himself from the men. He moved past cook fires, past mud-covered troops, past the food stores and to the perimeter.

It loomed in the distance. Hidden in the storm, but it was there. The walls of Hebron. The last holdout of the Anakim, the remnant of giants that had terrorized his people for a generation.

"Your enemies reside there, God of Moses," Caleb said. "I will kill them tomorrow."

As if in answer, lightning flared. Caleb saw the walls and the watchtower, the huddled figures of the sentries as they paced the wall. He smiled. Their commander had them out on a morning like this? Good. That means they fear us.

He glanced around and saw the boughs of a sycamore nearby. Sitting underneath it, he settled in and watched the gray light slowly enter the sky. Othniel would be looking for him. Some might worry that he was missing. But others would know where to find him. Nearest the enemy.

The sun was there, somewhere behind the clouds in the east. In this country he rarely saw it anymore. Winter hid its light.

But not in Egypt. There was no winter in Egypt. Only eternal summer.

He had not thought of Egypt in many years. Too much to concentrate on, too many challenges in building their home out of this land. The decades had buried it.

But now he was there again. The cool ripples of the Nile at his feet as he stood on a muddy bank. The stiff reeds as they bent in the breeze, their tips scratching against the stone pillars of Pharaoh's palace. The street vendors with roasted cobra on spits and luscious fruits grown from seeds gathered at the ends of the earth. The smell of perfume on the women, lavender and rose.

Caleb shuddered in the cold and wrapped his cloak tighter, stared at the gray sky and walls of the enemy, and thought of Egypt.

It was not long before Othniel found him curled up under the tree. He knew to search for him on the perimeter whenever he was missing, and this was the place that most afforded views of their target. It was simply a matter of trying to spot the huddled figure under a drab cloak, a cloak much cheaper than the one that such a great man could have afforded if he wished.

He saw the old man slouched forward with his chin on his chest, snoring so loudly that he could hear him even through the slashing rain and wind. He grinned to himself.

—— 4 ——

From Statues to Swords

I made my way through the masses of people in the streets of Memphis, searching for the man I was told to find: Akan the Stone Broker.

Mathea the Assyrian said he was a powerful official in the court of Pharaoh the god-king. Through him came the hiring of all workers who wished to create the carvings and paintings that made the nation great, that captured their ancient history and promised to advance the kingdom into the next thousand years with edifices that could never be destroyed.

But I had no way of speaking with the man even when I found him. The language was clattered and confusing to my ear. I could only hope to show him my work and let it speak for itself.

After a day of searching in vain, getting hungry and weary from my journey, I decided to try again the next morning and found the sign for an inn. I paid the innkeeper enough copper rings for a month's stay and was shown my way to a room at the top of the building that overlooked the Nile and the plateau of the pyramids.

As I ate my bread-and-oil dinner, I could not look away from the shining white mountains that towered over all. Their perfect symmetry, their golden caps. Thousands of workers moved up and down their steps, polishing and scraping away any imperfections on the limestone. Children slid down the smooth faces for play. It was apparent that they were the place of recreation for the entire city; the benevolent god-king's tomb where he could provide all for his people, even their enjoyment.

They were pagans, yes. An abomination to Yahweh. But you must remember that I did not know Yahweh in those days, so as I tell this tale to you, do not recoil with scorn when I express the admirations and feelings I had as a foolish young man.

I was consumed with thirst to know more about these people and their history of thousands of years. The first chance I got, I would go to the pyramids and climb their steps to watch the sunset. I would read every papyrus scroll in the libraries, not worried that I would make enough gold to pay the scroll keepers for access to the libraries, because how could a man not make his fortune here, the wealthiest kingdom on earth?

As I was sitting on the roof of the inn with the other travelers in the cool of the evening, finishing my meal, a man approached me. He was an Egyptian, clothed in a white linen gown, and I noticed that his eyes were painted with what I had learned was the black liner of the upper class. He was in his fourth decade then, still young and passionate about conquering his private empire.

"Are you the one named Caleb?"

"Yes," I answered.

"I am Akan the Stone Broker."

I was shocked. This important official had walked on his own feet into a common inn and sought me out? And more, he spoke my tongue?

"I am privileged, my lord, that you would come here, but I am afraid I am not worthy of it."

"That is true," the man replied. "But I was nearby and was told by Mathea that you would be of interest to me."

"My lord, a hundred pardons, but how do you know my language?"

"Men of Canaan have shown considerable skill here. Especially Kenazzites. Mathea has never led me astray when I have searched for talent, and he has brought me many of my best workers. I learned your barbaric language in order to teach you the proper language—the *Egyptian* language."

"Respectfully, my lord, I am not to be here as a slave."

His temper flared at me. "You will be a slave if the god-king wishes you to be so! You are here at his pleasure, and mine! If you do not mind your words when speaking with me, I will have you sent to Pithon to cut brick with the Hebrews. Then we will see what happens with your skill."

I said nothing, assuming he would calm down, which he did after a while.

"What you say is correct. You are not a slave . . . yet. If you want to earn your wages, though, you will do precisely what I require of you when it is required. If you produce, you will have more gold and women than you can imagine. If you fail, you will be sent to Pithon. Be outside my house in the third quarter, the Way of the Falcon, by the end of the first watch tomorrow morning."

Then he turned and left. I leaned over the roof and watched him depart into the crowded street to his waiting sledge. Four slaves hoisted him up on their shoulders, and a crier shouted, "Make way for the Stone Broker, servant of the god-king!" People shuffled away quickly as he approached until he was out of my sight.

As I grew to know him, I would discover that Akan was the smartest man in any room he walked into. Shrewd, calculating, arrogant, brilliant. I loved him in a way. Certainly respected him. I owe much to that pagan; may he burn forever in the fires of Sheol's depths.

And so my first year passed.

I carved and I drew for anyone who would pay me, in addition to whatever work I could get from Akan. I chiseled monuments to jackal gods, created maps for commanders, drew portraits for wealthy families. My name spread, and I was given gold.

But one day I learned that my destiny was warfare and not the arts. Some moments occur and a man knows that his life is forever changed. That no matter what he convinces himself about his destiny, it has been written for him and he cannot escape it, any more than he can allow his heart to escape from his body.

As I was walking through the streets of Memphis during a break at a site where I was carving stone animals to decorate a corridor of a wealthy man's home, I came upon an arena near a temple that I had never noticed before. It had short walls and seating for a crowd of only about one hundred, so one could easily see what was happening in the sand-covered pit.

A man was standing in the pit, challenging any from the crowd who would come and fight him. He was enormous, heavily muscled, deadly looking. Several bodies were lying near him. He was at least two cubits taller than any man I had ever seen.

I was confused, but many things had confused me since my arrival, so I simply waited to see what would happen. The crowd jeered and taunted someone, I could not tell who, until I saw a man stumble out of it and hold a sword up to the giant.

I leaned in and asked someone nearby what was happening, but I could not make out the answer.

The challenger approached the giant with the sword held warily. He had no confidence, no sense of bearing, no footwork, no training of any kind. The weapon may as well have been a cattle-prodding stick for all he knew what to do with it.

The giant laughed at him.

A woman was screaming above the clamor of the crowd. I tried to see who it was, but the people crammed in the streets had heard a challenger had come out and were closing in around me to see what happened. I was jostled around by food vendors, shoved by merchants, tripped over street children, but I finally caught a glimpse of the screaming woman.

She was poor, her rags of clothing filthy. She was screaming in a tongue I had not heard before, and even though I learned the language well enough over time, I cannot recall what she said. But they were words of torment and anguish. She was reaching out for the man who was challenging the giant, begging and pleading with him. Her husband?

With a mocking laugh, the giant brushed aside the man's feeble attempt at an attack and lopped his head off with a single hard cut from his scimitar. Blood sprayed. The sand became soaked with it.

The woman screamed even louder. She bent down, picked up the head, and tried to shove it back onto the stump of the neck. The crowd laughed at her.

My temper flared hotter than I had ever known it to. I pulled my dagger out and shoved my way through the crowd until I stood in front of the giant. The woman's sobs next to me were pathetic.

The giant turned away from the crowd where he was receiving his adulation and spotted me crouched in front of the woman and the headless corpse of her husband.

I did not know it yet, but this was to be my first encounter with Hebrews, and the first of many times I would fight a giant.

The dead man and his wife, along with the others forced to fight the giant in that arena, had been brought south from Goshen to be butchered in front of this crowd for their amusement and a few coins.

"You are a fool to stand before me," he said.

I said nothing, my anger at the injustice of the killing still burning inside of me.

The crowd started chanting for him to attack, and finally he did.

I was too furious to realize that I was battling a vastly superior opponent. Rage can get a man killed or it can save his hide. Yahweh chose the latter for me that day.

If I had crossed him with a sword I know I would have been killed. But my dagger was sly and quick. I rushed forward to meet his assault, then was able to move just enough out of his way to make a strike on his thigh as he swung and missed me. My grip was immensely strong after all of the stone carving I had been doing and I was able to hold on to the hilt as he passed, carving a deep gash across the front of his leg.

He stumbled to his knees. He would never walk on that leg again, and I learned more in that moment about fighting giants than I would ever learn again. Boldness and speed in the strike. Giants believe their size is so terrifying that their opponents are not able to concentrate. They are not expecting *you* to attack *them*.

I am not sure why I acted so decisively in my next move. Perhaps Yahweh gave me a nudge even though I did not know him then.

The giant was on his knees, clutching the wound on his thigh. The crowd had swollen and was roaring with delight at the unexpected contest. I let it wash over me. Their praise. My anger.

I was on top of the giant's back and driving the tip of my dagger into his ear. I shoved it until it could not go in further. He twitched and lurched forward with me on his back.

Dead.

The crowd screamed louder. I pulled my dagger out of his head and wiped the blood on his loincloth. It was exhilarating, but it did not last long.

I saw the woman bent over, completely oblivious to me, her savior, weeping into the headless torso of her husband. Grief and a sense of profound injustice hit me, and I lost all desire to hear the chants of victory the people were giving me.

I ignored the hands slapping on my shoulders and back as I walked through the crowd.

Akan was standing in the street next to his chariot. His arms were crossed as he listened to another wealthy-looking man gesture angrily while telling him something. I caught his eye, and he beckoned me over. As I approached, I heard the wealthy man saying, ". . . out of the street! Canaanites of that size are worth more money than you can imagine, Akan! I do not care if he is your man. I demand payment for my loss!"

"Why did you intervene?" Akan asked me coolly.

The wealthy man turned and thrust a finger in my face. "You have cost me a thousand pieces of gold, maybe two. You will pay it or I will have you thrown into the dungeons!"

"He killed a man without reason," I answered, holding his gaze.

"That is not your concern! He is my property!"

"Those exhibitions have been outlawed, Thebet," Akan said. "You would have lost him soon anyway."

"They were only Hebrews! There are plenty more where they came from."

We argued for a while longer before Akan said, "I will pay the fee if you will shut up and leave, Thebet."

I was stunned. To this point, Akan had maintained a cold and distant attitude toward me. I made him a great deal of money in commissions, so he left me alone, but he had never demonstrated any kind of loyalty to me.

He handed over a sack of coins to Thebet and then motioned for me to follow him. I stood below the chariot as he mounted it.

"Where did you learn to fight?" he asked.

"My father."

"Do you know the sword?"

"No, my lord."

"You will. I am sending you to the armies."

I was stunned. "But my lord, I am a carver and an artist. What use am I in the armies?"

"Plenty. If you succeed in the right regiment, your stature grows even more. According to the law of the new pharaoh, only those who have served in the ranks can build the new temple of Horus."

And now we came to it.

Akan was a clever man. He would be my patron in the armies, ensuring I was placed well, and when I made it through the training he would be there to place me as the chief stone-cutter on a temple, the highest paying of positions possible apart from working on Pharaoh's burial tomb. The new temple of Horus the warrior god was to be the grandest yet constructed. It was the talk of the streets that it would be built in Memphis, and all were converging to get the best positions. Slaves would haul the stones, but men like myself would carve them. It would be a job that paid more gold than the imagination could conjure.

I knew by then that for all their command of slave labor, the Egyptians needed my gifts. They had laws and could not force me into slavery apart from the decree of Pharaoh himself. There was no war I had been captured in and no contract I had violated, but they could pressure me in other ways. Akan could sully my name in the markets and deny me work if I refused him. I would not be hired by anyone if he was my enemy.

"A man of skill is valuable to me. A man of skill and renown more so," Akan continued. "In the crowd watching you was a member of the royal guard. I spoke to him after your victory but before Thebet accosted me. He was impressed and thought you might do well there. If you can join the Red Scorpions it will be a mark that guarantees a river of gold for us. Your skill as an artist is already there. If you apply for the chief designer position as a member of the Red Scorpions, it will be impossible for them to deny it to you, especially with my blessing."

"But what use am I to you dead if I am killed in battle?" I had no idea who the Red Scorpions were but did not care in that moment.

He shrugged. "There is that risk. But I take risks. It is why I am a wealthy man."

He rode off, ending our conversation abruptly. Before I could think about it any more I was surrounded again by admirers of my victory and tried to nod and acknowledge their praise. I looked for the Hebrew woman. She was gone. I never discovered what became of her.

I had killed the men at the well, and those had been the first deaths at my hand. The giant was the next. Only now did I finally feel the remorse of it. Of course he deserved to die, as did Bochba's guards. That changes not. But killing a man is killing a man. He had a mother somewhere. He knew emotions like I did, had thoughts like I did. It's different from killing an animal, and it took me a few wineskins in a tavern to get past it.

It became easier and easier after that.

Even that night, as I lay down in my quarters and the roads outside bustled late with activity and the scent of dates and spices and livestock wafted through my window, I felt the first pangs of yearning.

The decisiveness of my victory! The speed of it! The admiration of the crowd! I quickly forgot what had led me to attack in the first place—an injustice perpetrated against the Hebrew husband and wife.

I saw only the eyes of the beautiful Egyptian girls in the crowd who lusted for me, and heard only the sound of men yelling with admiration for me.

5

Training Master Horem

I would still carve, of course, and design with my charcoal sticks on papyrus my ideas for submission to build the temple of Horus. But after making his inquiries, Akan had heard that the selection for chief designer of the temple was to be made at the next year's Nile Festival, which celebrated the inundation of the river into the valley and covering it with the following season's silt. I had time to make the regiment and finish my designs in order to submit for it.

Akan had scrolls drawn up that secured a place for me to try out for the Red Scorpions regiment. I packed up what I thought I would need and it all fit into a single shoulder pouch. I only needed my money bag, my drawing supplies, and my dagger. The rest of my belongings I left in Akan's possession.

I took the journey by boat from Thebes to Memphis. It was an army ship that sailed with the standards of what I was told were the Hippo and Isis regiments fluttering above us in the hot breeze coming down from the desert.

"We have to travel with the Hippos because of Hapi," an officer growled next to me.

"What?"

The man glanced at me. "You're a foreigner."

"Yes."

"Hapi. The river god. The patron of the Hippos is Hapi. We cannot travel the river without a blessing from the priests of Hapi, who are funded by the nobility patrons of the Hippo regiment. We never travel together normally, but they were low on available ships."

I nodded politely, not understanding why this man was taking the time to inform me of these matters. My curiosity eventually got the better of me. "You are rivals?" I asked.

"The Hippos are the putrid, rotting flesh of Seth."

I had heard this curse before. Seth was their most despised god, the lord of the traitors and reprobates.

"I am joining the army," I announced naively. The man, whose face was heavily marked and scarred from years of hard living, looked at me with a smirk.

"Indeed? Which regiment?"

"The Red Scorpions."

"You jest."

"No. I had the papers drawn up by a noble. I am endorsed."

He studied me a moment, then laughed. "Make sure you enjoy your last night before entering the underworld. Most who try out for the Red Scorpions die long before they make it in."

I had heard that the Red Scorpions were selective, but I had not heard this. "They . . . die? They don't simply drop out?"

"They are the elite regiment, the pride of Pharaoh. The selection is so difficult that many die even when they are trying to quit. They have a training master named Horem, who is the most ruthless goat you can imagine. He doesn't allow anyone in who isn't hewn from rock and fire itself. He will especially hate you because of how you have bypassed the normal selection process."

"What process?"

"Most who join the Red Scorpions are required to have served in the regular ranks for three years before they are even considered for selection. No one is hated more than he who finds a way to avoid the process. I tried out for the Scorpions once when I was younger and prayed for death every hour until I dropped out."

He was a formidable-looking man, and it did nothing for my confidence to think that if he dropped out, how far would I get?

The desert had almost swallowed the sun by the time I finished climbing the long, rocky path from the Nile up to the top of the Giza plateau. I passed several Bedouin girls, who were carrying stacks of water pouches down to the river and filling them. They looked at me with hollow, gaunt eyes. Their lives were the hardest that I could imagine, worse than even that of slaves.

Many slaves in Egypt who weren't Hebrew could own land, conduct their own business affairs, even eventually purchase their own freedom. But these Bedouins would never see a life apart from the searing dunes of the west, where I would only sentence an Amalekite to perish among.

When I reached the top of the cliffs, the white tents of Pharaoh's army spread before me, gleaming in the golden evening sunlight in a vast ocean of martial order and precision. Oh, but the Egyptians knew how to encamp their men! Nothing like the filth we live in. The sanitation, the clarity of the ground, all of it was perfectly organized.

Men did not amble and wander through a forest of ropes and tent pegs; they walked down clean alleys and wide berths. The colors of each battalion and their patron god adorned the canvas, so I was seeing crocodiles, leopards, bulls, every animal in the world painted in exquisite detail. The tents of officers had standards mounted atop them that fluttered in the light desert breeze.

It had everything that would make it a city, and it stretched forever to the horizon in orderly rows. The only places where disorder seemed to reign were the civilian precincts. Pharaoh allowed the people from along the Nile to come to the camps to support their markets. Soldiers were not necessarily paid well, but their pay was direct from the coffers of the king himself and therefore steadier than the common riffraff, and that put them in the elite status.

Prostitutes did enormous business, as did bakers, menders, bronze workers—officers were expected to pay for their own weaponry maintenance—and falconers, for desert hare was a favored dish.

Cooking fires and slaves to man them, table merchants selling pastries, jewelers hammering at gold pieces and squinting at them to determine their weight and worth. Far to my left was an enormous oval, and I saw several dozen chariot teams swarming one another in mock drills.

I stared at the chariots and horses, awed by them just as I had been the first time I saw them.

Above it all were the pyramids, as white as lightning and tall enough to scratch the sky. Nearby too was that monstrous, hideously beautiful half-man, half-lion carving they called the

Sphinx. It was said to be over a thousand years old, but it was well-maintained and glowed in the sunlight. It leered at us like the pagan idol it was.

I was at a loss as to what to do next. All I owned was in the pack on my shoulder: a bag of gold and copper rings, my drawing supplies, my dagger, my carving blades, a pouch of date cakes, and my water pouch. That was all.

As I wandered near the camp, I was confronted by two roving sentries. These men wore only linen loincloths and carried their bronze swords in their hands. Nothing else, in order to be as light as possible in the event they had to pursue a spy peering in on the camp from a distant spot. Their chests and arms were as carved as the sculptures of the gods I had been creating.

"Where are you going?" one of them asked me.

"I am here to join the ranks. I am a foreigner. I was told to report here."

"Show your orders."

I handed over the papyrus scroll and waited while they read it. My referral had come from a house of nobility so I did not expect to wait long.

They stared at me hard a moment after reading it, then the other one handed it back to me and said, "The tent nearest the well is where your division will be assigned."

I thanked them and made my way into the camp with no idea as to how to search for the well apart from wandering to the center, assuming that was the logical place for it.

I found it and presented my scroll. The receiving officer studied my orders very thoroughly. So thoroughly that after a while I could not stop myself from asking, "Excuse me, sir, but what is written on there that is taking so long?"

As you have seen before, these were the days prior to my

learning respect and humility. I deserved much of the punishment I received.

His head snapped up, and he stared at me with pure hatred. "I am checking to make sure you are not the actual son of a noble lord or have family connections that would prevent me from killing you."

Again, I had not yet learned martial discipline, so I replied, "I do not need powerful family members to protect me; I can do fine on my own."

The officer glared at me, glanced down at the papyrus, then, faster than I could have ever expected, he jumped from his stool and punched me savagely. I swung a blow at him but he avoided it, much faster than the brutish, untrained giant had been.

My next feeling was a crushing blow across the back of my head. I went slack in the officer's arms, my world a daze of lights and pain. I felt kicks in my ribs, a fist across my jaw, relentless beatings all over my body.

A group of the Egyptian officers had joined in and were crushing my body in every way possible. My receiving officer yelled, "You will learn respect! You will learn it!"

After a while I passed out. When I revived, I could barely see out of my swollen eyes. Even my teeth hurt. I coughed, and blood erupted from my throat. Horrible pain in my chest. I knew I had several broken ribs. It hurt to even take a breath, and I coughed so hard that I nearly passed out again.

My eyes opened enough to get my first glimpse of a face that I would come to hate, and respect, above all others.

Training Master Horem seemed old to me even then, though he could not have been past his fortieth year. Like every other Egyptian soldier, his head was shaved to the scalp and he had no beard, but he had so many scars on his face that the white marks resembled one. The remnant of an old infection on his brow that had spread down his face left a horrific mark on his cheek, a black-and-red cavernous pit that seemed to burst into flames when he yelled, which he was doing now.

"Get up! Get up! Get up!"

I winced at the noise. Felt a hard punch to my face. I gagged and would have vomited if I had eaten any food that day, but instead I lay there heaving air from my gut while this new monster yelled at me and landed blows.

Somehow I found my way to my feet and tried to stand upright, an attempt that the man quickly ended with a punch to my gut.

"My name is Training Master Horem. Say it."

I tried to open my mouth but could not. My jaw had swollen shut.

"Training Master Horem. Say that name or I will cut out your tongue and feed it to the crocodiles."

"Tr . . . aining Master . . ."

Another punch.

"What is the matter with your speech? Say the full name."

"T . . . training Master Hore . . ."

This time the blow knocked me to the ground, and I could only lie there and bleed into the sand.

"Get my name wrong once more and I will slit your throat! By order of the mouth of Pharaoh, I have that privilege! You show up for my regiment without spending three years in the armies? A piece of worthless foreign dung? How did you bribe Lord Akan into getting you that letter? I will make sure you die with a lungful of sand and my foot in your—"

I squeezed my eyes shut and concentrated on saying his name correctly, searching my memory for it. All was a fog. A blur.

"Train . . . ing Master Horem."

No response from him. Perhaps I had said it right. I think I passed out again, because next I realized there was a wet linen rag on my face. It revived me somewhat.

It was Training Master Horem, kneeling beside me with a basin of water. He scrubbed my face roughly. It would not be mistaken for a bath given by a sensuous handmaiden.

"You have until tomorrow to report to the Red Scorpions regiment, first battalion, ready to train with the others. If you are not there, your name will be removed from the roster. If I get bored one day I might even hunt you down and kill you anyway."

After beating me nearly to death, and now personally wiping my face of the blood he had beaten out of me, I did not yet know what to make of Training Master Horem. I suppose I ought to have hated him on the spot, but I didn't sense that it was personal between us. He was doing his job, which was tearing out the rotten bones inside of a man and replacing them with fresh ones.

— 6 —

The Valley of Ra

I went to bed that night staring at the ceiling of my tent, believing I had made the worst mistake of my life. I was homesick. I knew I had the skills to fight desert bandits and other riffraff, but the orderly, disciplined fighting I saw displayed that afternoon on the training pitches was both intimidating and disheartening. I knew I could make it through the end of training if I did not quit, but the day was far off still. I could only see the endless weeks and months ahead of me. I did not know then how to see my life one day at a time, one challenge at a time, knowing that as each day and challenge was confronted, one more step had been taken toward the day of victory.

The next day at noon, I found myself standing with the other recruits and already exhausted. There were many ranks of us from foreign lands. We had been thrown together into a clash of languages, cultures, and personalities. On this morning, I am certain that every one of us felt as I did: that we had made the worst decision of our lives.

About fifty training masters prowled our ranks with whips. When there was not adequate response to their questions they cracked their whips across our flesh. If one was punished, all were punished.

We had been running across the hot sand, swum through crocodile-infested lagoons, and carried rocks up a sand dune that seemed to be as high as the pyramids, and that was just the first morning.

Now we stood at attention, sweaty and with multiple whip marks, our backs straight and our hands clasped to the hems of our loincloths.

"Forty days," Training Master Horem was saying as he paced in front of us. "Forty days and you will understand the meaning of suffering. You will know what it is like to peer into the depths of your *ba* and see what your fate will be. You will know which of the gods favors you and which of them wants you dead. If you are favored by a weak god"—he grinned widely—"your death will be painful, slow, and fun for me to watch. If you are favored by a powerful god, you will have riches and women beyond what your worthless mind can grasp."

Training Master Horem stood near me and glared into my eyes. I returned the stare, my eyes flickered to the red pit scar on his face, and suddenly I felt a heavy fist crack the back of my skull, delivered by another training master who had snuck up behind me.

I lost all vision and sound. I felt my face slam into the sand as my knees gave out.

My ears rung loudly.

He was saying something, but I couldn't understand it. I tried to lift my face to see his lips. Sound began returning, the ache from the blow flaring up.

". . . when I am looking at you. I vow by Ra and all the gods that if you ever dare to look in my eyes again, you rotting pus-filled baboon, I will have your . . ."

I lost the rest of it. My mind was swimming and surging as though it were caught in a current.

I felt the sole of a sandal on my back, pushing me down when I tried to stand up.

". . . this worthless sack of camel dung, this piece of . . ."

I turned my head and opened my eyes at last, and the effort was filled with agony.

". . . all spend the rest of the day barefoot, because you will fight barefoot on the sand. It will burn, and you will want to have your legs cut off, but find your manhood, because there is an enemy who hunts you . . ."

I felt the foot come off my back and, still groggy, stood up and felt myself pushed forward. We were running, my feet no longer had sandals, and it was bearable at first as the sweaty, reeking mass of us sloshed through the heavy sand for an hour until we got to a wide, flat plain that stretched from horizon to horizon. The sand had disappeared, and the dirt was compacted and smooth, as though ages ago there had been a floodplain here and this was all that remained.

We were overjoyed at first, because it meant we no longer had to trudge through the sand, but within a few steps on this new surface we shouted in pain.

The white ground was like an infinite baking stone, reflecting the heat from the sun so severely that our eyes clamped shut. The flesh on the bottom of our feet felt as if we had thrust them into a bed of coals.

Every man there, despite what he would admit to later, shrieked and cried like a woman as the soles of our feet blistered in the heat.

"This is the Valley of Ra!" Training Master Horem said gleefully as he ran alongside us, barefoot just like we were but utterly unfazed by the fire below us. "It is the hottest place we have found in the Upper and Lower Kingdom, an inferno without measure! Half of you will be dead before the day is out! Give my greetings to Lord Osiris and his pet Ammit for me when he devours your heart!"

They pushed us on in our ranks. I declare to you that that old jackal Horem was telling us the truth. I have never in the decades since experienced suffering like that day, nor have I felt heat anything like the Valley of Ra.

Men began to drop dead by late afternoon. The first one fell in front of me and went facedown in the sand and did not move. We simply stamped our feet on his back as we ran over him. Not a single one of the training masters even looked back at him as we left his body behind.

"Nekhbet gets her first feast!" Training Master Horem cried, referring to the vulture goddess.

Soon after, a few men broke ranks and tried to return the way we came, but Horem taunted them. "May you be favored in your cowardly escape! But know that you will not find relief by turning back. The nearest water is ahead, not behind!"

But the desperate men had become delusional and did not hear him. We never saw them again.

"Nekhbet will be too fat for her feathers tonight!" Horem shouted, increasing his pace until he was running around us in circles, singing the battle song of the Scorpions regiment. We hated him bitterly and yet could not help but admire him.

My feet were torn and bloody ribbons now. Every time I put my weight on one of them a hundred daggers stabbed my heel.

And the hours crawled on.

Once I tripped and fell, and they passed over me. For the briefest moment, I am ashamed to admit that I contemplated lying still and letting death embrace me. But I was stopped by Training Master Horem, who came up beside me after everyone had passed and kicked me directly in the kidney. The shocking pain woke me from my stupor.

"You are not done suffering yet, Kenazzite! I will not let you die until you have performed the Kiss of the Scorpion! Yes, that is a much better death for you!"

I was so thirsty and delirious that I couldn't fathom what he meant by the Kiss of the Scorpion. What fresh terror would that be?

The sun set and we did not slow down. I continued to run into delirium, hallucinating that I was swimming in a cold mountain pond, and that I would get out, shivering, with a tray of cold berries laid out for me, and I would be fed those berries by an attractive woman as my head lay in her lap.

Sand in my eyes. I dug at them. No pond. No cold berries. No attractive woman anywhere in sight.

Men died all around us.

My anger at Training Master Horem was deep, and I believe it was the only thing that kept me alive that night

All that night we ran, until daybreak when Horem let us stop at a well and have a drink. Slowing down even for a moment made me pass out, as did the others, and we were kicked in the face, and punched, and struck with rocks until, bloody and gagging, we stood up again to keep running forward into the endless cursed desert.

The sun rose. The heat grew more intense fast. There seemed to be nothing left of my feet to run on, only bloody stumps of bone.

At some point that next day we arrived back in the camp. Of the original group, only fifteen remained. Everyone else was left in the desert for dead.

We fifteen who still lived were allowed to drink from a bucket of day-old goat's milk that had already curdled in the heat. But we did not care. It was liquid and it was nourishment, even though we immediately retched it back up.

Training Master Horem walked up and stood above us. His shadow cast over my face, and I looked up to see him grinning wickedly.

"A Red Scorpion must know how to find his way in the desert. There are three pillars of rock out there"—he pointed in the general direction we had just come from—"and you must find them all by tomorrow morning. They are pillars of three different types of rock, so we will know if you are lying by what you bring back. Bring back rocks from all three pillars and we will know that you succeeded. Fail to bring them back by the end of the first watch tomorrow and you will be sent back."

My weak mind finally let me comprehend this. What about directions? How was it possible to find these pillars if they had no training—?

Wait, I told myself. The others did have training. They had spent three years in the armies and learning many skills. This was simply an extreme test of those skills. I had none of that training, however.

I staggered to my feet as Horem watched me.

"Good fortune to you, Kenazzite," he sneered.

With no idea as to where I should run, no water and no food, I simply headed into the west.

A high point. Find a high point.

I squinted against the harsh glare and covered my eyes.

A dune rose in the distance. I decided that if I could make it to that dune I could at least get a bearing.

I don't remember how long it took me. I don't remember anything about the rest of the day. I only know that I reached the top of the dune after passing out from lack of water several times, and then wandered back into the desert looking for a pile of rocks.

I woke up in the middle of the night, my face buried in the sand. When had I fallen asleep? I sat up and blinked at the stars above. A cool desert breeze passed over my skin, reviving me a bit.

I felt something in my hand and looked down.

A black stone was clenched in my grip.

I had no idea how I had gotten it. Did I reach a pillar and not remember it? When? Where was I?

Something skittered through the sand nearby. I searched for it a moment but saw nothing. How I longed for at least a viper to slither past me so I could kill it and drink its blood.

The skittering sound again, and I turned and saw that it was indeed a viper making its way across the sand nearby.

I gagged as I tried to swallow, my mouth too dry and swollen to allow it. I clenched the black rock in my hand and held it in front of me while I approached the snake.

It seemed to sense me and increased its speed. I fell several times as I chased it. I was making it angrier by the moment, until finally it coiled up, turned, and erupted toward me.

I don't know what I was thinking pursuing it so closely, for I was lost to delirium by then. I had no time to react to the strike. I only survived it because its fangs struck against the rock I was holding instead of my hand or arm.

Terrified, I cried out, yet all I could think about was getting something to drink. I began seeing the viper as a tube full of water and not a deadly adversary.

I had to defeat it. As it slithered away from me after its strike, I moved in from behind, reaching out to grab it by the tail when I tripped and fell directly on its back.

It snapped up and bit toward me, and this time I knew I was dead. But Yahweh spared me again, as the viper had already emptied its poison sacs after the first strike. It, too, was short of water and could not replace its poison fast enough.

The fangs dug into my forehead. I frantically pulled on the creature, but its curved fangs were hooked into the flesh of my head. I panicked and pulled it so hard that the fangs tore out of my skin.

I kept attacking it, much like the giant, and smashed against its head with the black rock as hard as I could. We were on sand, and I had nothing solid to strike the head against, but I flogged and flailed and then made a solid enough blow with the rock that the snake appeared stunned and rolled over several times.

I raised the rock high, took careful aim, and smashed its head with it. The snake finally went still.

I tore at its scaly hide with the sharp edge of the rock until I saw blood and hungrily sucked at the opening. The warm, rancid blood made me retch and gag, but it was liquid. It was *something*.

After I sucked all I could out of the snake, I felt sick in my gut, but it had given me enough of a push to try to find my way to the next pillar.

I searched all around me. Everything looked exactly the same. No landmarks. No pillars of rocks. Just an endless desert night.

I positioned myself facing Thuban, the northern star. Finding it, for I knew at least that much of navigation by starlight,

I knew if I could walk straight to my right, I would be heading east for the river, wherever it was.

I would find some water, revive myself, and go back out and find the pillars. I staggered onward for hours. I began to panic that I had not reached the river yet. Dawn was coming and then the end of the first watch. If I didn't have all three stones, I would be sent away. I could not bear the shame.

The sun rose, and I finally reached the plateau above the river. I rushed down the side of it, rolling many times and cutting up my arms and back as I fell. I ran desperately to the river.

At last I reached it and plunged my head below the surface, caring nothing for crocodiles or anything else that might be there. I took deep drinks, retched them back up, then paced myself with slower sips. I could have swallowed the river, I promise you that.

I was revived immediately and, drinking as much as my stomach could handle, was back on my feet and running for the desert like a drunken man.

I saw and heard no one else. I climbed the bluff over the river and scrambled up the highest dune I could find.

I shielded my eyes and searched the horizon for any sign of a rock pillar.

Nothing.

The sun was rising fast. There was no way that I would make it back before the second watch began.

I was heartbroken. Devastated. I'd had no possible way to succeed in joining the Red Scorpions. It was designed to fail for people like me, who had never even been taught the basics of navigation on land.

I was surprised at how bitter I felt. That moment of glory in the market where I had killed the Canaanite giant had infected me more deeply than I realized. I *wanted* that praise, *craved* that attention. It fed me as a young man. It was the very air around me. I did not know at the time how dangerous and flighty a mistress it could be.

No, at the time I was furious with myself. I had no choice but to simply return to the camp and get my gear. Lord Akan would be upset that I had failed, but I did not care anymore. No one would be more upset than I.

I trudged back to the camp. Now that I was near the river again I knew exactly where I was. Soon the pyramids loomed ahead, taunting me with their white sparkling beauty.

I walked into the camp and to the tent of the Red Scorpions. Inside, I found Training Master Horem and several other instructors.

"Do you have your stones?" Horem asked me.

I shook my head and held out the black one. "I only found one. I will go and get my things and be gone."

Horem stared at the rock in my hand. So did the other instructors. Their expressions became outright shock.

"How did you get that?" Horem asked me, standing.

"I . . . found it out there."

"Who did you bribe?"

"Bribe? What do you mean?"

Horem turned to the others. "Is that one of the stones?"

One of them picked it up and studied it.

"Polished. Cut like an arrowhead. The pillar is believed to be covered in the sands of the centuries. Only the help of a god could have brought it here. It cannot be found without the help of the gods."

Horem studied me carefully. "In all of my years of selection for the Red Scorpions, no one has ever found the black pillar. No one."

I was utterly confused. "But you said there were three pillars we had to find—."

"The other two pillars do not exist. We send everyone on a fool's mission just to see who quits. Only the black one is out there, and . . ." His jaw clenched. "And it is said that whoever finds a stone from it is favored by the gods."

Of all the stunned people in that tent, none was more stunned than I. I searched my mind for any memory of finding the pillar. I remembered nothing, of course. Only the thirst and heat and the wandering among the eternal shape-shifting dunes.

I put the black stone down on the table in front of them. "So then I pass this challenge? Where are the others?"

"All of them failed like you were supposed to, but they gave up hours ago. They are by the well, waiting for the next selection."

Training Master Horem handled the stone a moment himself. He handed it to one of the other men.

"Take this to the generals. They will want to know about it and consult the priests." He looked back at me, his expression once again stern and angry. "Get back outside with the others. I will be out for the next challenge."

—— 7 ——

Kiss of the Scorpion

Over the next forty days, we knew only suffering. We ran endless distances. We carried things until our arms nearly fell off. We were thirsty. We slept nights under the stars with no shelters—even when the *khamsin* blew through, its wall of sand and darkness and wind obliterating everything in sight. Training Master Horem stalked me like a devil after the black stone incident. But he was hard on everyone, not just me.

I will not bore you with the rest of it. Our armies have done the same, more or less. I have trained them much like the Egyptians trained me.

There were two more experiences that I will tell you about before I made it to the end. They taught me much about myself. About my ability to endure, to handle fear and pain, and therefore the lessons that I apply to our own troops as we conquer our promised land.

About halfway through the forty days, I found myself in the ranks at full attention near the chariot pitch. There was a tent canvas fully stretched out on the ground in front of us. We were standing around it, waiting for the training masters to appear.

Training Master Horem emerged from his tent and walked to the edge of the canvas.

"This is the Kiss of the Scorpion," he said, as easily as if he were telling us it might rain later. We looked at him, then at the canvas. There was nothing there. I laughed to myself.

Training Master Horem heard me laugh and walked over to me. He leaned in and touched his forehead to mine. I stared straight ahead and did not move.

"Caleb will be our first volunteer," he said, leaning against me as he shouted loud enough for all to hear. "We will see if he is indeed favored by the gods."

I had not been able to lose that hated title. The others used it to mock me, none more gleefully than Training Master Horem. They were convinced I had cheated somehow.

He stepped back and gestured for me to walk into the middle of the canvas.

I stepped cautiously onto the canvas and walked to the middle. Everything about this experience was warning me that danger was extreme and imminent, but the scene could not have looked more tame and unassuming.

I crouched into a fighting stance and waited for whatever was going to happen. My short sword was up and poised. Were they going to attack me all at once? I looked at the line of faces around the canvas, some of them my fellow recruits, some of them training masters, and above them all on his platform like an enthroned god himself, Training Master Horem stood with his arms crossed.

At one edge of the canvas the group parted. Two men carrying a wide brass basin walked forward.

They turned the brass basin over on its side and dumped out

the contents. I squinted to see what it was . . . and then felt my insides grow cold with dread.

Hundreds and hundreds of scorpions, that fiend of the desert, crawled over each other in a pile. Immediately the training masters took hold of the edge of the canvas and pulled it up, then jerked it down quickly, snapping the cloth and sending the entire mass of scorpions flying toward me. I turned and tried to run out of the way, but all of the men were lifting their end and I found myself facing a slope of canvas all around me that I could not climb. I slid backward—right into the middle of the canvas where the scorpions awaited me.

Hold still, I begged myself. Hold still.

It did no good. Their tails reared up and lashed out at me, and I felt a dozens stings on my legs and torso. One stung my forehead before I could stand.

Rivers of pain. Oceans of it.

Their poison flooded into my blood and I knew I was a dead man, but I did not care because death was far preferable to this pain.

More stings.

I somehow got to my feet. My mind was dim.

The sword. I still had it.

I plunged the tip down into the canvas and ripped a hole in the bottom while the men continued shaking the edge of it, bouncing the scorpions all around me.

I could feel myself blacking out. I knelt and crawled through the hole I'd cut, swatting away scorpions with my hand. I crawled under the canvas handbreadth by handbreadth. My eyes were now swollen shut, my throat constricting.

Without seeing it, only feeling it, hands finally grabbed me and pulled me up.

My breath rattled and wheezed. It felt as though my lungs were being crushed. The stings were like smelting rods from the furnace that had been shoved under my skin.

I heard someone saying, ". . . has more of them on him! Get them off—"

I felt a splash of water hit me, then another. Someone was throwing it on me.

I felt rough bristles of some kind of brush scraping against my torso and face. My eyes were still too swollen shut to see anything. A burning hot oil of some kind splashed down my head onto my shoulders. The pain was so intense that I finally had to kneel down.

Then I passed out.

I remember dreaming. It had to be the scorpions' poison, but it was a dark nightmare that I began having in those years, and it was always the same. I have had it from time to time ever since, but I understand it differently now.

In the dream, there is a blood-red sunset in the west. I am walking into a lagoon of the Nile. The water is perfectly calm and warm. I make no ripples as I submerge, still walking forward, the liquid covering my ears.

I hear the underwater sounds of reeds swaying. Hippos shuffling through mud. Crocodiles splashing as they enter to hunt. I continue walking.

Deeper underwater I go. I do not feel the need to breathe. No, air is meaningless down here. Only darkness matters.

The water grows colder. Something massive passes nearby, but I do not see what it is, only feel the current ripple in the black.

There is no light anymore. I move forward willingly.

Soon I am standing on the bow of a boat. It is built with black wood and is draped in black linen. But the boat is underwater, like I have been, and not on the surface where it should be.

Why? I do not even think about it. I only stare ahead as we plunge the depths, the dark ship passing through darker waters.

Into the night we go, and I begin to see strange things. The water turns a deep red around me, it smells foul and I wince at it, suddenly realizing that I am underwater and feeling the urge to gag and gasp for breath and claw my way to the surface. What is the red water?

But before I know what it is, the water turns black again, and I am passing through . . . frogs. Endless hordes of them kicking past me and scurrying to the blackness behind. Then smaller creatures, tiny insects, I cannot tell what they are, suffocating me. Then larger insects, black as the water, their buzzing dimmed and muffled by the water.

The insects pass, and the river is filled with immense shapes swirling in the current. I hear the sounds of lowing and bleating . . . the sound of suffering. But it is too dark, I cannot see them, but they are there. Cattle? Sheep?

Then my skin is on fire with pain, the pain of the scorpion stings, the pain of hot coals pressed into my flesh, and eruptions of disease appear everywhere on my skin and in my eyes, and when the agony cannot get worse, the water bursts around me with flame and cold.

Flame? Underwater? But there it is, everywhere, a river of red and orange fire that is consuming all. The boils are gone, my flesh now burning from the flames. I will die soon, I know it.

But it is relentless, this ship, taking me where it must.

It occurs to me vaguely that I must be in the *Duat*, the Place of the Dead, the River of Night the Egyptians always speak of. I am on the journey of Ra, god of the Sun, crossing through the trials. But none of these trials are familiar to me.

The flames are upon me now, burning me alive. Things strike me. Sharply. Solid objects like rocks being hurled are gashing me. I swing at the blackness wildly. Fire rages. I feel my flesh tear from the rocks, which are icy cold.

Then the fire is gone, and more insects come, and the ship sails ever darker. Their buzzing overwhelms me, their legs crawling in my ears and mouth. Locusts? Here?

They are everywhere, and eternal. They have no end or beginning. The locusts will devour me even before I get to Ammit, the destroyer of souls, who waits for me at the end of the Duat under the watchful eye of Osiris, god of the dead.

But then they are gone. The locusts disappear, and the silent darkness of the flowing river returns. I sense nothing. Feel nothing but the pressing of the water against me.

The darkness grows. Profoundly it grows, until it is everything. Too black and too dark for me to breathe. Too oppressive to be borne. The river has become night swallowing night.

What is this part of the Duat? It is nothing like the priests have described!

Darkness. Blackness. All is one.

And then the worst of it comes.

Low, in the distance, I hear the screaming. It is one voice, a woman, muffled by the water but clear enough to hear her suffering. It is not the cry of pain. It is the cry of ultimate loss. The piercing wail of the underworld, of spirit wraiths, scarcely human. Her voice is joined by others. All women. Who are they? For whom do they weep?

Their screams well up in my ears, and the ship plunges

into them with determination, the black sails rippling as we pass deeper and deeper. Suffering is all I know. Suffering is all I see. The sound of . . . mothers. Mothers weeping for their lost children. That is the only sound it can be. Nothing else is as terrible.

Rumbling ahead. The water is shaking. I stagger for the first time, grabbing the railing of the ship to remain standing.

The water is roaring now, sloshing me and the ship back and forth, until I feel the ship breaking apart beneath me, its black wooden planks ripping away and disappearing, and I am flailing in the deadly current, suddenly gasping for breath, not realizing until this very moment that I cannot survive under water and must breathe now, immediately.

I thrash for the surface, but the water roars louder.

And then it parts.

Yes, it parts.

As though a blade has sliced toward me and cut it in half, the water splits away and I am hanging in the nothingness of an endless night . . . and then my feet stand on solid ground.

I gasp for breath. I am in the desert. Nothing else is around me. Cold stars twinkle overhead.

In the distance I see a light on the horizon. It shimmers and dances, and it looks small from here, but I realize that it is larger than the sky itself, I only have to move toward it. Red flames and golden flames. It moves off, and I find myself following it into the vastness of the wilderness. . . .

It was this dream I was having, and it was the first time I had it, when I finally roused after being attacked by the scorpions.

The swelling around my eyes had lessened, and I could blink

them open. My face still felt heavy. A dull ache throbbed everywhere in my body. Every joint felt stiff and mortared into place. My very eyes hurt to move.

I was in a tent. Nearby sat Training Master Horem. Instantly I wanted to sit up and come to the position of respect, but my body was sluggish and I ended up only lurching onto my side.

"Lie still," Training Master Horem said. I obeyed.

"What god do you worship?"

I didn't answer. I had no answer.

"I asked what god you worship," he repeated, very calmly.

"Marduk," I said. It was the first god name that came to mind. Training Master Horem frowned.

"I do not know this one. Where is he?"

"The north, Training Master Horem."

The scarred man studied me a while longer. "No one has ever thought to cut through the canvas. That was clever."

I did not know how to answer. Was this a trap?

"You also did not die, even though you were stung over fifty times that we could count."

My curiosity got the better of me. "Do many men die when they do the Kiss of the Scorpion?"

"We only do it to one recruit, because he always dies. It is supposed to strike fear into the others. We usually pick out the recruit none of the training masters like. But you lived."

I could not tell whether he was setting me up for something else or actually engaging me in conversation. I remained silent.

But he simply stood and walked out.

I was puzzled at his behavior. I was even more puzzled at my dream.

— 8 —

Khufu's Horizon

The tallest and grandest of the pyramids was known by the Egyptians as Khufu's Horizon.

Khufu was the king who had commissioned it over a thousand years before, and he had left instructions that it was to be a place where the people through the ages could ascend and worship his glory, looking out across the lush green Nile Valley and be assured that this was the center of the world, the only place that mattered. That was why it was called Khufu's Horizon; after seeing it, you were left believing he was time's greatest king, and this was time's greatest kingdom.

We were at the fortieth day of selection. To say we were tired insults the idea.

Out of the tent came Training Master Horem, followed by several of his subordinate training masters. His pitted scar was florid with his temper.

"On me! Now!"

We rushed over in a mass of sweaty, sandy bodies. Dread

silenced our chatter. I don't know when the last time I slept was. My broken ribs from the first day had never really had a chance to heal, and they ached still.

"You have made it through the first cycle. Welcome back to those who have been here before. I assure you, it gets worse from here." He smiled at us, that smile that always left us wondering whether he was truly happy or was eager to see us die.

Gets worse? I thought it was only the forty days, and this was the fortieth day. Another mind game?

"How many are here now?" he asked a training master behind us.

"Fifty, Training Master Horem."

"We only have room for thirty more to pass through. So the first thirty who touch the golden cap"—he pointed to the top of Khufu's Horizon—"will be allowed to continue." And with that, he walked away.

We stared at each other. Was that all?

Run. Now.

Once more, I did not hear a voice. I only felt it. But I knew to obey it right away.

With everyone still standing there, confused as to their instructions, I darted out of the ranks and started running as fast as my legs could push me through the sand.

I heard exclamations behind me as the others started giving pursuit. I lowered my head and only thought about running as hard as I could for the base of that pyramid. Training masters appeared ahead of me, and at once I saw the challenge in full.

The army training grounds were set apart from the main complex surrounding the pyramids, which was actually a city of tombs. I told you before that the Egyptians worshiped death, and so the places of the dead were the busiest sites in the land.

Hordes of people hauling, pouring, chiseling, shouting, laughing, livestock lowing—it was a teeming, bustling mass of humanity hurrying their king on his way toward death by building monuments to it.

There was a staircase that cut up the pyramid's center that led directly to the top, where the brilliant gold capstone, as large as a horse's head, glinted in the sun all day long. I had seen many people going up and coming down the staircase to pay homage to the gods.

We had to run through the crowds that worked on the burial sites, reach the staircase and climb to the top. But the staircase was emptier than normal, and this was because training masters with whips were positioned the entire way up to the golden capstone.

I left the army complex behind, crossed a blank patch of sand and reached the tomb city, ducking and leaping around men and equipment, carts and children, needling through the bustle until I reached the base of the pyramid itself.

A quick glance behind me told me that the others were gaining ground. I could not climb the staircase. It would be impossible with those whips lashing at me. But the white casing stones, polished and shining, were too smooth to find purchase. And as I touched them I discovered they were also terribly hot from baking in the sun all day.

Frantic, I searched for another way up. Some of the others were taking their chances with the staircase, and I heard the crack of whips and the sound of men crying out in pain as the barbed tips bit into flesh. I panicked because I thought I had chosen poorly. Maybe the training masters were just going to whip them, and if a man was tough enough to withstand it, he could reach the top.

But no, for even as I watched, training masters were crowding around the recruits and kicking and shoving them back, hitting them on the heads with long staffs, doing everything possible to prevent them from gaining any height on the narrow staircase. The recruits who had just arrived for this cycle were faring better because they had not been through the weeks we had just suffered, but they could not fight their way past the training masters, who seemed utterly intent on ensuring that no more joined their ranks.

There was no other way. I had to climb.

I closed my eyes and calmed my breathing. I was thirsty again. Eternally thirsty. I squinted away the sweat as I studied the casing stones. They were fitted together perfectly in their lines, and the polish on their surface had been done without blemish. I could not help but admire the craftsmanship.

Forcing myself to be patient, I ran my fingers along the lines, searching for something. The pyramid was built many centuries before, and although it had been maintained with extreme care, I had to believe it would expose a fault to me—the place where the chisels had long ago been used to fit the stones together when they slid in. Perhaps they had eroded enough from the wind and pounding of sand and occasional storm.

My finger found a notch on the upper right side of a capstone. I instantly glanced above it to the same spot on the stone above, and my trained eye caught the defect in that one. Then the one above it, and then the one above that. It was barely anything, and I could not even fit a toe into the groove, but it was all I had.

The training masters continued to fight and berate and whip the recruits trying to climb the stairs. In sheer desperation and numbers they had managed to force their way up a few more steps. Eventually they had to make the top. I had no more time.

Assuming that the stones closest to the ground were the most well-maintained because they were easier to reach, I aimed my fingers for a casing stone several cubits above my head. With a running leap, my bare feet managed to find purchase on the angled stones just enough to let me catch the chiseled groove I had spotted. I touched it, but my fingers did not hold and I slid back down.

I ran at it again and missed it again.

It took me three tries before my finger caught the groove, and I clung to it with all my strength. My feet slid around trying to find a place to catch.

Frustration and hopelessness filled my heart. What was I thinking? The pyramid capstone was endlessly high above me. There was no way I would be able to repeat this three hundred or so more times.

In desperation I pulled up on the fingers that held the groove and . . .

A chisel.

I let go immediately and slid to the ground.

A crowd had stopped working and gathered to watch us, cheering us on. It was clear that this challenge was a routine entertainment for them.

"Tools!" I called out. "Tools! Stoneworker tools!"

A stonecutter nearby said, "What will you pay to use them?"

"Five copper rings," I said, glancing back at the staircase and trying not to scream *Hurry up!* at the man.

"Ten."

"Ten. Please!"

"Witnesses?" The stonecutter looked around, finding the necessary people who would help him hold me to the debt. Hands raised in excitement.

He held out his bag to me, and I dove into it, grabbing two chisels with sharp heads. I called thanks to him and raced at the angled surface of the pyramid. My feet found several steps of purchase before they started to slide, but my chisels were out to catch me. I jammed them into the highest casing-stone gap I could reach, and they caught.

The crowd burst with cheers and chants behind me, and again I felt that exhilaration that can only come when you are being watched and admired by the throngs. Oh, that temptress, she can bewitch you.

I pulled up on the chisels, found a groove to stick my toe into, held myself against the pyramid with my legs, and found another gap to stab the chisels with, this time one that was slightly larger and easier.

The noise of the crowd must have drawn the attention of the other recruits and the training masters, for the recruits had gathered below me and were trying to climb like I had. The training masters whipped at them and pulled them down. I saw Training Master Horem running up the stairs to my left, about fifty cubits away, shouting and gesturing at me.

It occurred to me that this may have been another impossible challenge that was simply testing our will to continue. It was not designed for someone to succeed. If I had found the black rock and also managed to reach the capstone of Khufu's Horizon, how much more would Training Master Horem detest me?

"You have violated the rules!" he shouted at me.

"You gave none!" I shouted back. "You only said to touch the capstone!"

I saw him draw a bow that someone handed him and aim an arrow at me. I froze against the pyramid wall. This was it. My death.

I thought about letting go of the chisels to save my life, but I was young then, braver than my own good. I would rather have died than quit in front of all those people. Yahweh have mercy, how foolish the young are!

I flattened myself as much as possible but kept my face toward Horem. I would die like a man, staring down his arrow, hating him.

He released, it flew toward me, and at the last moment I winced with my eyes shut, expecting the arrow to slice deep into me and cut apart my insides.

The arrow struck me full in the side, and it felt like someone had taken a stone hammer and pounded my ribs with it. I lost my breath and tried to suck air back into my lungs. I released one of the chisels and hung by one arm, somehow keeping the presence of mind to hold on while my world ended in the pain of what had just hit me.

Several ribs were broken. That was certain. But I saw the arrow clatter away down the side of the pyramid, one of the big, heavy longbow arrows that were sent over the heads of your own ranks to reach troops attacking you. Why had it not cut through me?

Training Master Horem was loading another arrow, knocking it into the string with a cold glare at me. I reached back over and grabbed the other chisel, my ribs piercing me with a sharp pain as I moved.

I pulled my legs up as he let the next arrow fly. This one struck me on the shoulder, and I finally grasped that he was loosing blunt-tipped arrows at me.

So that was it, then. He wasn't going to kill me. If I could withstand the pain, I could make it to the top.

Fresh resolve flooded into me. I looked below and saw that

others had followed my lead and were haggling for tools. Some had acquired them and were already trying to pick their way up. Others, learning from what they saw happening to me, ran along the base of the pyramid until they were well out of bow range.

Discouragement again. Another arrow struck me, this time on my thigh. It was immensely painful.

It was too far. I would be struck unconscious by an arrow. I had to drop down and move farther over. I cursed my stupidity bitterly. I'd given up the advantage.

I pulled the chisels out and let myself slide down the face until I hit the sand and then turned to run. But my world went dark as a whip cracked across my skull.

No sound, then the roaring of the crowd came back.

I did not see the training master who hit me. I simply stood back up and told my legs to run forward again. The crowd parted at the base of the pyramid as I stumbled forward. The whip cracked behind me, missing this time.

I ran again, past the rest of the recruits. Every step made my ribs pinch. I couldn't take a deep breath. And I was still so thirsty.

The crowd followed me, cheering for me. I let that noise power my leap with the chisels. I caught a gap in the casing stones, and even though I had lost my early jump on the other recruits, I quickly saw they were not sure of what my strategy for gaining height had been. The ones who had found picks and chisels aimlessly struck at the gap between the stones. I knew exactly where to strike on each stone, the small groove where a craftsman like myself a thousand years ago had once driven his tools in to make sure the stone was a fit.

The higher up the wall we climbed, the wider the gaps in the stones became, and soon I was pulling and stabbing in a fluid motion, only hampered by the ache in my side.

Stab. Set. Pull.

Stab. Set. Pull.

Up the endless mountain I climbed. The crowd noise was growing dim below me. I heard the *chink chink chink* of the others as they pounded their chisels into the casing-stone gaps.

Once in a while one of the men would lose his grip, sliding down the surface faster and faster until he hit the bottom, shattering his knees and legs. Some tumbled when they could not keep their loincloths against the surface to slide on. Those men died.

Of course, it occurred to me that I would reach a height where, if I let go, I would slide to certain death no matter how far up I was. But I ignored that warning as well. All for the glory.

The people came to the pyramids and slid on them for amusement frequently, but that was far down below in a set apart area. Only those polishers tied to ropes lowered from the top had ever seen where I was.

Stone by stone I climbed. The heat of midday bore down on me, burning my skin without compassion.

I let myself grow angry to focus my efforts. I would win. I would get there first. I would not merely be one of the thirty chosen.

The face grew steadily narrower as I neared the top. I chanced a look upward to see how much farther I had to go. The capstone was visible fifty cubits above me. I saw some heads near it leaning over and looking down the face I was climbing. Those would be the training masters who had ascended the steps and were looking down as I climbed the other side.

I had been up this high before. I had climbed the pyramid and looked out across the Nile Valley as it snaked away to the north and south, and saw the jagged land of demons that stretched east and west. The green strip of the Nile, the dull brown of the desert. The scene was staggering even from the safety of the small stairway that had been chiseled into the face.

Now the wind blasted against me as I neared the top. My arms ached. Only panic of death kept me hanging on.

Stab.

Set.

Pull.

A few more cubits. The heat was unbearable. The wind was going to knock me off. I hated Training Master Horem for hitting me with those arrows.

Stab.

Set.

Pull.

The apex of the mountain was near. I could see the face of Training Master Horem as he leaned over the side only five cubits away. His glare was murderous, but he did not draw his bow.

Stab.

Set.

Pull.

The top.

I slapped my hand on the golden capstone as I held on to the other chisel. It was not over yet. I had to get to the staircase. I could not descend the way I had come. I'd realized that halfway up.

I dug my chisels in side by side and crept along the base of the capstone. My muscles started shaking like they knew the end was near, and the fright and anger that had powered my climb was giving way to reality.

I reached around the sharp edge line and searched for a place to secure my grip so I could pull myself to the other side.

A strong hand clasped my wrist and pulled me before I could stop it from happening.

I found myself standing on the top of the steps, Training Master Horem beside me. He was beaming. The crowd below had erupted with delirious shouts and cries. Someone must have told them my name, because I heard it chanted over and over, even above the wind at the summit.

"In twenty years of being a Red Scorpion," Training Master Horem said in a calm voice, "I have only seen a few men reach the top. I was one of them." He turned to me and smiled. "But *we* all came up the stairway."

9

The Gold of Honor

I was branded with the emblem of the scorpion on my leg. You can still see it here. I keep it covered up, of course.

I celebrated with the other men, who made merry for several days along the riverfront. I am not proud of what we did, but I was a young fool then.

I saw Training Master Horem once in a while. It is good that I hated him, and I am glad he is dead now. We might have become friends.

Even if they survived Yahweh's wrath, the men from my old regiment are long dead from old age. I learned much from those days, and learned even more from Training Master Horem. If I am honest, I would have loved his counsel from time to time while training our own armies. No one knew better than he what the limits of a man's body and courage are. He would have been the first in the breach against the city of the Anakim, I assure you.

None of that matters. What matters is that I was chosen for the chariot teams.

I reported for duty in Thebes at the arena I had seen near the pyramids when I first arrived. I had not yet ridden a horse, although I had seen them. My first day among them could not be described as easy; I did not have a natural way with them like other charioteers.

And yet the sight of the men rushing around the arena at speeds that were impossible created a desire in me that was profound. I vowed to pour myself into my training.

Oh, the beauty of it. How the cart edged into a smooth turn. How the driver gave the animals their heads at just the right times to either accelerate or stop. The dust cloud that billowed behind their wheels, showing how fast the driver was going and how you could never run away from it.

You know little of chariots, because we have no use for them in our fighting. Joshua and I rode them in battle long before you were born, after we left Egypt. I will tell you of that soon.

These mountains are too steep and narrow, and there are too many rocks for chariots. They are entirely useless to you and this army. But one day you may find yourself on the plains grappling with the Sea People, and if you do, you must know how to fight them, for they are chariot masters of the first order.

First, what they cannot do. They are terrible if there is any type of uneven ground or hidden rock fields. I burst many spokes in my wheels on sand-covered stones.

The horses tire quickly, so you have to plan attacks knowing that you only have a short window of heavy battle in them before they must rest. Many eager charioteers were lashed because they drove their horses to death needlessly. Men are replaceable. Chariot horses are not.

The animals can be ornery. The training rubs your hands raw as you hold the reins for hours in the hot sun, sweat beading on your forearms and running into your grip. You only get about an hour of fighting before you have to withdraw from the field. You miss most of the battle because your part is so short.

But, oh, that hour of battle.

Yes, when the wind is tearing across your face and the wheels are running smooth, the horses snorting and whinnying with battle rage, and the look of fear in the eyes of your enemy.

When you are spread in the hawk formation with two long wings on either side of you, the electrum-coated chariot shining so brightly in the sun that it hurts the eyes, the archer leaning over the side to bring a terror-filled death to those you hunt.

The rig itself is wondrously simple and yet it has sophistication that we can only dream of creating. A joint from the front post sits in a notch that absorbs the shock of the terrain as the wheels bounce over it, wheels that are spoked and sturdy and can withstand high speeds. The balance is perfect.

And so I learned to master the chariot. I alternated between handling the reins and holding the bow.

I will sketch for you the hawk formation, for it was unstoppable. We were never defeated with it.

One chariot was in the lead. This was the commander. The rest of the unit stretched back from him in a line on his left and on his right, forming the shape of an arrowhead.

As we approached the enemy's infantry lines, we swerved one direction, allowed the archers on that side to release their arrows, clearing the way in the enemy ranks for us to then turn head-on into them, cutting them like a blade and tearing their front ranks to pieces with our bladed wheels before swerving at the last moment to the other flank and letting the archers who had not yet loosed do so.

We struck hard and violently, then wheeled away before the

enemy could know what hit him. Chaos and fear were our weapons as much as arrows and blades.

May Yahweh forgive me if I miss those days. Riding hard until sunset, the Nile glittering below us as we wore down the training pitch on the bluffs above. The nights we went to town and celebrated a day off.

I loved battle. I loved seeing my blade drenched with the gore of a man's guts. I loved the wineskin shared with comrades around the evening fire as meat roasted on the spit. Wine, women, and war. Those were our life.

I had two friends closer than all. They were the men in my fighting team, the ones I trained with every day for endless hours. We hated each other one hour and wanted to hug like lovers the next. We grew so sick of sleeping in the same small campaign tent, smelling one another and rolling on top of each other that we woke up every morning with murder in our hearts.

"Elbows in faces, and faces in legs!" That was the motto the training masters used to shout at us as they described how we were to fit three men inside a tent built for one.

"We disguise the size of our forces this way," they would yell as we shuffled and grunted inside the crammed spaces. "The enemy watching us on those hills only sees tents for five hundred men, when really there are fifteen hundred! If you want to kill Amalekites or Nubians, you need to sleep with your face in another man's legs! They don't tell that to you when you are being recruited, do they?!"

The names of the two men in my fighting team were Amek and Senek. They were pure-blood Egyptians and treated me like dung and called me foreign filth, until I whipped them so badly in sparring that they ran from me in terror. Then we became the closest of friends. That is how men begin relationships, Othniel.

We trained in small unit formations from the rising until the setting of the sun. Our hands no longer knew blisters because they had become as hard as the leather in our shield straps. We drilled and drilled and drilled. So many hours. Senek was the left, Amek was the right, and I was the point. We trained blindfolded to prepare for if one of us lost our eyes to a blade. We went two days without water and then trained for two full overnight watches until the sun rose and we were almost dead from thirst. We chased women and they chased us, unable to resist our toned and hardened bodies and well-paid army purses.

The stories of those first battles on the frontier with the Red Scorpions are for another time. Perhaps in other chronicles when I am willing to share in a moment of weakness. We must get to when Moses enters my story.

But there was one battle that I will tell you of, because it helps explain how Yahweh used it in my idolatrous heart to finally turn away from the false gods, and how I was so intimately familiar with the events when Moses and Aaron emerged from the wilderness and brought their God with them.

The highest award in the Egyptian armies, even in the kingdom itself, is the Gold of Honor. And I won it.

Presented by Pharaoh himself, it is reserved only for those who exceed every understanding of courage and valor in battle. It is a simple gold chain of links that can be worn like any other necklace, with the exception of the hawk seal emblem on it that marks its identity.

The Gold of Honor presents the bearer anything he wants in the kingdom. You move to the front of every line, win every negotiation, and are generally treated like a member of the royal household.

You will still be outranked in the armies, but even every great general must bow to you when he first sees you, even though he may give you orders in the next breath.

It is rarely awarded. I know of only three others in all my years in the armies who won it.

It was early in my career as a soldier when my opportunity arose. I sensed it as a man can sometimes sense his destiny. Humility was difficult for me in those days. I was exceptionally gifted at everything I tried. I thought to myself: Why would I not distinguish myself in battle?

These events occurred some years after I finished selection with the Red Scorpions. Pharaoh had come to visit the Red Scorpions and train amongst us for a moon cycle. He had only recently been rid of Queen Hatshepsut, the female pharaoh who had so offended everyone by her very life. She had been Thutmose's regent, and upon her death he set about destroying as many references to her as he could.

He was obsessed with the martial disciplines, and his first years of engagement were spent with the foot soldiers. When he wanted to learn the chariot, he came to the Red Scorpions because we were the best riders in the two kingdoms.

You cannot imagine how remarkable it was that the god-man himself, the King Who Would Reign Eternally, would actually come amongst his fighting men and train with them. Sweat with them. Bleed with them.

I had ascended rapidly as a training master in my own right, and Akan the Stone Broker had ensured that I would be the king's instructor on this day. Many jealous eyes followed me as I rode the designated royal chariot to the edge of the tent where his majesty was staying. Amek and Senek were there, and my comrades teased me with jealous humor because they would be staying behind to make room for the king.

The king came out of the tent with a spirited attitude. He was young; he could not have been more than his third decade. Eager to prove himself to the men he ruled.

The chariot was coated entirely in electrum, an alloy of gold and silver with traces of copper. The effect was a dazzlingly bright reflection of Ra's light that marked the chariot as belonging to the king. His men could see it anywhere on the battlefield. This was a mixed result, of course. His men may see him and be inspired, but he also attracted every archer's aim.

As he approached, the ranks of the army and his personal guard bowed low. I did so myself, and he stepped into the chariot and beckoned me up with him.

He leaned against the railing, his royal war headdress perched on his shaved head. I then struck the horses and we were off.

There would be one squadron in this training run. None of the pharaoh's guards would come with us. There was not room in the chariots, since he wanted to know what it was like in a battle-ready rig with a driver and archer, and he had ordered the guards away, which I found remarkably brave and provided the first instance of begrudging respect we gave him.

We were to take him out at full speed, let him get his first feeling of the rushing torrent of chariot battles by feeling the wind in his face and the lurching and creaking of the rigging, but we were to preserve the royal safety above all.

I was nervous in the extreme. There, next to me, the king of Egypt. The royal court that normally surrounded him and exalted his majesty was falling far behind us. It was only the desert and our squadron of twenty chariots.

As soon as I had brought the horses to a gentle trot and was guiding them to the desert road that led to the nearest training pitch, the king, who had been silent to this point, suddenly said, "Take me to the farthest pitch. My training masters tell me it is the one with the most difficult obstacles."

My blood went cold. The fifth pitch, the one he was referring to, was an hour's ride away and was the most advanced pitch in the regiments. It was dangerous to anyone who had never been on a chariot before. His eagerness to prove his valor to us was admirable but entirely foolish.

But I could not tell him no. He was the all-powerful ruler who could command my death instantly just for looking at him without permission. And yet if harm came to him in my care, I was dead anyway. I searched for any kind of reason to speak and possibly dissuade him.

"Great Egypt," I said, "I will take you directly to the fifth pitch. Would you spare one moment of kindness to your servant and allow him to ask you if you are aware of the name of the fifth pitch?"

"Do not speak that way to me," he said evenly. "Out here we are fellow soldiers. What is the name of the fifth pitch? They did not tell me this."

I was stunned at how casually he wished to engage with me. Glancing behind me to see if we could be overheard, knowing certainly that we could not, I cleared my throat and said, "It is called the Ring of Horus."

"Similar to the Ribs of Horus?" he asked.

I nodded. The Ribs of Horus was an obstacle course that the elite foot soldiers conducted near the riverbank. Horus was our falcon-headed war god; we named everything after him.

"Similar, your majesty, but men are allowed to attempt it

much sooner than we allow our chariot soldiers to attempt the Ring. And we don't have anyone attacking us; the course is dangerous enough."

The king looked at me eagerly. "Take me there directly!"

I hesitated for effect.

"What is it?" he asked. "Take me there now."

"I will take your majesty, if you will absolve me of any wrong-doing in whatever your fate may be. Otherwise I ask permission to end my life immediately."

It was a horrific gamble, but I had no choice but to ask. It had been both my honor and my terror to host the ruler of the Great Realm this day.

It worked. He was now so desperate to know what lay in the fifth pitch that he raised his hand dismissively. "Yes, I absolve you. Now tell me what is there."

And so I did. The entire hour it took to get to the fifth pitch, I told him of the challenges we would face by running the course, and of my own experiences drilling there and fighting bandits on the frontier.

I was a natural storyteller, and he was enraptured by my tales.

When finally we arrived at the Ring of Horus, we had two different reactions. His was of awe and excitement, mine of trepidation.

It was not just the course that worried me, for it was danger-ous enough. A wild, uneven road that traversed thirty leagues of rocky desert, on narrow trails and with hidden snares, it was a course that had to be taken at full speed in order to qualify under the time limit of one hour.

A charioteer had one hour of battle at maximum speed for the horses and therefore one hour to run the Ring of Horus.

What worried me more was that there were fewer security

patrols out here. It was on the edge of the territory controlled by the Amalekites, desert bandits who swooped in and raided our lands and disappeared before we could send anyone to stop them. The Red Scorpions spent too much time dealing with them. They were a nuisance, but a deadly one.

We pulled up, and the king dismounted. The other chariots behind us stopped as well, and all the drivers and archers jumped out and bowed low before him.

He impatiently waved them up. "Out here we are brothers! Leave that for the court and in front of the population. Here we bleed together!"

I knew immediately that he had just commanded their loyalty for life. Everything about the king they had been taught—his godhood, his aloofness—had made them think of him as a distant figurehead who had great power but ultimately had little to do with them. Now here he was, wanting to be one of them? Offering to bleed with them? But gods did not bleed. Even if it would be a long time before he was as skilled as us, it was his intent that mattered.

"I will attempt the Ring of Horus," he said.

Smiles faded. They did not want harm to come to the king they had just grown to love moments before.

". . . but as a passenger!" he finished.

They all laughed in relief.

"I want all of you to ride as hard as you can and try to defeat my rider," he said, gesturing to me. "And if you do, I will know who is the best charioteer in my armies. To him I will award ten lakhs of gold!"

Silence. Then a roar of approval from all of us. Gold was the way to a soldier's heart. Ten lakhs of it meant women and drink until the end of his life.

He bounded back up into the chariot, and I scrambled to take my own place. I have said how bizarre the whole situation was, the great king and divine man acting thus. It was bizarre also to have everyone line up side by side for this road.

We all should have known better. We should have spoken up, even at the risk of our positions. The Ring of Horus was supposed to be taken one at a time, not in a mass formation.

I knew it as certainly as it could be known: men would die today. Risks would be taken to get to the front, and bodies would be flipped and crushed, chariots mangled. Horses would break legs and need to have their throats slit. But he was the king, and we dared not deny him.

I had described everything about this course to the king during our ride over, so he knew right where to point when he said, "The time stone's shadow must not reach the next notch before we return, or we will fail. And I do not like failure! Lashings if we fail. Gold if we win! Does that sound like a reasonable wager, my brothers?"

We yelled and cheered, including me in spite of myself.

We waited a few more moments while the shadow of the sun reached the next starting notch. As soon as it touched, we would unleash our horses in the most desperate ride of our lives.

For all the glory. For all the honor. And for gold, of course.

We were men who worshiped ourselves and only paid prayer service to the gods.

Then we were off, all racing for the same place, the side of a barren cliff that had a ledge we called the Narrows—where the way through was only as wide as the chariot's wheel base. No room for any error, or the punishment would be a fall of a hundred feet onto the *wadi* floor below.

I cracked the reins hard and leaned in. His majesty gripped the rail and let out a whoop of excitement.

"Defeat them! I command you, defeat them!" he shouted.

I glanced right and left to gauge my distance. This electrum-coated chariot was noticeably slower than the others, so my only chance to win was to find the perfect angle of every turn, but more importantly, to be the first one through the Narrows.

The ledge approached. We were going far too fast, yet no one seemed to care. The king was there, and gold awaited.

I knew I had three rivals. Their names are unimportant because this is the only time they appear in my story.

In truth, I have forgotten their names. I am old.

Instead I will call them Red, Blue, and Green—for the colors lining their chariots. Every chariot master painted his rigging to reflect himself to others and display the number of enemy deaths.

Red, Blue, and Green were gifted riders. Any of them could have been the one driving the king that day, but they did not have the benefactor that I did in Lord Akan.

And yet I was the best. No sense in hiding it.

They closed on me, knowing I was going to get there first. Wheels shrieking with the speed, the wind roaring in our ears, the line of us bore down on the cliff, and with an odd exhilaration I knew that several were about to die because there was no way they could slow down in time.

"Come on, my beauties!" I cried to the horses. "You must win!"

Their heads lowered and reached the gap first, and all at once came the clamor of men shouting in fright and wheels snapping as they struck the cliff directly, killing their horses, tossing men into the air and over the side of the wadi. I pulled forward faster and let out a bloodthirsty cry despite myself, for I wanted nothing more in life than to see my rivals vanquished, even if they were my battle brothers. The king yelled a war cry on his own, as he knew he had escaped death while others had not.

I could not look behind me yet but had to concentrate all of my skill on guiding the horses, letting them slow just a bit so that we did not slide down the edge of the wadi but needing to keep the speed up. In my mind's eye the shadow crept faster and faster to the notch that would end the trial.

The Narrows narrowed even more. The heat of the midday started to turn that cursed electrum chariot into a furnace. Sweat poured down my face as the king cheered me on.

Then we were past it and onto the open plain, where I was able to take a deep breath and finally turn and look behind us.

At least five men and their chariots had been destroyed at the entrance of the Narrows. Yes, Othniel, we were that callous about the loss of life. I thought little of men dying in those days. There were always more who could replace them, and you must remember that we were obsessed with the afterlife and almost eagerly awaited death, where we believed we would see our comrades again and raise drinks and kill more enemies.

I gave the horses their heads again, and we surged forward. The next landmark was a dark pile of rocks a few leagues ahead. There was no outline of a road out here, only the landmarks and whatever side you had to pass them. Cheating was not possible, because normally there were lookouts posted at the guide points to ensure the Ring of Horus had been fairly run. Today we did not need them; we would be keeping an eye on each other.

My slower chariot soon began to lose ground to the fleeter, lighter rigs behind us. I saw Red, Blue, and Green flank me.

Frustrated, I tried to angle us enough to cut them off. It was our only chance to prevent them from using their speed to beat us.

It worked. Red backed away. I angled to Green, but he managed to speed up just enough to get his team out in front of mine and so I had to back away.

The king seemed to sense we were being less aggressive on his behalf, and he shouted to our rivals, "Any man I catch taking it easy on me will get fifty lashes!"

That did it. Motivated by gold and given the chance to let this be a full initiation ritual, complete with the danger, Red, Blue, and Green seemed to become maniacal in their lust for victory. Their archers held on desperately as the chariots lurched right and left, bumped over rocks and went flying, barely landing upright, and then we were onto Seth's Flat—the field of deep sand we knew was coming but still always caught us off guard—and every horse stumbled to its knees, jerking the chariots to a stop. We all went flying through the air.

I was ready for it and landed on my feet, looking quickly around for the king and finding him lying on his face. I was terrified that he was hurt, until I saw his sandy face look up at me with a devil of a grin. He was quickly on his feet and running back to the chariot with me.

As we mounted, the others were clambering over their rigs, calling out to the horses, shouting angrily at each other, everyone furious that they had been tossed like a bunch of green troops. Several wheel spokes in the ranks of the contenders had broken, throwing them out of the race.

I pleaded with the horses to get moving, but they were spooked. I sang the Red Scorpions' regimental song in a clear, loud voice. That seemed to work. They calmed down.

"You must rock back and forth with me, your majesty!" I shouted to the king.

Together we leaned left, then right, then left, right, back and forth like that until we had a rhythm of motion that allowed the wheels to raise up just enough as the horses strained against the deep sand to get us moving again. Progress was agonizingly slow, and there was nothing we could do about it but the hard work of rocking it side to side, side to side.

Red, Green, and Blue had regained their mounts. They were the only ones to do so. I nodded. It was as it should be. Only the best remained, racing for victory.

The horses wheezed and gasped as they fought the maddening sand. You have walked on it before, Othniel, and know how frustrating it can be to appear to make no progress, even though you are working twice as hard for your steps. Imagine the state of the horses by the time we made it.

It felt like forever, but we finally reached the end of Seth's Flat. The horses sensed the hard ground and responded to it, jerking us ahead. I whipped them furiously to gain as much ground as possible, chancing a look over my shoulder at Red, Green, and Blue as they struggled to get to the end of the sand pit.

The rock pile ahead grew larger. I will not name it for you here, but you can know that the name was inappropriate. We rounded it on the far side. I started detecting the effect of the run on the horses. Their turns were more sluggish, and foam began pouring from their mouths.

The Spring of the Duat was ahead, a marshy swamp that sprung up out of the desert on the other side of the rock mound, which could only have been placed there by the hand of a foul god as an evil prank, for the water was fetid and would have sickened the horses and killed any man who tasted it. This was the most difficult of all the obstacles yet, because I would have to keep them from stopping to satiate their natural urge to gorge themselves on water.

The smell of the swamp assaulted our nostrils as we approached. Nothing grew but a green slime over the mud.

"Brace yourself, your majesty!" I shouted, and then we struck the mud at full speed, sending clumps of it flying all over us, drenching the king's new white linen kilt with muck, but he could not have been more delirious with happiness.

"You are the best in my army! I shall make you commander of ten thousand!"

Absurdly, in spite of the danger we were in, I looked at him and felt my face blushing with pride. Commander of ten thousand?

I was not watching the horses, and they suddenly skidded to a stop and plunged their faces into the water, realizing at last what it was.

"No! No!" I shouted, yanking on the reins as hard as I could. "Majesty, pull out the bow!"

The other three chariots were behind us. I could hear them.

The king took out the bow and waved it at me.

"Break off the arrowhead!"

He did not question me but simply executed the order and snapped an arrowhead away from the shaft, which he'd plucked from the quiver. I was impressed by his discipline.

"Now shoot it into their hide! They are trained to run when they feel an arrow strike them!"

The king raised the bow in one fluid motion and released it, and the blunted arrow struck the horse's hide directly, startling it into a frightened whinny.

I cracked the reins, shouted "Kah! Kah!" the sharp-edged command I knew they would heed, the command that ordered flight from battle, and the horses finally reared up and ran again.

I looked back. Red, Green, and Blue were doing the same thing.

"Kah! Kah!"

The interior of the chariot no longer gleamed, and neither did the exterior. We were covered in the rancid dark mud. The king kept laughing, and I remembered the first time I knew I was going to finish the Ring of Horus, the thrill of it unmatched by anything else.

We were going to win if we could just be the first chariot back to the Narrows.

We flew past the other broken-down chariots, whose riders paused a moment in their frustrating efforts to repair their rigs and harness their horses to let loose a war cry of respect for us. The king, muddy and bleeding from where he had collided with the ground, raised his arm in salute, and they erupted for him, their predicament forgotten.

The Narrows approached. I could feel victory. *Feel* it. I had no way of knowing exactly where the shadow lay, but I knew we were going to beat it back.

We rounded the first turn in the terrain where we would glimpse the finish.

The cliffs were there. The Narrows path . . .

The path was blocked. By at least twenty men.

I was confused at first. They were not our men who had crashed earlier.

Then it struck me.

They'd seen the electrum chariot, knew who was in it, and bided their time until we were alone against them.

"Majesty, we are going to be attacked," I said as calmly as I could. "Did you learn the wedge formation with the infantry yet?"

The king's face fell. "Who are they?"

"Amalekites, your majesty. They will capture you for ransom. We must fight them until help can arrive. I cannot turn this rig around. Did you learn the wedge yet?"

"The wedge is for three people!"

"You can fight it with two," I said, now desperately. "I will cover the rear. You be the left flank!"

The king nodded, his bravado gone. But his courage was still there, for he drew one of the bronze swords from its scabbard and held on to the railing with it raised, waiting for me to stop.

"I am going to send the chariot at them, and then we must jump out the back. Do you understand? Then we run and try to get back to the men. If they catch us, we fight in the wedge."

I did not wait for his response; we were too close now. I pulled out my own sword, grabbed some arrows and the bow, and we both leaped out of the back of the chariot.

The Amalekites looked stunned that we had not slowed down, thinking us unwilling to fight them. They dove out of the way of the careening chariot.

The horses felt lighter and knew to turn back to look for their rider, and when they did so at too fast a speed, the chariot swung wide, broke from its fastenings and tumbled toward the bandits, its weight and momentum dragging the team with it. It had the effect of a broad cut from a scythe, sending the bandits scattering and crushing a few of them.

"Run! Run!" I called to the king.

We kicked off our muddy sandals and sprinted barefoot back to where the other members of the squadron were coming.

Red, Green, and Blue had seen the whole encounter and raced past us to put themselves between the bandits and the king.

We had been rivals moments before, willing to kill each other for gold, but now we were once more the Red Scorpions who must defend their pharaoh.

As soon as they passed, I saw the archers in the chariots raise their bows and release a few arrows that made the bandits duck. But these were fearsome desert warriors and knew to avoid arrows when they saw them.

Like a smothering horde of locusts, the Amalekites swarmed down on the charioteers we had been racing. I heard the sound of them being slaughtered as we ran, their sheer numbers overwhelming even the Scorpion troops.

On my right came more, emerging out of the sand. They had circled us, and there were dozens of them who had hidden under cloaks covered with sand and now emerged, swords raised, their war cry shrieking from their lips.

I called to the king, "Form the wedge! We have to fight our way through!"

Thutmose, the king, fell in next to me. He had been a good student of the art.

Three men rushed us from the front. I raised my sword to engage them while also searching quickly around for an escape route.

There, through these men. A small pile of rocks we could climb, leading along a ridge.

The three men were on us. My sword whirled and flashed in the sunlight. They were good fighters. My attacks were blocked and anticipated.

Our only hope was to kill these three quickly before the others reached us, and they were closing fast.

I concentrated on one of them and got my blade ready, and then I saw him lurch forward as an arrow hit him in the back, breaking his ribs and spine with its force. A heavy arrow, an arrow that could only be drawn by . . .

My friends Amek and Senek appeared on the ridge above us. They must have followed our column without being allowed, desperate to be a part of the king's ride. I had never been so happy to see their ugly faces.

"Cover us, we are coming to you!" I shouted. Amek only nodded and raised his great war bow again. He drew back a thick bolt of an arrow, the arrows we used in massed skirmishes that could penetrate through thick hide armor and shields.

"Majesty, this way!" I pulled the king with me, thinking wildly that I was touching his royal person and how that could have me killed under any other circumstance.

We climbed the ridge under the cover of Amek's and Senek's arrows. I glanced back. The Amalekites on the open plain were cutting down my squadron.

Reaching Amek and Senek, I gasped, "We need to get back to the main—" I was cut off by a burning pain in my thigh. An Amalekite arrow cut me as it passed and clattered on the rocks. Blood everywhere. But it was shallow. I sensed it.

"We need to get him back," I tried again.

Amek loosed another arrow down the ridge toward the pursuing Amalekites and stood up. Senek stood as well, and after several quick arrows the initial band of Amalekites who had followed us retreated, deciding we were not worth the risk.

"They believe the king is in the main body of our squadron," I said. "Else they would not give up so easily."

"Don't they see him with us? Didn't they see his chariot?"

"They believe it to be a decoy," Thutmose himself offered.

Amek and Senek bowed down low before him. They had not had the chance yet.

"Majesty, if I may ask, how do you know this?"

"They knew I would be here. That means someone told them," Thutmose answered simply. "Normally I use a decoy, so they would believe I did it again. And I certainly do not look like Great Egypt right now," he said with a grin.

"We need to move. They will discover us if we do not get back," I said.

"Follow me," Amek said as he stood.

Amek and Senek were not tired from running the Breath of Horus and moved easily over the ground. Pharaoh Thutmose and I struggled behind them, my leg bleeding heavily.

"Ra departs from the heavens. We will not be able to make it back before dark," Thutmose said.

"We will press on through the night, your majesty," I said.

And as the sun set we kept moving onward into the desert until night was full and the stars appeared. Over knobs and across narrow wadis we followed that ridge. I do not know how many hours we traveled. Our hearts were heavy for the dead and wounded we had left behind, but our mission was indisputable: get the king to safety.

It was late. I remember that we had been walking in silence for an hour or more, anxious that we would be discovered, when we heard a clattering of rocks below us on the ridge. We all dropped instinctively to our chests and held still.

I closed my eyes and strained my ears. A light breeze dusted the rocks, but nothing else. We kept waiting.

Another clatter, a small one that we would not have heard if we had been walking, but there it was plainly ahead of us.

I turned and made eye contact with Amek and Senek. With hand signals we communicated:

Men?

Yes.

How many?

Many.

Somehow the Amalekites had gained on us. Perhaps they discovered that the king was not in the middle of the squadron faster than we hoped. Which meant that all of our brothers were . . .

I shook my head. Time to forget them.

The others waited for my orders. I looked around and squinted my eyes to focus them in the dark. The ridge we were moving on stuck up like a spine in the desert, and we had been moving along its crest. Not on the very top in order to avoid being silhouetted against the sky, but high enough to be able to hold the high ground in any engagement.

But if they had somehow encircled us, we were doomed regardless. How had they moved so fast? Were there so many that we were encountering a separate group?

I thought hopefully that perhaps these were more of the Red Scorpions from the camp, come to search for the king. But that could not be true; reinforcements would be coming from the road, not stealthily along the ridge.

I wanted desperately to act. Hold still, though. I needed to hold still until I knew more. How many? Could we fight through them?

A clattering noise again. Why were they moving so carelessly?

They were not moving carelessly. They were signaling each other.

A cry rose up from all around us as dozens of Amalekites emerged from the darkness and swarmed our position.

Amek and Senek started sending arrows while I grabbed the king and pulled him in the only direction I could spot that had no enemies advancing on us.

"We must fight them!" he protested.

"We will, your majesty, but from a better position. Amek! Senek! This way!"

I had seen a break on the ridge, a dark spot that could mean what I hoped it meant . . .

The Amalekites rushed toward us furiously. They had to run across loose shale and slid and stumbled on one another, slowing their attack and giving us time to make it to the black shadow that grew larger as we approached.

The king fell, and I heard his wrist snap as it wedged between two rocks. I cursed. He did not cry out in pain but was back on his feet instantly. I pulled him along, admiring him in spite of our situation. But he would now be of no use in defending our position.

We could not outrun them all. We had to find a position of strength where our small number would be an advantage, a position like a cave . . .

. . . which was what we saw open up in front of us. I shouted, "Inside!" to the others as I helped his majesty along and Amek and Senek released their arrows with steady, disciplined aims.

I was the first through the cave entrance. It was as wide as three men standing abreast, and the roof was two or three cubits over my head. It was completely dark, so I could not determine how far it went into the mountainside. Larger than I preferred, yet it would have to work.

"Lord king, stay behind us and use your good hand to stab through our gaps. You have learned infantry?"

"Yes."

"Attack low. Hit their ankles and the tendons below the knee."

The Amalekites were getting closer. We could hear the rocks and pebbles sliding as they neared the entrance. Amek and Senek took their positions on the left and right side of the entrance and pulled out their short bronze blades and readied their small crocodile-hide shields.

"Ignore the more tempting targets like their torsos or heads," I continued. "They will be guarding those areas, and every blow matters."

Figures were just outside the entrance now and closing in.

"We will grow tired and so you *have to fight with anger!*" I shouted as my time ran out and the first few Amalekites burst into the cave in a full charge. Amek and Senek braced themselves against either wall and drove their blades into the two men closest to them while I knelt and hacked at the legs of the one in the middle.

Three Amalekites down at once. They screamed in pain, their blood spraying our faces from the arteries severed. And it flared up in me again: lust for killing. Death in my taste. Anger at who would *dare* attack me. I roared in hate and picked up a nearby rock and came down with it with all my strength to crush the Amalekite's face, silencing his screams.

The Amalekites must have realized that we had a defensible position because they then tried to kill us with hails of arrows from the outside of the cave. We ducked back against the walls of the cavern and winced as the tips clinked and snapped against the rock. One hit my knee, but it was only a graze.

The arrows ceased, then came another charge. Ten this time, stacked up against each other. They had a smart commander. He did not want to send them in in small groups at a time to be cut down by the pharaoh's elite troops.

Thutmose leaned forward and put his hand on my back to balance himself. Amek and Senek crouched. I held the blade up, felt the darkness around us, listened as feet struck the gravel at the entrance. They were upon us again, and I stabbed with hard, steady thrusts.

The first one collapsed after three cuts, but he kept fighting as he fell and even after he hit the ground. The second was a huge man who stepped on the back of his comrade and hacked at us with a club, catching Amek on the shoulder before swinging toward me.

I blocked it, but another man appeared behind him, then another, until soon we were surrounded by them in the tight space, elbows flying and breaking against teeth, blades stabbing. I kept finding flesh to penetrate, then panicked because it was too dark to see who was who. The smell of sweat from everyone, and blood, blood everywhere. My head scraped against the stones, and I cried out for Thutmose, yet he did not reply.

Cries of meaningless words, grunts, and shouts filled the cramped space. They would not die easily, these wicked men from the desert with their tattoos and self-inflicted scars on their faces, which made them look like monsters of the afterlife.

I remember that it was so very dark and hot in that cave, and somehow I kept surviving and cutting at legs, and then somehow I found a way to shoulder myself next to Amek, shouting one of our regimental war cries "Sting and move!" to let him know it was me. We fought them back to the entrance, tripping over corpses and wounded men, who bit at our ankles and gashed their teeth deep into our legs.

Men do not die easily or quickly. You learn that.

In the confusion, Senek lowered his head, grabbed both Amek's arm and mine, and shouted, "Shove them out! All together!"

I lowered my head alongside his, and we pressed forward with all our remaining strength. The Amalekites were fearsome, but they were thin, worn down by the ravages of a barren desert diet, and we were able to push them back through the entrance until they stumbled over the bodies of their dead, and we laid into them, hacking at their flesh till it quivered and shook from the death tremors.

An order in their tongue was shouted and the half dozen remaining in the cave suddenly withdrew outside into the desert night and disappeared.

Amek, Senek, and I gasped for air, our muscles shaking with exertion, our eyes wild and searching the opening for any sign of an arm or a leg we could attack, but none emerged.

"They . . . are regrouping," I said between breaths.

"How long until they return?" Thutmose asked.

"I . . . do not know. They will not leave while you are here, though." I shook my head. "They did not anticipate us giving them such a fight. We are isolated and far from our army. They know they can just wait until we come out in surrender because we are nearly dead from thirst, then cut us down while they take you captive, your majesty."

"We will not surrender. We will wait and see what fate the

gods have for us. If it is to begin our journey on the Duat, so be it," Thutmose said calmly.

Amek and Senek smiled, as did I. Finally, a warrior to lead us! After years of being led by a false pharaoh. A woman, even!

"Grab those bodies and stack them at the entrance," I said.

The entrance was narrow enough that it only took a pile of seven of them to block the passage to waist level. One less defensive posture we had to worry about. Now the Amalekites had to attack us by climbing over the pile, and we had free lines of sight on their legs.

"Why do you attack the legs?" Thutmose asked as we piled bodies. I was impressed again at his willingness to get his hands dirty with the work.

"A wounded man is far more valuable to us than a dead one. He screams in pain and makes his comrades upset as they listen to him. He writhes and thrashes about and gets in the way of their attacks."

"You mentioned the other targets on the body."

"It is instinct to stab a man in the torso. That is also where his armor tends to be if he is wearing it. You may get lucky and kill him after a single blow, but"—I gestured to the corpses at our feet—"most men take multiple wounds before they die. Better to hamstring them and make it impossible for them to fight, and then listen to them squeal and frighten and get in the way of their friends."

We waited and watched until late into the night. We could hear voices outside in the harsh, guttural Amalekite tongue.

Thirst. That was the horror that soon became everything to us. We had lost our water pouches when our chariot was attacked, and we had been on the run in the heat of the day and then fighting off attacks all evening in the suffocating cave.

I even considered drinking the blood of the dead, but I had learned that it would only make me thirstier.

In the middle of the night, the tension was broken when Amek said in a weary, cracked voice, "If I survive this I am going to drink myself to death."

We all laughed.

"I will provide the wine," the king said.

"What about your woman?" I asked. "What use are you to her as a drunk?"

"She drinks more than I do."

It continued this way. No one wanted to think about how we were eventually going to die. That we did not have a prayer at withstanding another attack.

Just before dawn, Amek died.

He had been silent for a while. The rest of us had carried on our conversation and assumed he was sleeping. We had divided up the watch, though no one could sleep and so we kept each other company by talking about old things.

When I reached over to prod Amek, he did not move. I poked him harder, then smacked him with the flat of my blade. Nothing.

When I touched his neck I knew instantly he was dead.

I pulled my fingers away and exhaled heavily. "He is gone to the Duat."

Senek sat up. "What? How?"

"It is too dark. I cannot tell. Perhaps he had a deep wound and bled out without our knowing." I said these things as though I were describing the weather. I felt numb. Hollow. A shell of myself.

Amek had been almost flesh to me. He, Senek, and I were closer than brothers. I would grieve bitterly when this was over.

In the dark, I heard Senek draw a sharp breath. I knew this sound from him. It was rage.

"Senek, do not do anything—."

But he was up and running for the cave entrance. I leaped up and tried to catch him, shouting, "Wait, you fool! Wait!"

I managed to seize him by the legs and trip him as he was climbing up the stack of bodies to get outside.

"Do not! You will be cut down!"

"Come at me!" he screamed as I tried to hold him. "Your mothers are all whores! I will have every soldier in the regiment ravage your women and take the very rags on your back! I will feed your naked carcasses to Nekhbet!"

He ranted and yelled, his voice echoing loud in the cave. Thutmose joined me in holding him down.

"I command you to silence!" the young king said, and Senek was startled at this. He regained himself. He nodded to me, and I released him slowly.

When he spoke, he had great pain in his voice. "Apologies, my king. Amek was our brother."

Thutmose nodded. "I will make a sacrifice for him and give him gold for his journey to the afterlife."

Silence returned. We waited. All I could think about was finding something to drink. We'd already scoured the corpses for any water pouches, but Amalekites were known for fighting all day with no water and so none were carrying any. They would have a supply camel nearby, a tactic we also used.

"The gods are testing me," Thutmose said after a while, and his voice cracked with thirst.

Senek and I did not know how to respond. In the fighting, I

had almost forgotten that we were with the son of Ra himself, the god-man who communicated with the divinities. In spite of my suffering, I was worried I had not been showing him the proper amount of deference and respect due him.

"They test me and they will find me in the full measure of manhood," he continued in the darkness. "And when I have survived this insult, I will ensure that every man of Amalek will have his eyes cut out and forced down his throat. They will be tied to oxcarts and torn apart, and their entrails will be used to smear their blood on my throne. I will send their women to my loyal Red Scorpions to be ravaged for the entire Nile feasting season, and then they will be impaled on spikes until Nekhbet comes and devours their eyes under the hot gaze of Ra as my sacrifice to my brother gods. Their children I will torture to death one by one. They will be thrown into pits of cobras and lagoons of crocodiles after they have been ravaged by my army like their mothers. I, Thutmose, the third of that name, declare this to be so."

With the king being as weak as we were, his words did not resound in the cavern like they might have in his throne room. But his conviction was chilling to me nonetheless.

At some point that night I was stung by a scorpion. The irony of it was not lost on me. It got me on the ankle as I was pulling Amek's body to the back of the cavern.

"By Seth's rotten breath!" I shouted, then swatted the insect. The pain was intense and irritating.

"What happened?" Senek asked.

"Scorpion," I said with a grimace. It was a small one, yet those are what cause the most damage internally. I could even now feel my lungs closing and my face swelling. "I will be all right," I added dismissively.

Oh, how the gods must have enjoyed that comment, because right after I said it, we heard the sudden thumping of feet on bodies. Instantly the cavern was filled with Amalekites who had rushed in, taking us by surprise, and as my breathing became more labored I felt the jolt of panic energy that comes when your life is threatened. My sword flew up. I could see the outlines of the men against the pale gray light of early morning.

A blow struck me. I tried to counterattack the figure above me, but two more appeared next to him. I could not even shout orders, the surprise was so complete.

I blinked away the tears that my treacherous, swelling eyes were producing. Thought about pulling back further. No. No advance for the enemy! The king. Where was he? I rolled to my left. Feet kicked at my ribs, blades cut downward, but by some unknown power they kept missing me. I was completely vulnerable. There must have been a dozen of them inside the cavern with us. My eyes were swelling shut now from the scorpion poison. Helpless, I waited for the killing blow to my chest, thinking how I had failed my god-king and my comrades, how my journey into night would be filled with terrors, and how Ammit would devour my soul when it was found wanting.

But why had they attacked? Why risk more dead when they could just wait—?

Then I heard it. Outside the cave.

The roar of the khamsin.

I barely had a moment to glimpse through the bodies at the gray morning sky before it was swallowed by sand.

They had seen it coming and were searching for any shelter they could find. I imagined their forces outside scrambling over each other, wrapping heads in blankets, desperately seeking anything that could shield their mouths and eyes from the terror all were familiar with.

Like the breath of Horus himself, sand rushed into the entrance on the wings of the wind and flooded our cavern, pelting our bodies with such ferocity that the Amalekites, who had been standing over us, were blown forward and on top of us.

Darkness. Roaring. Screaming.

I acted without thinking, already nearly blind from the swelling, punching my fist into any flesh nearby that I could find.

I sensed that I struck a neck with one blow and then kept striking that spot until I felt the windpipe break under my knuckles.

Another man was stabbing wildly at my thigh with his dagger. It penetrated my flesh twice deeply before I caught the hilt and tried to shove the tip back toward my attacker.

I strained, pushed, the man shouted, the shouts muffled in the sand that was filling the cavern, and I made the mistake of taking a full gasping breath, the first thing you are taught *not* to do when suffering through a khamsin.

My mouth filled with sand instantly. I clenched my jaws and could feel my teeth grind against it, soaking up any remaining moisture on my tongue. I gagged and coughed as the sand swarmed down my throat into my lungs.

The tip of the Amalekite's knife found my thigh again. He was turning my leg muscles into a pulp.

My only advantage was that my swollen eyes were allowing hardly any sand in through my lids. Somehow I managed to see a flash of movement from my attacker's arm and avoided his next blow, found his skull with my hand and dug my fingers into his eye sockets. He flailed and shrieked in pain. Then someone fell on my head and crushed my face, but I did not relent on my grip, digging my fingers in as deep as I could, willing them to penetrate all the way through to the other side of his head.

My rage was complete. Pain, suffocation, all of it subsided and I could only think of killing every Amalekite within my reach.

We grappled in the dark like animals. I could hear only grunting and gagging and the roar of the khamsin.

Despite this, I had an idea.

"Outside!" I yelled in our tongue. "We can escape their army in the khamsin!"

Senek did not answer.

"Senek! Senek!" I shouted. "Majesty! Are you there?"

I wrenched my hand away from the skull of the man I had been blinding because he was no longer struggling. I sensed my elbow pressing against something metal. My blade.

I pulled it out and shoved it into the torso of whoever was on top of me. I hoped it was an Amalekite. His guttural curse told me it was.

"Lord king! Are you alive!"

"I am alive, soldier," he called from the other side of the cave.

The sun had risen fully, and while it was still quite dark inside, I could make out what was happening as I got on my feet again. The Amalekites had stopped searching for us and were huddled against the cave walls, covering their faces with cloaks. Sand had drifted up to our waists, covering the corpses entirely.

"Run to the entrance as soon as you can break free!" I called to the king.

"Madness!" he answered back.

"It's our only chance to evade their army; we can escape in the storm. Senek! Where are you?"

"He journeys through the Duat," the king said over the roar.

I felt the punch of this news deeply. "Are you certain, your majesty?"

"I am certain."

I allowed myself to the count of five to grieve my comrade. Both of them gone. Amek and Senek. My brothers.

"Majesty, run! Run for the entrance!"

We began staggering toward the mouth of the cavern. The sand sprayed us, and the wind howled like spirits of the underworld across the entrance. I felt an Amalekite's hand reach out to stop me. I swung my sword down heavily, nearly cutting his arm off. The hand released.

Thutmose and I waded through the sand drifts and emerged at last from the entrance. The wind buffeted us, nearly tossing us back inside. We lowered our profiles.

Of all things, the scorpion sting hurt the most. Not the knife wounds in my leg, not my possible broken ribs—nothing hurt like that creature's little stinger. Oh, how it irritated and angered me. My lungs rasped and wheezed from the poison. But my swollen eyes continued to be an advantage, keeping out the windswept sand. I could not see well, but I could see.

I stripped off my tunic from my waist and wrapped it around my face. Now I could breathe slightly better, as the cloth protected my nose and mouth.

We pushed our way through the sand. I was immeasurably tired and thirsty. The king collapsed several times; he did not have the endurance I had from all my training. I had to pick him up each time he fell.

I did not know where we were going. My leg ached. I remembered Amek and Senek every few steps, suffering grief for them heavier and heavier. How had Senek died? An Amalekite blade? I kept trying to ask the king if he knew, but my mouth would not form the words. I was growing delirious. I saw ships sailing in front of me on the Nile and I believed it to be so, until another hour of walking toward them brought me no closer.

The khamsin's wind finally started to die down by late afternoon, leaving a dull brown haze all around. Visibility was limited still, but at least the sand was not being sprayed against us anymore.

I made out formations of rocks that looked familiar. We were still on the ridge, now much farther along. By the will of the gods, or so I thought then, we were being led back to our men.

By evening we were in Pharaoh's camp. He was swarmed by caretakers and physicians and priests and dozens of others in his court. I made my way to the nearest campfire, seized the largest waterskin I could find, and drank until I could hardly see straight, all while my brothers in the regiment crowded around me to hear the tale and learn what happened to the others who had gone on our ill-fated chariot ride.

And when it was late and my leg and other wounds had been cleaned and bound, I sank into my bedroll and wept and wept for my friends Amek and Senek.

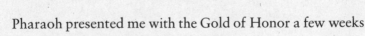

Pharaoh presented me with the Gold of Honor a few weeks after we returned to Memphis. He declared that my courage and heroism were to be admired and emulated by all.

I knelt down before him and his entire elegant court of nobles and ladies, who applauded for me. But the entire time I knew everyone was thinking the same thing. *Why is a foreigner receiving such an honor?*

The Gold of Honor opened the doors of the kingdom for me. As long as I wore it around my neck, I would be given whatever my heart desired. Merchant partnerships. Women. The best food harvested in the fields. The best wine from the best vineyards. Adulation from the masses who would gape at me in astonishment.

It was everything I could have hoped and prayed to the gods for. My pleasure was complete.

But soon enough, in the quiet corners of my heart and mind, I began to wonder if it mattered at all.

— 10 —

The Wife of Youth

You are wondering whether I ever met a woman. I sense it. A natural question.

My Hebrew wife is gone to Sheol these twenty years. She was good to me and raised my children. I loved her. But it is not yet time for her to enter my story.

I had a woman in Egypt as well. Golden eyes and golden skin. Soft and painted. A pagan, yes, but then I was a pagan too. What I thought was beauty was what she had.

I met her while on leave from training with the pharaoh's guards. Normally on the last evening of the week, the soldiers stood outside in formation and listened to the latest guidance from our commanders. They warned us against the health dangers of the filthy women in the wharf district and said that because of who we were, we were always the targets of spies from neighboring kingdoms. We were not to drink wine and share secrets.

So, naturally, when the men were released from formation

they promptly found the easiest and cheapest whores in the kingdom and got so drunk that they spilled every detail about palace life to anyone who would listen. By rights, our pharaoh should have been strangled in his sleep every week by a foreign assassin because of these security lapses. Perhaps Yahweh spared him just to have him on the throne when Moses came.

It was after one of these instructions, as the others clamored away to begin the carousing that soldiers are known for, that I made my way with my friends to a quiet tavern where the officers usually met up. Yes, we would engage in shameful behavior as well, but in a manner more dignified. More controlled.

We paid for our wine and drank it calmly. The prostitutes who came to officers were of the higher class. They and the men who owned them knew we had more money than the common troops.

None of them appealed to me that particular night, though. I was too tired from training to concentrate on them.

I left Amek and Senek early in the evening—this was long before the battle when I won the Gold of Honor—and made my way down to the wharf. I liked sitting by the water on nights like that one. Waves lapped gently against the posts holding up the docks. A cool breeze came from the south. Rowdy and bawdy noises drifted from the city behind me. I didn't mind them. It helped me to feel less lonely.

I'm not sure I knew it at the time, at least not directly, but what I was longing for was a woman. The warmth and satisfaction of her body, yes, and also more. I had had women available to me ever since I won a position with the Red Scorpions, and yet it was never satisfying. My physical thirsts were quenched, but the cistern I wanted to drink from was deeper.

I wanted someone to collect my pay from the paymaster.

Someone to fold my bedroll for campaigns. Someone to miss me when I was gone and be joyful to see me when I returned.

Most men, even among our own people, only value the company of women for physical satisfaction and how they can be served. That is understandable. It is also incomplete. No matter how much of a rogue a man believes himself to be, he has a heart, and that heart yearns for the companionship that only a woman can provide. As much as I loved my battle brothers, they were not women. I could not dip my face into the soft flesh of their necks or let them stroke my forehead while I lay in their laps and they listened to the things that troubled me.

None of that was on my mind as I sat on my favorite dock on the wharf and listened to the warm night around me. All I knew was my loneliness—which was interrupted by a female voice in the darkness behind me.

"I like to come here as well," she said.

I turned and searched for the source but saw only the shadows cast from nearby huts, the city behind them.

"Reveal yourself," I said.

"That would spoil my fun."

The voice was playful. Feminine.

I tilted my head to discern where it was coming from. I heard a giggle. There . . . in the shadow of a hut to my left.

My first instinct was to stand up and walk away. I have always been awkward around women; even those who were paid copper and gold rings to keep me company. You are likely marveling at how forward this woman was for addressing a stranger. I was used to the forthright behavior of Egyptian women by this point, but even still, I was hesitant to move.

Then, after a few moments of silence, I decided to leave.

"I am sorry. Please forgive me." The voice had moved, and now I heard it coming from an alley between the huts.

"Are you a deck whore?" I asked loudly. It was a fair question. Harlots roamed the wharf for fishermen and sailors fresh off the barges with rings to spend. But I saw how my question may have been too abrupt.

"Certainly not," she said indignantly. "And you would not be able to afford me even if I were."

Playful again. I cleared my throat and fingered the dagger in my waist belt nervously, then marveled at what I thought I might do with it. I had already called her a deck whore. Why not stab her as well?

"I can tell you are a soldier by your build and demeanor, and by your complete inability to speak with a woman who was not paid to speak with you."

I had always thought myself skilled of tongue, but I was completely unable to give her a response.

"What is your name, soldier?"

"Caleb, of the Kenazzites," I stammered.

"The very same?"

A figure emerged out of the alley. Slender, covered in a shawl, not out of modesty—the Egyptians had none—but because of the night chill.

"He who wears the Gold of Honor?"

I was used to this by now. So few had ever won the valor prize given by the god-king that their names were spoken of in reverence from the delta to the cataracts.

"Yes," I said. That was all I said. Very eloquent, I know.

She walked up close to me, and I saw her face for the first time. She was attractive. Not the most beautiful woman in the

Two Kingdoms, but . . . the way she carried herself, held her hands behind her back, tilted her head as she looked at me, her dark eyes and skin—all of it was alluring to me.

I felt a need to say something. Nothing came from my mouth. I looked past her to find somewhere else to direct my eyes.

"I heard you saved the king himself," she said, stepping even closer so that I smelled the perfume I came to love the first time.

"The king is a god," I replied. "He did not need to be saved."

She smiled. Her mouth was lovely. Her best feature. "I did not know that Amalekite arrows could recognize the flesh of a god-king and know to avoid it."

I could not help but laugh. Perhaps it was because I was nervous. It occurred to me then that I had never really spent time around intelligent, poised noblewomen. For that was what she had to be, I knew it instantly. The common women did not have time for the idle pleasure of sitting by the shoreline on an evening's lark.

Her bearing informed me as well. She had been trained in posture and language. Her grammar was eloquent, free of the abuses and slang of common speech.

That was it, I thought. That was why I felt so uncomfortable. I was not used to a lady of her kind.

"My lady, please allow me to escort you from this place. It is not safe for you to be here alone."

"I frequently come here alone."

"Then the gods have been generous with you. I cannot imagine that they will do so forever. You will be captured and sold."

"What price do you think I would fetch?"

"By whom?"

"My captors. Their ransom price. Do you think it would be high?"

"Well . . . yes, I do. I think you would be worth at least a lakh of gold if your father is nobility."

"What makes you assume that he is?"

"Your bearing speaks it. A river rogue would see it in you immediately. A lakh."

She nodded. "Would you pay that for me?"

"I do not understand."

"You certainly do understand. Would you pay it for me?"

"I need to take you home."

Even for an Egyptian, this woman's forward manner was disconcerting to me. But of course I was intrigued and did not want her to leave.

Women. There you have it.

"I will allow you to take me home, Gold of Honor winner," she said. "No other man would be worthy of it."

Flattery. I sensed danger in it, knowing never to trust a woman's flattery. But she smiled so easily, so honestly, that I could not hold back a grin of my own.

"Is that it?" She was staring at my neck. I reached up and fingered the gold chain and nodded.

"May I handle it?" she asked.

I nodded. She ran her fingers over the chain. I tried to ignore my longing for them to move to my skin. I do not believe it was lust for her in my heart then. Longing, yes, but not lust. I was lonely. She was there. We were alone.

I gently pushed her fingers away. "I must take you home now. How far do you live from here?"

"Not far."

She walked in front of me, and I searched the corners and shadows as we walked, wary of anyone who may have been following her and waiting for the chance at ambush.

"Why do you come down here?" I asked.

"I like to sit and think and be alone and watch the Mother River for signs of my future. It appears she answered me and delivered a heroic warrior who commands the adulation of the kingdom."

I chuckled to myself, feeling more at ease by now.

"Is something funny?" she asked.

"What does a woman think about?"

She glanced back at me. "The same things as men, I would assume."

"Not likely. You do not want to know what men think about."

"Now I am curious. Tell me."

"We think of wine, women, and war."

"I like wine. I do not know war. I am a woman, so I suppose I think about them."

"Not like a man does. And be glad you know nothing of war."

"Do you have a woman, then?"

"I do not."

We walked a few more steps in silence.

"Has a man claimed you for marriage yet?" I ventured.

"A few have challenged for it. My father has not given his permission. He will give it to you, though. You wear the Gold of Honor."

I shook my head. "Egyptian women are very forward. You assume much."

"Do I? Describe the women in your land to me."

"The truth is that I did not know them very well. I came here as I reached the age of noticing them."

"And what do you say of Egyptian women?"

"That they are forward."

"It saves time, does it not? You find me pleasing to look at?"

I noticed movement ahead and studied the spot, then saw a cat run into an alley. "I do."

"I find you pleasing to look at as well. And you wear the Gold of Honor. You must have every wharf whore in Egypt tossing herself at you."

"I have not had the time."

"Nonsense. Soldiers have needs."

"The ones who wear this have no time for needs. Only training."

This went on for a while as we ascended the embankment from the river delta to the district where the nobility lived. We passed ever larger alabaster homes with exquisitely detailed paintings and carvings. I had provided some of them myself. We passed a lion I was particularly proud of, carved above the doorway of an estate owned by a fat old nobleman who had a fleet of fishing boats and spent his days getting fatter and more idle while his young wives pleasured him. He did not strike me as worthy of the lion carving.

"We continue to climb the hill. That means your father is important," I said.

"He is of minor importance. He does have money."

We arrived at the gate of her home, a large place I recognized from having worked on the estate across the road from it.

"I carved that eagle," I said, pointing up at the gateway image. She turned on me in surprise.

"That artist was you? We have often commented on the eagle above that gate. Wondering what slave forged it."

"I am no slave. I am highly skilled and highly paid." My foolish young man's arrogance is shameful for me to think of now.

She smiled again as she looked up at me.

"Caleb of the Kenazzites, you have much to boast of. I expect you will put some of those earnings to use and offer my father a fair bride price."

"You assume much."

"I assume you like to look at me and be in my company. To continue to do so, you must pay for it, and far more than the wages of a wharf whore."

She turned away and walked through the gate, which her servants closed behind her.

Women. There you have it.

We were married, of course. Yes, I paid the hefty bride price to her father, a shrewd little man who knew what she was worth but gave me just enough of a reduction in price to make it possible since he wanted to be able to tell the other nobles that it was his daughter married to the Gold of Honor winner.

Perhaps it was foolish. But I had to have her. That was that.

May Yahweh have mercy, that woman gave me joy. Her smile and speech made me drunk with love for her. I found myself looking for chances to skip my duties on the training pitches to be with her.

I went on long searches for various ornamentations for her hair or our home, spending all of my money on foolish woman's things.

The kitchen maids she brought to our home cooked well. My friends in the guard noticed my fuller waist and poked at me and teased me relentlessly.

I loved watching her in a crowd, especially at the banquets held in the palace by Thutmose, his excuse for drinking wine with his men. He was restless between campaign seasons and loved the release of an elaborate party that must have cost the treasury untold fortunes.

Debauchery. All of it. Yahweh, purge me of the memory. But not of my memories of her.

Much has faded in those years, but I remember her walking through the crowds of soldiers and wives and nobility and carrying herself with exquisite dignity, making eye contact with me in subtle ways as she moved among the tapestries and cushions and drank from the golden goblets of the palace banquet halls, gathering the gossip and ensuring my name was on the tongues of everyone who mattered.

And I would take her home late at night and feast on her. She gave of herself willingly and eagerly, and together we knew the joy that comes from union.

She was, as Moses used to say, the wife of my youth. I took great pleasure in her and did my best to treat her kindly, and when I was away for the campaign seasons on the frontier, expanding the empire of Thutmose, I ensured that my letters were filled with professions of my devotion to her and my desire for her.

Her name? I have not mentioned it, perhaps because it is difficult for me. This memory is among the most anguishing to recall, Othniel, for reasons that will soon become clear.

Maia. Her name was Maia.

You wish to know what happened to her.

I will tell you, and then we will move on with my tale, leaving the past to be the past. Do not ask me of it again.

Several years into our life together I was given orders to go to the north and oversee the security of the building of a new palace for the king. Construction pits were havens for thieves and robbers waiting to club and steal a laborer's wages. Slaves did not get wages, of course, but many of the workers were journeymen like me. If they were beaten and robbed by bandits, the palace would not be built in time. If the palace was not built in time, then the king would be displeased. And that would have been unthinkable.

The king declared that it would become our permanent home and desired for me to move my household there while the palace was being built. It would be located on the river island of Yebu far to the south, near the lands of Nubia and just downstream of the first cataract, traditionally the edge of our sunlit kingdom and bordering the barbaric and mysterious lands inland. Thutmose wished to spend a few years conquering farther south and exploring for more gold and jewel mines. This would be the base from which he could campaign for weeks and then afterward return to his harem and banquet hall to rest.

At this same time, Maia became large with child and gave birth to a boy.

I see the boy now. Curly, dark hair right from his first day. He loved to play with my Gold of Honor when it dangled from my neck, and touch my nose and chin whenever I held him. We named him Ramose. I adored him like nothing I had ever been given. My heart swelled for him and his beautiful mother, my joy enhanced because I had been permitted to take them with me to the new home.

We packed our modest home quickly after his birth, for we were to depart before the end of the week with the next caravan. We had slave women and a wet nurse for the boy. He screamed for his mother steadily through the entire process of loading our things into the oxcarts, and when Maia would tend to him, he would scream for me, then the wet nurse, then a slave woman, then Maia again, and it all went on so robustly that I nearly lost my sanity. Children do not care about a man's plans!

Finally we departed our home. I was eager to move on from Memphis to experience new adventures. I had a young man's wanderlust. Maia was spirited as well; she had never seen the lands outside of the city. Women had no need to travel anywhere but the markets and the temples.

"What kinds of men are the bandits?" she asked me as we rode away from the city. Ramose had fallen asleep, having exhausted all of his pleas.

"Some are workers who lost their trade and are desperate. Others are profiteers who organize wandering vagabonds into parties. The rest are nomads who strike from the desert."

"Will we be safe?"

"Yes," I answered. These types of questions had been asked of me many times in the past few days. Maia was like a child in her eagerness to experience this adventure.

I went for a walk after the fire was made. Maia oversaw the servants while they made bread and began roasting the desert hare we had snared that afternoon.

I climbed a slope nearby to admire the desert evening, to where the watchmen had taken up position. A ribbon of pink cloud hung in the west, dark purple in the east. The moon was a thin sliver. I tried to spot the point where it turned sharply again, but it was too far in the distance.

The guard on the first watch was one of my own.

"Do you have enough water for the night?" I asked him.

He nodded respectfully. "I was supplied, sir."

"I will have some of the hare brought up for you to eat."

"I am grateful, sir."

"This is a dangerous land."

He nodded, looking unsure of how to have a casual conversation with me. I noticed his eyes flickering from me to the edge of the wadi down below us.

"We campaigned here years ago. The savages were hard men. They will fight to the death if we encounter them."

"I will be ready, sir."

I clapped him on the shoulder and watched the sunset in silence with him. I searched every shadow, every crevice, every dark corner for movement.

Maia and my son were sitting next to the well. I remember that she was wrapping him in fresh cloths, and I could hear his cries piercing the camp even from where I stood.

My back was to the watchman. It was the mistake I would regret forever.

I heard the swish of his tunic as he leaped for me, and it was the only thing that saved my life. I did not even turn; instead I jumped forward desperately to avoid the blow I could feel coming, and the dagger he carried missed the top of my back where he swung it down but sliced into the flesh of my ribs, biting deep and hot. I caught myself with my hands and pushed off, rolling to my left, this time facing up at him and seeing him striking downward with the dagger, this time at my chest.

All I could do was raise my hand, and the blade punctured straight through my palm, buried to the hilt in my hand.

I punched him in the face because he was off-balance from the strike. He missed my second swing and had his knees pinned against my torso to keep his profile low. He had been trained well. I had trained him.

I shoved my elbow into his neck to keep his face up and tried to withdraw the dagger still stuck in my palm, but he forced the arm down and pulled it out himself, swinging the blade at my neck.

I felt it slice deep into the muscles near my spine, but Yahweh spared me then, I do not know how, and it missed my breathing pipe and was only flesh-deep.

It was the movement I needed to regain my balance. I kicked my left leg high and hooked my knee around his neck, jerking downward until I had his face in the sand. I grappled for a nearby rock, raised it up and struck him on the jaw, breaking it with a soft crunch. In hate, I struck him again on the temple and tore away a piece of flesh, exposing his skull and spraying blood on my arm. And I only wanted to hit him again and again until that skull was crushed into pulp and my rage was satisfied.

I realized in that moment that this was not a random attack from a guard who had been paid to assassinate me but the beginning of a larger raid, for as I looked up I saw the hordes of Amalekites rising over the edge of the wadi and racing for our camp.

I had been the signal, I knew in an instant. The watchman knew I would come to check on him, and the chieftain of the Amalekites would be watching for him to attack me on this hill and then send his men in a flood to massacre us.

There were at least a thousand Amalekites attacking us. The largest army by far I had ever seen them assemble. We had but one hundred men, enough to hold off the usual bandit raids that occurred on the trade routes, but not nearly enough for the battle facing us.

Their chieftain was in the front. He had skulls dangling from his saddle, and I could hear them clacking against each other as he rode a war camel and cried out in an unearthly, guttural battle cry. Like all of their kind, his skin was splotched with hideous tattoos and carvings on his flesh. He had foot soldiers with pikes and scimitars, but those were not the weapons I saw that made me catch my breath in fright.

In front, tearing across the sand in golden blurs, were two black-maned lions.

Trained hunting lions were common to the royalty of Egypt. I had been with Pharaoh Thutmose when he had used them to run down gazelle in the desert. Raised from birth, they could be tamed. But you were never to give them man-flesh. Once they tasted it and realized how soft and tender and available it was, they turned on their masters violently. Thutmose had tried to use them in war once; the lions ate their handlers as soon as they were set loose.

But the Amalekites kept them chained and fed them man-flesh until their appetites craved only that. Then before a raid, they starved them for days. When it was time to attack, the lions somehow knew that the easiest flesh would be what their masters directed them to, and their hunger made them relentless killers.

Their heads hung low with their breath coming out in grunts, the hunting charge, as they rushed for the camp.

Amalekites were child sacrificers and raised their young to know only pillage and rape and destruction. They drank the blood of dead enemies to appease their war gods. They were the most wicked people ever to exist, more animal than man.

And I knew, even then, as I watched the barbarians with their war camels thundering over the sand toward our camp, the starving lions running the fastest in the front, that I was going to lose all that I cared about in this life.

I stood, the gashes from the dagger bleeding and biting me in pain, and stumbled down the hill toward Maia and the boy. My feet felt as heavy as baking stones.

"Maia! Maia!"

She looked up and saw me. Then she looked where I was pointing as I ran to her. She raised her hand to her mouth in terror.

I do not know what I thought I could do. We had soldiers, but they were outnumbered so vastly. My mind became confused as I ran. Where had they come from? How had they assembled so many so quickly? Was there a city of theirs nearby that we did not know of?

Maia snatched up Ramose, who was screaming as shrilly as before, and her instinct was to run to me. Screams and shouts came from the camp.

"To arms! Create a line!"

I was a good commander. I had chosen our camping ground well, on a hilltop where it could be defended from a raid such as this one. But again, there were too many, and we had no walls to protect us.

I glanced at the attackers. One of the lions had peeled away from the other when it spotted Maia running.

"Here, here!" I shouted as loud as I could, waving my arms at the lion. "To me! To me!"

The lion paid no attention to me but was focused only on the small woman running with her shrieking bundle.

It was the moment of ultimate helplessness. The power of my sword or the aim of my bow had abandoned me, and I was a shattered man even before I saw the animal leap into the air with its paws raised, its throat releasing the roar that still finds me in the darkest nights.

Every man was slaughtered but me. All the women who had been with us were raped and carried off for enslavement.

I lived only because they thought I was dead.

I threw myself at the lion as it was destroying my world and tried to get it to consume me as well. I beat it with stones and shoved my hands into its mouth to get it away from the bodies of my wife and son, but it would not release from them. You cannot imagine the power of those creatures.

I had no thought to rally my soldiers. They were dead men. I did not care. I only saw the fur of the creature covered in the blood of my family.

The lion finally did turn to me and swiped me with its powerful paw as I tried to put my hands into its mouth. It struck me on my head with the force of a war axe and sent me into oblivion, and I was swallowed in darkness.

I had the dream again.

A river of blood and a black ship that sailed through it. The descent into ever-deeper waters. The sounds and images of terror. I struggled to raise my arms and swim through it, but did not feel resistance like liquid normally provides. Only heaviness. Imprisonment. A dungeon of blood and cold fire.

The black ship sailed on, and I with it.

I awoke late that night. My vision was blurred as I gazed up at the stars. With every heartbeat I could feel bludgeons of pain in my head. Two thoughts emerged in the fog of my mind. One was that the cruel gods had preserved my life. The second was that Maia and Ramose were gone forever. Only a blood-soaked patch of earth remained.

I sat up. My throat burned for water, but I had no will anymore. No desire to even stand and search for the drink that would sustain me. I only wanted death.

"May Seth take you, Ra!" I shouted at the sky. The worst curse in Egypt, beseeching the foul god to have victory over the divine sun.

I gained my feet and wandered into the camp, looking for a blade to fall on. It was empty. Completely empty. No people. Empty tents flapped in the desert breeze. No other sounds.

The gore of the lion kills was everywhere, as was the gore of the Amalekites. I saw fragments of humans. That was all.

The Amalekites had taken all the weapons. I looked for anything sharp to gash myself with so that I would bleed out for good this time, but there was nothing.

Finally I was able to pull out a tent peg and walked back to where my wife and son had been devoured. I held it to my neck, feeling the jagged prick of bronze against my flesh, and took a deep breath.

One hard thrust and I would be with them in the underworld. We would stand before Osiris together and mock Ammit as he stood in the corner of the chamber waiting to consume our hearts. But the scale of Osiris would that our hearts were lighter than his feather and we would be permitted to pass into light.

I held it, ready. My muscles tensed.

And I could not do it. My beloved would go unavenged.

In this life, their killers walked the earth. I closed a portion of my soul forever as I sat there on the sand under the stars. In its place, an obsession was born. A desire to kill every single Amalekite I would ever encounter.

Hebrews and Amalekites are blood enemies, Othniel. Countless deaths of our people by their hand. As you hear my story, so there were and are many more who can testify of worse. Children murdered, women raped and killed.

For generations to come, our heroes will be those who have

killed the most Amalekites. They will have tales written of them and songs composed of their deeds.

But in that moment, I cared nothing for Hebrews. I only wanted to fill the hole in me with Amalekite blood.

The king changed his mind about the palace. It was eventually built, and I assume it was used by other kings, but Thutmose never went there while I knew him. It was his right. He was the king. The affairs of his kingdom made my life trivial. What is the loss of one woman and child to a soldier?

I returned to Memphis a hollow man.

I flung myself at the enemy in the desert relentlessly. I volunteered for every dangerous mission and even resorted to begging Amalekites and Nubians or whoever we were fighting to slice at my neck, but my rage to kill them always overcame the gesture and I lived on.

Praises came. Adulation was mine. The nectar of my soul was the admiration of crowds and I drank it in. And I feasted on hate. I went for long runs in the desert at night, wearing nothing but my sword and sheath on my back and trying to blister and tear my feet because I needed to feel something, something that could satisfy the emptiness in my chest.

PART II

— 11 —

Defending the Widow

Othniel watched his uncle. The old man was staring at the ground. He grieved for him. To see one's wife and son perish in such a way was . . .

He sighed. No more of this.

Othniel shuddered in the cold. Runoff had leaked into the tent and dampened his back, putting him in a foul mood, as he had to strip off his tunic and dry it next to the fire. He did not mind being wet, but he hated being cold and wet.

"All this talk of the desert is making me miss it," Caleb huffed. "One thing I can promise you is that we never had trouble staying dry, and we never had to delay an attack because of the rain."

Caleb fell silent and closed his eyes. Othniel let him take his breaths in peace.

"Uncle, we can be done. There is nothing more for it today. You need your rest."

Caleb shook his head. "You must be wondering when Moses will come into my story."

Othniel said nothing. It was precisely what he had been wondering, but he did not wish to appear overly eager.

Caleb stared ahead now, his eyes vacant. "What do you remember of Moses?"

"Not much, Uncle. Vague glimpses in my mind's eye of him. I remember his beard and how white it was. White like the ice on a northern lake."

Caleb chuckled. "You are the poet, aren't you?"

"I do not presume."

"You are too modest. Moses was that way as well. Never thought he could weave his words to move men."

"You can do the same, Uncle."

"Not like him. Although he did not say much when I first saw him."

Othniel waited patiently. It was true that he only knew Moses from a distance, glimpses of the white beard as he stood before the assembly, his rich voice resonating across the rocks and bramble of the wilderness. Born of the generation that came after the departure from Egypt, Othniel knew he was a different breed than that of his parents—a fickle, heartless, spineless puddle of humanity that saw the wonders of Yahweh with their own eyes and yet turned from them.

"Let's go for a walk along the perimeter."

"Uncle, we checked the perimeter a couple of hours ago. The officers have it in hand."

"We shall check the perimeter anyway. There should never be an hour of your life where you are not checking your perimeters."

"Will you always speak in riddles and lessons?"

"Yes."

Leaving the tent, Othniel fell in behind Caleb as he made his way through the thicket. A path had finally been worn down from soldiers walking from one location in the camp to another, and Othniel was grateful that Caleb was not going to have to force his legs through the undergrowth. The old man did not cry out in pain, but his face was a constant grimace whenever he had to walk through thickets. The motion of it was brutal to his knees.

Caleb scowled as they passed troops moving along the same path as them. In the light of day, his men could easily tell that it was him. He was the only one in the army with a walking stick. They gave him a wide berth. One soldier pitched himself off the path into the bushes when he caught Caleb's eye. It made Othniel think of something the training masters always shouted on the drilling fields. *"Generals should not know your name for any reason other than your being a hero. If they know you from anything else, go ahead and throw yourself at the enemy and pray he kills you before the general does."*

Ahead was the clearing with the cooking tents. The wood being soaking wet, the smoke was thick and billowing through the forest, creating a heavy fog. The smell of roasting meat made Othniel's stomach tighten.

"I am hungry," Caleb said, and Othniel could have rejoiced. Caleb turned aside from the path and strode into the nearest cook tent. Women made the meals for the army, and they bowed low to the ground as he approached.

"Who is your husband?" he asked an older woman.

"I am the widow of Shamez the Miridite, my lord."

"I knew him. A good man. You are cared for?"

"Yes, my lord."

"What is the best thing that you make?"

"Fig cakes, my lord. They are the best in the land."

"I desire for you to prove that to me."

Caleb sat down and crossed his legs with effort. Othniel sat beside him while the old widow frantically summoned her maids to help her prepare the cakes.

"I do so love a fig cake," Caleb said with a sigh.

"You were going to tell me about Moses, Uncle."

Caleb scowled. "You have worn me out already, boy. I will get to Moses in my time."

It was not long before the rumor that the great general was in this part of the camp spread around the mountainside, and already the line was beginning to form outside of the tent. Commanders were coming for instructions, bringing him disputes to resolve, punishments to hand out, scouting reports, the overwhelming problems that faced any army of this size, especially one caught in the highlands of an unknown land during a storm that would be written about for decades to come.

A few voices called out for Caleb, and the old man shook his head. "Tell them I will do absolutely nothing until I have eaten the best fig cakes in the land. Tell them to remove their mouths from their mothers' breasts and use them to order their men to their proper courses. I will not be around forever to be their handmaiden."

"You wish for me to tell them exactly that, Uncle?" Othniel asked, suppressing his grin.

"Exactly that."

Othniel walked over and poked his head out of the tent. He blinked against the rain and made out over a dozen figures huddled under their cloaks. "The general said to remove your mouths from your mothers' breasts and use them to give orders to your men instead. Solve your problems on your own. He will not be around forever to be your handmaiden."

From inside the tent, Caleb said, "Never mind. Tell them I will live forever and bury all of them and their sons."

Othniel had to smile at this. So the old man had heard the rumors in the camp that he had struck a deal with Yahweh to live forever to torment his soldiers. This generation had never seen a truly old man, one who had reached his ninth decade, apart from Moses, Joshua, and Caleb. Moses had gone on to Yahweh in glory. Joshua still presided over their lands. Caleb still attacked walled cities. Every single one of their parents and grandparents had perished in the wilderness. It was not unreasonable for them to believe that Caleb might live forever.

Othniel relayed the message, and the men walked away grumbling.

Caleb's voice, sudden and piercingly loud, resonated through the storm. "If I look through that tent flap and see any of you, I will decide that those are my volunteers to be the first troops through the breach."

There were some stouthearted men in that group. Othniel recognized a few of them. But no one ever wanted to be the first ones through a breach. The sound of their sandals scuffling through the forest receded.

Othniel returned to Caleb's side. The cooking fire had produced its coals when they had arrived, so the widow's fig cakes, mashed and cut, were already roasting. Othniel could not prevent himself from staring at them with raw desire.

Soon the old woman scooped them up with her cooking blade and flipped one of them to the goatskin eating mat spread before Caleb.

He eyed it skeptically. "It does not look like the greatest fig cake in the land, old mother."

The woman's wrinkled face twisted in a scowl at first; then

her eye twinkled. "You have judged the beauty of the bride by her veil. Peer under it and discover her delights."

Caleb chuckled. "I enjoy your company, old mother. However your fig cake tastes, I desire for you to become my cook."

"It would be my pleasure to serve you, my lord. I would bring my maidens."

"You may."

Caleb prodded at the cake with his finger before raising it to his lips. He sucked on it with his eyes closed. He did not move for a while, and then he opened his eyes and looked at the old woman. "It is the second greatest fig cake in the land. Only my wife made them better."

The widow's expression softened. "If that is my only comparison, my lord, I will accept it. Her gentleness and kindness was known everywhere. I can only assume that her cooking matched it."

Caleb's own face fell a bit as he heard this. He paused before taking another bite of the cake. The old woman brought one to Othniel, and although he had never known his aunt's cooking, it was hard to imagine anything better than this.

The two of them ate in silence. The tent they sat in had a large gap between the main post and the lashing, allowing spurts of rain inside with every strong gust of wind.

"Your tent was not tied down properly," Caleb said.

"We had to do it on our own and lacked the strength to tie it securely, my lord."

Caleb stopped eating and grew very still. "You built your own tent? In my army a widow never builds her own tent. I will run these men so hard that they will want to die!" He beat his fist savagely on the ground and glared at Othniel. "Assemble every man in this camp! Every one of them!"

"Uncle, the storm—"

"Assemble them! Now!"

Othniel did not argue further but walked outside and shouted, "Assemble on me, every man and officer! Orders of the general!"

It took half an hour for everyone to believe that this was not some sort of jest and to emerge from their various tents and shelters. Othniel counted a battalion's worth of men, not anywhere near their entire army. But it would have been a fool's errand to assemble all the camps on the mountain during a siege when the enemy was looking for an opportunity for a counterattack.

No, this camp would do. Each battalion had its own encampment. Word would spread from this one to the others quickly. Caleb could make his point here.

When they were assembled, Caleb, who had been standing in the rain watching them, raised his voice.

"It has come to my attention that this widow, the wife of a brave man who was killing pagans before all of you were able to feed yourselves, had to tie down her own cooking tent. A hundred strong men all around her, and a feeble old woman and her handmaids pitched their own tent in this storm." Caleb spat at the feet of one of the men, and without anyone seeing it coming, his walking stick lashed out and struck the man on the side of the head, splitting open his flesh and sending a spurt of blood across the face of the man next to him. The gashed man staggered backward and collapsed, groaning.

Caleb spun and struck the next man in his line of sight, sending him reeling with a blow to the shoulder. Everyone watched, stunned. No one rendered aid to the wounded men.

"I am Caleb, the son of Jephunneh the Kenazzite! I saw the hand of Yahweh heavy against the Egyptians! I saw his hand strike the oceans and toss them onto dry land. I was there when the Nile turned to blood. I was there when fire fell from heaven and consumed the desert. And after decades of walking his warpath, I know that there are few things he hates more than the widow neglected!"

He moved into a fighting position and beckoned to Othniel, "Nephew, bring me my sword, for I will strike down every one of these men, and may the adversary devour them in Sheol."

Othniel forced himself to move to obey the orders. The men were soaking wet from the rain, but their shivering and gasping was not caused by the weather.

Caleb hobbled forward with his sword and staff to the next man in the line. The soldier, an officer, immediately broke.

"War chief, forgive us! We did not know!"

"You are an officer in my army! You need to know the fate of every locust that makes its home among us; how much more the widows who cook your meals?"

Caleb swung the staff even as he spoke, and the man's jaw shattered with a sickening crack. His screams of pain were like a dog with a broken leg. No one knew whether to try to move to stop the old man, who had become a raging bull. As he moved to the next one in line, the cries for mercy rose up. They were afraid to break ranks and risk angering him further, yet were too frightened for their lives not to speak up.

Caleb paused as he stared at the next officer. It finally occurred to Othniel that Caleb was targeting officers. The leaders of the men who should have known better.

Caleb's expression was flooded with cold fury, enhanced by the streaks of water running from his mangy white hair. His voice rose again above the rain. "Do you all wish to live?"

"Yes! In the name of Yahweh, yes!" came the cries.

"Will you have mercy on the widow from this day forward?" Caleb roared again.

"For the love of our land, we will! In Yahweh's name, have mercy!"

Caleb cut them off with his upraised staff. "I want every man to run to the bottom of this hill as fast as his legs can carry him and pick up the heaviest rock he can carry. Then I want him to bring that rock to me, and to keep doing it until he has vomited out his last three meals and I feel as though he has sufficiently apologized to this widow! The rocks will be made into a memorial for her husband, Shamez the Miridite, who was more of a man in his smallest finger than all of you and your generations before you!"

The soldiers let that settle in their spirits. No one made a sound.

Caleb continued. "You will then take down all your own shelters and stack them in the forest, and for the rest of this campaign you will see no covering for your heads and will sleep no peaceful night."

This was devastating enough, but Caleb saved the worst for last. His anger had not yet abated; his eyes flashed with deadly rage.

"Your battalion will fight no longer in this siege. You will now be the women of my army! You will cook for your husbands who will be fighting. You will also cook for the women who normally cook for you. You will have the duties of women but suffer the hardships of men. May the Lord strike me down if by this time tomorrow you are not all crying for death in your shame!"

It was the ultimate punishment, and Othniel shuddered as he considered it. Doing the tasks of women when there was a battle raging? Not being a part of the plunder of a city? The songs sung and tales told of the cowardice of a battalion would live forever. The legacy would be eternally tainted. Generations from now, men would hang their heads in shame when they were assigned to such a unit, to be taunted by their fellows assigned to nobler stock. The tribes of every man would be noted and shamed as well. Fathers would wear sackcloth and mourn the lost manhood of their sons.

All of these thoughts descended upon the battalion. Better to have all died in battle against the enemy than this.

Caleb let them ponder it all in their own time. He said nothing for a while, then in a softer tone said, "If you can build this widow her memorial before the sun sets, and every stone is no less than one cubit—and reaches the height of ten cubits—I will consider letting you fight in the siege."

Every back stiffened with resolve. They looked to Othniel like eager boys desperate to gain back their manhood.

"Begin!" Caleb said, dismissing them.

There was a mass scramble of bodies down the mountainside, until eventually they all disappeared into the forest.

Othniel moved next to Caleb. "I have never seen you so angry, Uncle," he said quietly.

"I have rarely been so. It is as though they have learned nothing of the ways of Yahweh."

"You must continue to be their teacher."

Caleb sighed, returned to the tent and sat down facing his now-cold fig cakes. The elderly widow approached cautiously.

"You do me too much honor, my lord. A worthless old woman like myself should not be responsible for sullying the reputations of a thousand men for generations."

Caleb paused in his eating and gazed at her. His eyes softened, and he leaned forward and clasped her hands in his own.

"Good lady, the reputations of a million men are worth nothing when compared to a single command from Yahweh. Many of the songs of victory that we sing are about the Lord our protector. None need his protection like the widow, and he joyfully defends her."

The woman lowered her face, and a tear trickled down her cheek. Her maids could be heard sniffling as well.

Caleb finished his fig cake, then gestured for Othniel to follow him back outside. Othniel thought about protesting this for the sake of the old man's health, so that the continued walks in the weather did not give him the coughing sickness that so frequently killed the elderly, but he knew it was of no use.

As they departed, the first of the soldiers, lugging a stone on his back that weighed as much as he did, was making his way to the spot Caleb had designated for the memorial. The man dropped the rock, and it sank a handbreadth into the mud. It seemed to occur to him anew just how long and arduous this task would be. But he nodded to Caleb, his eyes respectfully downcast, and trotted back down the hillside.

"Bring him to me," Caleb said, and Othniel caught up with the man and summoned him. When he was standing before his general, he kept his eyes locked down at his feet and his hands clasped behind his back.

"Your name, soldier?" Caleb asked.

"Heliphet, son of Japhtha, my lord. But I have shamed that name and will no longer bear it."

"How have you shamed it?"

"By ignoring the widow's plight. By eating her food and not thinking to care for her. I desire to die with honor in the building of this memorial, my lord, if you would grant me even that small attempt to spare my son my fate."

The young soldier was clearly strong, being the first one back with his rock, and he had a sincerity in his appearance that Othniel found impressive.

"You have a wife and son?"

"A wife of four years. One son, another child on the way."

"Where is she?"

"She keeps my tent farther down the ridge."

"You bring a pregnant woman on campaign?"

"My lord . . . she is no ordinary pregnant woman. She would have been harder on my indiscretion than even you have been."

Caleb smiled. "That is good. A man can rally from his fate with the help of a strong woman. Continue your task, and your honor will be restored."

Heliphet could not hide his grin as he bowed and ran back down the mountain.

Caleb walked through the forest until they came to a ledge of rock that stood above the treetops banking down the hillside. Just visible through the low-hanging clouds was the streambed at the base of the hill where the battalion was gathering rocks. They could make them out as they worked, struggling to carry the weight, slipping on the wet undergrowth.

"Watching labor like this reminds me of those days," Caleb said.

"Which days, Uncle?"

"Egypt. Our people under the yoke of Pharaoh. They are nothing alike, of course. The training and instructing of soldiers is not the same as our people in bondage. Being worked to death in the quarries to build idols. Having the flesh torn from our backs and the backs of our children by the spiked whips of their overseers. None of that is comparable to a bunch of troops needing their thick skulls cracked."

Othniel marveled again at how Caleb referred to the Hebrews as "our people." But he did not press him. More would come in time.

Soon enough, Caleb said, "I live with the guilt of it, you know."

"The guilt of what, Uncle?"

"I was never a slave. The Egyptians made me a wealthy man. I knew nothing but glory and honor in their courts. What right do I have to lead Yahweh's people?"

"Joshua leads the people, Uncle," Othniel said delicately.

Caleb seemed relieved to be reminded of this.

"That is true. The right man leads them."

"But you lead us."

They watched the battalion struggle for a while longer, and then Othniel prevailed upon Caleb to return to his tent. Caleb reluctantly complied, suddenly seeming his age once more. He gasped as he followed Othniel back to his tent, where he took his time stripping the wet garments from his frame to dry them on the fire rack.

Caleb reclined on the cushions, his bare torso wrinkled and scarred but still full of muscle. Othniel admired him, silently praying to Yahweh that his own torso would look so good in the decades ahead.

Caleb went still and silent so quickly that Othniel thought his uncle had fallen asleep. He was about to creep out of the tent when the old man's voice rang out.

"You asked me about Moses."

"Yes, Uncle."

"Very well. It is time that he enters the story."

— 12 —

The Two Hebrews

Before we go further, you must know some things about the Egyptian rulers and why Yahweh struck the king in the manner he did.

The king of Egypt was not known by the title of pharaoh until recent times. The name means *Great House*, for he is seen as the personification of his kingdom. You must understand: the king is Egypt, and Egypt is the king. His divinity is beyond question to the common people.

The kings of Egypt in our time are very different from the kings who greeted Abraham and Joseph. In Abraham's day, the king was kept in a cloud of comfort far away from the people. Nearly all of his subjects never saw him in person, including many who worked in his own palace. It was thought to be far beneath the dignity of the god-man to be seen among us mortals.

That changed after the Hyksos invaded and their golden kingdom was razed to the sand and their women impregnated with the seed of barbarians. In their long exile from their river paradise, the native Egyptians realized their new dynasties must become warriors and lead their regiments on the battlefield. They must perfect their skills with spear and lance, bow and chariot. They must be master tacticians and be schooled in the fighting arts, as well as the governmental and administrative functions. Incompetence among advisors is intolerable and swiftly dealt with. This is how Moses was raised, and many of his skills from that time delivered us during our hard years in the desert. Mine as well, if I may be so bold.

Thutmose III, the pharaoh of the events I am telling you about, the king who was once the young ruler I saved from the Amalekites, was of the line descended from Kamose and Ahmose. They were the greatest kings of the age, and Thutmose III spent his entire life trying to live up to them. Perhaps part of his stubbornness during the plagues Yahweh sent us came from his refusal to appear weak in his line.

I once read the *stelae* written for Kamose about his exploits. The Egyptians are not known for modesty, but the kernels of truth I picked out were remarkable. He came from the south and attacked the Hyksos armies with astounding valor and tenacity, driving the shepherd kings out of the land and establishing the rule of the Egyptian race once more over their land. Kamose's son, Ahmose, extended his father's legacy and succeeded in destroying the Hyksos threat forever. It was this line of kings that Thutmose was well aware of, and why the thought of letting another Semitic people like the Hebrews escape was unthinkable.

I confess that my heart still aches when I think of him. I know these words could have me stoned by the priests, who see the adversary of Yahweh as all that is evil. They are right, of course. He rots in Sheol and rightfully so.

But he was a great warrior. His men loved him, as did I when I knew him. He could have been such a noble king. He could have listened to the voice of Yahweh through Moses and allowed the Hebrews to leave in peace, and perhaps his name would be written in our records favorably, much like the pharaoh who appointed Joseph head of his kingdom.

We shared a chariot together in the ferocity of battle. We slew the Amalekites and the Amorites side by side. I was nothing compared to him in status, but he loved fighting with his men and always treated me with respect. Such experiences cannot be easily forgotten.

You must remember that I had very little dealings with the Hebrews. They lived in Goshen, far to the north of where I served in Pharaoh's guards in greater Thebes, where the cities of Luxor and Karnak merged into one colossal, sprawling city. The journey down the Nile by boat to Goshen took seven days with a good captain, ten and the risk of your life with a bad one.

They slaved in the building of the cities Raamses and Pithon. Egypt was a large kingdom, and the king had many slaves. The Hebrews were kept to the north, where they could not rise up among the Egyptians in the more valuable cities and cause trouble.

During those later years, after I had been in Egypt for seventeen summers, the king started spending his time in Memphis, which was closer to Goshen than Thebes. He wanted to be centrally located to strike out at Canaan or the western trade routes to the Red Sea if necessary.

The kings were divine in the eyes of the people and supposedly able to defeat Egypt's enemies with one prayer to their brother Ra, the sun god, or to Horus, the god of victory and armies and the wind. Horus could conjure up the great khamsin from the west and wipe out any threats.

It was fortunate for Moses, then, that during the days of pleading the case of our people, he had ready access to Pharaoh in the palace of Memphis and could move between Goshen and Memphis with the ease of a few days' journey.

Now to Moses.

The best place for me to introduce you to Moses is to tell you what was told to me shortly after he arrived back in Egypt after forty years away. My first encounter with him was a memorable one, as it was for all who witnessed the events that were to come, and I will tell it to you soon enough, but first you must hear about the origins of the old dust-covered man who stood before us in the clean alabaster courts of the most powerful king on earth, demanding that his people be released from their bondage.

As I left the meeting hall where Pharaoh received his audiences, unnerved by what I had witnessed, I pulled aside an elderly eunuch I had befriended named Lanath. He had always been kind to me, and I to him. I brought him back gifts and wares from my campaigns, and he provided me with information about what was happening in the court of the king. I asked Lanath about this man Moses, and why some of the older generation knew of him. Over his favorite wine, this is what Lanath told me.

Moses grew up the scion of Pharaoh's daughter and a possible heir to the Divine Throne of Ra. A Hebrew, the lowliest of those in all of Egypt, the heir to the Serpent Flail? It is an impossible tale if I did not know the truth of it.

They said she found him in the waters of Mother Nile, in a river reed basket sent by the river goddess Hapi. She consulted with the priests of Hapi and Osiris, and it was determined that such a sign could not be ignored. The child was special and had a god's destiny, that much was certain.

Not much is known of his life before he fled from Egypt. Moses did not write of it, and I never heard him speak of it. But Lanath said that he grew in stature and favor among the Egyptian royalty. He became skilled as a warrior, as well as in the literary arts. He was popular with the people, and his name became renowned.

And yet his heart was stirred for his people. The Hebrews were slaves and suffering under hardship like we cannot imagine.

Moses was gone for forty years. No one knew what had happened to him. Most of those who remembered him were dead or as old as he was. We know that he was in Midian, of course, and that he had married. You know of the bush that burned, which commanded him to return to Egypt. Moses himself told me about it, but more on that later.

All of that being said, it began when Moses came to the meeting hall at the palace of Memphis with his brother Aaron, requesting an audience with Pharaoh like the rest of the foreigners who came to pay obeisance or plead their cause. Pharaoh took these meetings frequently; he liked to hear what was happening outside the borders of the kingdom with his own ears. His spies were everywhere, but they could be bought, and he never knew what was trustworthy information.

They had waited for a month for their audience with Pharaoh. I was posted on duty in the court when Moses entered with Aaron, and what I noticed first was how unkempt they both appeared. Their garments had not been cleaned in many a fortnight and were caked with sand and tattered like those of a shepherd.

Oddly, he did not open his mouth to speak, but it was his brother who spoke on his behalf. Moses stood silently, his staff in his hand, and watched Pharaoh's face as Aaron spoke the word he was compelled to deliver. I thought nothing of them when they passed me to go before the king. Just another cluster of rabble from beyond the desert and not worth my attention.

I had recently been named to the palace guard. It was the highest honor a soldier could have . . . and the dullest. The king seemed to know this and eased the burden by training with us personally in the courtyard and training pitches. To pass the time I continued working on the design of the temple of Horus. Construction still had not begun, even all these years later, because the king had diverted the treasure away from funding the temple into building his army.

We did not complain. The Red Scorpions were the tip of the blade for Egypt, and the more we conquered the happier we were. We fought, we won, we lived. And now at last the greatest danger many of us faced was whether a viper had slithered into the gilded halls.

The columns of the palace were decorated with the colorful banners and drapes of the upcoming festival of Osiris. A hundred nobles reclined in the hall on their couches, fanned by slaves. Marble floors, marble statuettes, gold- and silver-plated ornaments. The gods of the pantheon looked down at us from their painted walls. Hippos. Vultures. Hawks. Serpents. The torches made the sculptures appear to coil and writhe. Paintings from the Book of the Dead covered every space, the Egyptian obsession with death prominent. One such image was a heart being torn from the chest of a Hyksos ruler and devoured by Memet the crocodile god.

It was a room designed to impress its visitors. The decadence and wealth of the kingdom of the ages for all to see.

Pharaoh himself sat on the golden throne, the red-and-white colors of upper and lower Egypt festooned about it. His crown was the crown of red and white. His flail a red cobra, his scepter a white hawk. Slaves lay at his feet with their faces pressed to the marble, awaiting his desire to stand. These were not common slaves but the former nobles of other kingdoms who were sentenced to be his footstools. He would walk across their backs out of the hall when he decided to depart, with them scrambling around each other to ensure his feet trod upon their flesh like Egypt trod upon its conquered nations.

Amidst all of this show of wealth and power were the two figures of Moses and Aaron, who stood before the god-king like red ants might stand before a lion.

And yet they were refusing to prostrate themselves. They did not touch their foreheads to the ground. Did not grovel before him as supplicants, but kept their backs stiffened.

This was an outrage to us, the ultimate insult. Pharaoh was Egypt itself, the personification of the glory of our people, for by that time I had become fully one of them. I and the other guards screamed at them to pay the proper respect, yet they seemed impervious to the commands.

I moved up close and reached out to grasp his arm to force him to his knees, and he turned his head to look at me.

I was frozen. No muscle of mine could move, so enraptured I was in his stare.

I had patrolled the six regions in a single month. I had hunted crocodiles with my sword to cut my own shield and armor skins. I had slain Bedouin warlords and Amalekite chieftains and drunk wine over their corpses.

But that stare. I knew even then, and from that moment on, that he had seen . . . something. Something eternal and powerful, something I had never known, and all of this I took in one glance from him.

The eyes made me think of Seth. I had carved an idol of him once and had found it so lifelike and disturbing that I vowed never to carve another one, so wary I was of bringing that god even into my mind. This man was the living embodiment of that idol, I knew it in an instant. Was he Seth himself?

I stepped back, stunned to silence.

Moses glared directly at Pharaoh. Aaron, who appeared to be his mouthpiece, stepped forward. His beard, caked with the fine sand of the desert, quivered as he spoke in the Egyptian tongue.

"We have come from the wild lands of the east," Aaron began, "where we have been before Yahweh our God. We wish to sacrifice to him with our people, Israel. Yahweh, the God of Israel, says to Pharaoh, 'Let my people go, that they may hold a feast to me in the wilderness.'"

It was such an odd statement, and so presumptuous that no one moved or answered for a long moment. The priests, sensing their presence would be requested because a foreign god had been mentioned, edged closer to the throne of Pharaoh.

We all watched his face, expecting him to respond to this outrageous violation of protocol when addressing him.

The king himself was now approaching his fiftieth year. His chest was broad and muscled under his garments, a chest that had been filled out by pulling the great gold-plated war bow since his youth.

He was the mighty Thutmose, the third of that name, conqueror of realms. I had fought with him. I had ridden in his very war chariot as his lancer. For twelve of the seventeen years since he had ascended the Serpent Throne without a regent I had been there alongside him as we slaughtered the barbarians of the west and east and explored up to the third cataract of the Nile. When he chose to speak, it was always with the certain clarity that his words were final and that he was not interested in discussing anything.

And so I could not have been more shocked at what I witnessed next.

When Pharaoh was holding court he wore all the elaborate garments and face paints to make him look more like a statue than a man. Behind his painted face, his emotions hidden under the kohl, Pharaoh said, "You are Moses, correct?"

The gray-haired Hebrew nodded.

"I have been hearing about you from my overseers in the north. They say you are raising up a rebellion against me."

"We raise no rebellion, Pharaoh. This was once the homeland of Moses, as well as yours. Your throne is not in peril. We desire only to lead our people out of it according to the commands that Yahweh has given us," Aaron said, speaking on behalf of Moses.

"Does Moses not speak for himself?"

"I am his mouth, great king. That is the will of our God."

Pharaoh inclined his head ever so slightly toward his vizier, who leaned in and whispered something. For a long time no one moved, waiting on this private conversation to conclude.

Finally, Pharaoh said, "You were banished from this kingdom forty years ago, in the reign of my father. Why do you return now?" His tone was casual, almost as though he merely wanted to have a simple conversation among friends.

"Pharaoh, as we have said, we have come to bring our people into a desert place so that they may make sacrifices to our God."

"That is why you return after forty years? It is a weak reason. I would instead believe that you have come to raise a rebellion. You know our secrets, have studied our arts. You grew up in this very palace. What I say is true, is it not?"

"What you say is true about his learning, O king. And yes, he did grow to manhood along the Nile and in sight of these walls. But he does not come to raise a rebellion. Yahweh will deliver his people from your grasp," Aaron answered.

"The Hebrews are one nation among many that serve me as slaves. Why are they important?"

"They are important to the Lord God, Pharaoh."

Pharaoh studied him a moment longer. The corners of his eyes seemed to turn up as if he was smiling slightly under his mask of paint.

"Who is this god you call Yahweh that I should let the Hebrews go? I do not know him, and I will not let the Hebrews go."

The conversation was over. Pharaoh had spoken.

Moses did not kneel and touch his forehead to the ground before sulking away like a kicked puppy like we all expected him to do.

Pharaoh was fast to dismiss anyone who did not interest him or who had been given a firm no to their request. But Pharaoh only watched them, unmoving, as though he were challenging them.

I could not have been more stunned or confused throughout this entire encounter. This filthy Hebrew had come in without bothering to cleanse his beard, which meant he had ignored his appearance after waiting all day outside to be received and carelessly let the west wind buffet him with sand, even though he was about to enter the courts of the divine king.

He had failed to bow to the ground before Pharaoh when

failure to do so meant instant death, and yet Pharaoh had not summoned us to strike him down on the spot. They were sparring in conversation like old acquaintances instead of god and mortal. Most shocking of all, there was talk of this Hebrew having grown of age among the palace walls? Learned the Egyptian arts?

Aaron said, "You make a mistake, great king, in angering our God. You will know his wrath. For Yahweh, the Lord our God, has said that his hand will be heavy against Egypt until the people of Israel are released."

Now there were echoes of laughter all throughout the hall. The nobles and their wives whispered and giggled to one another at the absurdity of the god of a nation of slaves overpowering Great Egypt.

"We lived under the yoke of shepherd filth for a hundred years, Moses," the king said. "The Hyksos were your kin. Semites from the north. I had my historians present me with the report."

He made a gesture with his flail, and a priest moved close with a scroll and laid it at his feet.

"We drove them out of our land so that their stench did not offend our gods any longer. I have spent my life chasing them wherever they went. But the Hebrews were allowed to stay. Do you know why?"

Aaron did not answer. Pharaoh raised his voice a bit so that the assembly hall could hear him.

"The Hyksos called themselves the Shepherd Kings, and indeed they behaved like kings. They were warriors and conquerors. But the Hebrews behaved like livestock. Tame. Docile. Ignorant. Choosing to live in their own filth. We let them stay because we learned that while shepherds can cause trouble, livestock pose no threat. They take their beatings and continue to work."

I noticed Moses wince slightly at these words. Pharaoh continued.

"Go back to working among them. They have become numerous, and I cannot allow them to stop working." He paused and smiled broadly. "Not even to sacrifice and hold feasts to their god in the desert."

The room was silent and still as we waited for Moses to respond. He shook his head, glanced at Aaron, and turned his back to leave.

All of us gasped. I stepped forward and withdrew my sword, but then I saw that Pharaoh had raised his hand to stop me. I was so confused and furious that I had to turn my head to the ground so that I did not glare at my own king.

"You have chosen to come back and rejoin your people, Moses, and your people are my slaves. I will tell my overseers that the Hebrews must be idle, for they have the time to request permission to go have feasts! Let their work increase threefold and they will not have time to listen to lies from you."

Moses and Aaron paused and looked back. They appeared to be upset, though their stance was still defiant. All of us turned to Pharaoh and awaited his next words. Many in that hall had already heard him speak more in the past few moments than they had ever heard him speak since he had assumed the throne.

Pharaoh waved the crook and flail in a dismissive gesture, and the foot slaves fell facedown before his throne, forming steps with their bodies to the base of the throne pedestal. Pharaoh stood and descended from the throne by stepping on their backs, the meaning of the gesture even more emphatic after what we had just heard. It was then that I noticed I had not seen these particular slaves before.

They were Hebrews, and Moses looked at them for a long time before departing.

When the two men had left, Pharaoh dismissed everyone else. I fell in behind him as he walked away, it being my turn to provide his escort to his chambers. When we were out of sight of the hall and moving along the corridor to his private quarters, he raised his hand and summoned me beside him. His gait became loose and easy, the same as when he walked among his army and not trapped in the politics and show of the palace.

"My king," I said.

"I wish to hear your impression of Moses, old friend."

I had to force myself to speak through the confusion in my soul. "My king, the entire encounter baffles me. I confess that I am slow-witted and cannot fathom why you would have wasted your time speaking to him when he was so disrespectful of your throne. I cannot fathom how he lived in this palace once. And I certainly cannot fathom why you would care in the slightest about my thoughts, your majesty."

We passed a veranda overlooking the palace gardens. A hundred gardeners worked with tiny blades, removing every out-of-place shoot of weed or grass. The flowers were so fragrant that we could smell them all at once, even from inside the walls. The bull god Apis and dwarf god Bes, the fertility deities, stood in silent watch over the plants, carved by my own hand. The windows had been designed to channel in the breezes from the garden, so that the king would never be without a pleasant scent. The Nile sparkled in the distance. Barges glided on it with full sails.

"You are from the northern lands."

"Yes, your majesty, the Kenaz."

"You came to us and have served me well. You have carved our idols and designed temples with skill never before seen. You have fought my enemies bravely. You wear the Gold of Honor for battling with me."

"I have contributed a pitiful amount, your majesty."

"You know the Hebrews."

"Majesty, I do not. I have never had dealings with them."

"Still, I wish to know the thoughts of a Semite barbarian from their homeland. They are not native to Egypt. They came to us the same way the Hyksos did. The same way you did. From the north and east. Have you heard of a people who worship one god?"

"I have not, your majesty. It makes no sense at all. One god cannot fulfill all that is required of gods."

"How did you worship in your lands?"

"We had gods of the mountains and the desert, the rain and the crops. But none like the Egyptian gods, divine Pharaoh."

The king waved the others away with his left hand, and the group of servants and guards who followed us all bowed to the ground, touched their foreheads, and backed away from us. One never turned his back on the king.

We paused at a balcony that provided an even better view of the river and the gardens. Thutmose reached for a golden wine goblet that had been placed on the balcony in the event the whim occurred to the king that he would like a drink. I knew the royal wine steward. He patrolled the halls as much as I did, but instead of looking for threats he was looking for potential refreshment points for the king.

I took a sip from the goblet to test it for poison, as was the duty of any man or woman who was near the king when he took a fresh drink of wine. I felt no constriction in my throat other than the constriction of my nerves. We had fought together and forged a certain bond, but he was still the divine pharaoh and I a lowly servant.

"They will not be going away," the king said thoughtfully. "Moses was raised the heir of Hatshepsut. He would have ruled Egypt if I had not been born. His name was renowned among our people once, and I fear that it will become so again. A man popular among slaves is not a threat. But a man popular among Egyptians as well as slaves, who knows everything about us . . ." He shook his head slightly.

Before I could answer this stunning piece of information, he continued. "We do not know how it happened precisely, but she took him in and raised him as her own from infancy. She was always an insolent, stubborn woman. But she was very clever and ensured that Moses's heritage as a Hebrew was overlooked by the court. He has an Egyptian name, after all, and it resembles my own. My scribes tell me that he was exceedingly gifted in the sciences, as well as the arts. That he was the greatest charioteer in the upper kingdom."

There was a long enough break in his words that I sensed an opportunity to ask, "Great king, why did he leave? And for forty years? Where did he go?"

"The scribes tell me that he killed a man. An Egyptian. That would have been overlooked for a man of his stature, the heir to the throne, but he was renounced. The records have been purged from that point on. The scribes cannot find any more on him. He disappeared from our lands without any trace, and then suddenly my spies tell me that he appeared in Goshen a month ago with his brother, ranting to the people about their god delivering them. That is why I need you to follow them and discover how they are going to try to rally the Hebrew slaves against me."

Now my confusion began to abate. He could have simply dismissed them and had them killed and been done with it. A tilt of his flail to me and I would have found the courage to grasp them by the hair and slit their throats, eyes of the storm god or not.

But I understood now that the Hebrews had become so numerous that even the slightest rumor spread among their camps at Goshen would cause us no end of trouble. Pharaoh wished to stamp out any rebellion before it could occur by shaming the name of Moses and the power of his unknown god of slaves. Then, to the Egyptian and slave alike, his name would mean nothing.

As if to confirm this, Pharaoh said, "I do not have enough men in place near Goshen to quell an uprising of a million people, and if they hear of their leaders being struck down, they might ransack the very cities they are building for me. The Hebrews have been docile for generations and suddenly they are agitating against their overseers. I will move carefully."

"Majesty, I will do anything you ask of me."

"The overseers ensure that the Hebrews speak our language so that they cannot plot against us in their tongue. I will send instructions that they are free to meet in assembly with Moses and his brother. Their new burdens to make bricks without straw will distract them enough. This will quiet down over time, but I want you to keep your eyes on them and report to me."

"Yes, Great Egypt." I bowed low and touched my forehead to the ground and slid backward, away from him.

Follow them I did, all the way back to the land of Goshen.

I had been there before during passages to the Way of the Sea for campaigns in Canaan.

As you read in the records of Moses, they returned and told the people what Pharaoh had told them. And the people grumbled and complained, and I thought for certain that Moses and Aaron would be stoned.

But that is not necessary for me to expand upon. We do not have the time now. What happened when they returned is what I wish to tell you about.

His name was Nembit, and he was the king's chief magician when I was there. He fashioned himself as Yahweh's adversary when the terrors began.

He had no left eye. It had been torn from his skull when he was a young priest apprentice by a vengeful and jealous lover who attacked him in his sleep. His right eye was clouded with cataracts, so I am sure that he could not see through it either, but he made his way around the palace without difficulty. They said he could see with the eye of sorcery.

He was older than anyone I knew, his shaved head wrinkled and blotched by ancient sunburns that had never healed. Two great scars crossed his temple in parallel lines and went behind his ear, where he had once ripped through the flesh of his head with the fangs of a cobra during a conjuring ceremony.

He had a limp. A crocodile bite, he said. We believed him.

They said he allowed himself to be poisoned so many times, in perfect doses, that he was completely impervious to snakebites.

He consorted with young boys and even younger girls. He took delight in gruesomely torturing slaves, those who had been sent to him for punishment by their masters, claiming he was experimenting with them to find a better way to judge the rising and falling of the Nile by their bodily reactions to his tests. It was believed that Mother Nile was a living being, a channel of lifeblood flowing from the dark heart to the south into the velvet green lowlands of the north. Nembit claimed that Mother Nile could be known much like a human body could be known, and so he tested them.

It was this man that Moses and Aaron stood before.

— 13 —

The Terrors Begin

Moses and Aaron departed Goshen to return to the king. I arrived back at the palace in Memphis well ahead of them. I had time to go before Pharaoh and share what I had seen, and he listened with great interest as we walked through the gardens toward the training barracks. The king loved to train with his men as often as he could, and I was honored with the privilege of sparring with him on this day.

"So they are returning to me then?" he asked.

"Yes, my king."

"And their elders are upset with them?" he asked me for the third time.

"Furious, my king. It would not surprise me if they meted out a death sentence to them upon their return to Goshen."

Pharaoh nodded. That had been his intent all along.

"Their magic trick with the staff was the best they could do," he said.

We reached the pit, where a ring of soldiers handed us our

weapons. It was alongside a cool, green lagoon of the Nile surrounded by pillars, which were painted with the specific maneuvers of the infantry and the chariot. On one pillar were the paintings of figures engaged in hand-to-hand grappling, and it appeared as though that was the format we were to train on today.

The training master who stood next to the pillar fell to the sand and touched his forehead before Pharaoh when he was summoned.

"I see you have come across new movements," the king said as he studied freshly painted figures on the column.

"Yes, your majesty," the training master answered.

After stripping to only a loincloth, I took up my position in front of the king, bowed to him, and we began practicing the maneuvers under the eye of the training master. Soon our torsos were caked with sand as we threw one another around. I did not hold back; it could have been fatal for me. Thutmose was a great conqueror and only wanted the most realistic training that could be provided. He had killed many slaves simply by working on a new technique with his spear or bow that had been created.

We fought to seven draws, and it was clear to me the king was becoming frustrated that he was not mastering the maneuver quicker. He beckoned me forward for another round, and we locked legs, knee to knee, trying to throw each other into the neck hold we had been taught.

He managed to flip me onto my side, and I was about to reach up for his head when I caught sight of Moses and Aaron standing on the edge of the pit.

"Majesty," I managed to gasp while pointing. When the king saw them, he tightened his grip on me, and I decided the best move for me at that time was to allow him to complete the throw. I put up enough resistance to make it appear to him that I had tried to maneuver out of it, but my body hit the sand in what had to be a satisfying thump for the king to hear.

He stood over me panting, his muscles glistening with sweat and dirty with sand, a grin on his face. He looked up at the Hebrews.

"You have returned to me, Moses. I was expecting you later."

"We were brought before you as soon as we arrived, Pharaoh."

The king reached out a hand for me and pulled me up.

"What have you come to demand this time? More food for your people?"

I could see Moses look at Aaron quickly before answering, as though to gain confidence. "The Lord our God says that you are to release the Hebrews and let us go into the desert to make sacrifices to him."

Thutmose smiled and shook his head. He reached out for a linen towel that a slave had rushed forward to provide and wiped his face. I did the same.

"The staff was not sufficient? You return to humiliate yourselves and your god again?" He walked to the bank of the lagoon and dove in, rinsing himself.

Until this point I had mostly dismissed the trickster god of the Hebrews. He had no empire of men serving him, no monuments.

But when Pharaoh dipped into the Nile that day a second time, I had my first doubts, and the earliest sense that perhaps my world would be coming to an end. For when Pharaoh broke the surface of the Nile, as he came up for breath, a cascade of dark blood erupted in the water around him.

At first I thought there had been a crocodile that had snuck into the lagoon, somehow getting past the netting that had been strung to avoid its entering. I immediately called for the weapons masters, and we all plunged into the water desperate to reach the king.

But as we drew close, we saw the blood rush toward us as though it had been released from a spring in the earth, filling the entire lagoon. The air thickened with the stench of rotting death.

I managed to reach Pharaoh, who was standing absolutely still, watching the blood fill the lagoon all the way to the beach, then past the narrow entrance that led to the main body of the river.

Like a scarlet cloth being unfurled over a banquet table, the blood spread across the river, passing under barges, under fishermen who staggered back from pulling in their nets, all the way across to the far western bank, where the setting sun above the cliffs made it look even more sinister.

None of us could take a full breath, not only because of the stench in the air but because we were in shock.

I looked at the king, waiting for that familiar smile to break out, the expression of a hawk circling a mouse, but he could only clench his jaw and stare like the rest of us.

"Pharaoh!" Aaron thundered from the riverbank behind us. We turned to face him. "I am warning you. Do not put Yahweh to the test!"

Thutmose seemed to gather himself at this and whirled about on his priests, who were standing on the riverbank, looking every bit as confused and terrified as we were.

"What is this?" he called to them.

The magician priest Nembit knelt by the bank of the lagoon and dipped his fingers into the blood. He smelled them and examined them closely. "It is blood, great king."

Pharaoh punched the surface of the lagoon in his anger. "I know that, you old fool!" He stumbled out of the lagoon to the bank, and I followed him. "Make it stop!"

"Great Egypt, we will consult the gods," Nembit said, motioning the others to bow low with him and back away. As they turned to leave, I saw his eyes darting to each of them as if searching for answers.

The king raised his arms to the courtiers, who had come to watch his combat demonstration, which now seemed pitiful.

"Return to your homes," he said, finally regaining some of his royal decorum. "I will go and sacrifice before the gods myself and restore the river."

Everyone was so shocked by what had happened that it took them a moment to respond, but eventually they filed out of the lagoon, and it was only the king, myself, a few guards and slaves, and the two Hebrews left standing there.

The king walked up to them and appeared genuinely terrified, dripping from head to toe with blood. His kohl eyeliner was running down his face. He moved in close to Moses and stared hard into his eyes.

"You conjure tricks that shame me. I would order you tied down in the scorpion pit this very moment, but I wish to crush the name of your god in front of your people, so that their men will always be laborers and their women whores for my soldiers."

Moses held his stare. For the first time, he spoke himself.

"Great king, the Lord will humble you before the nations of the earth, and he will defend his people. Whatever it takes."

***

That night, at the temple of Nute, I watched the priests cleanse themselves in the golden baths and sacrifice three bulls to the goddess of the river. Their incantations and chants were guttural and heavy; occasionally one would stand up, sprinkle more blood across the altar, and then return to the group.

I got in a skiff and rowed across the blood river to the temple of Osiris, where those priests were sacrificing to their patron. Up and down the banks of the Nile, torchlight shone from every temple great and small, from the smallest dwarf god's idol to the grandest corridors of Amon Ra. I wanted to see every one of them. Wanted to experience everything I could of the efforts that the king was making to thwart this foulness.

Remember, the river was one of our gods. As I rowed across it under an endlessly dark sky, the smell of putrefying flesh made me vomit over the side of the skiff until I had nothing left in my belly.

Hippopotamuses, crocodiles, pike, snakes, frogs, turtles, every living creature that swam in those waters had died and was floating on the surface. The furnace sun of the desert did the rest, speeding up the decaying process, causing intestines to bloat with gas and burst, spraying excrement and flesh across the fetid surface of the once-beautiful river.

There was no fresh water to be found in the land. Every vase, every cistern was full of rotting blood.

I had to pull hard on the oars to move the skiff through the blood. I looked at the sky as I rowed, trying to get my mind off what I was rowing through. Amon Ra would emerge on his fiery chariot in the east in a matter of hours, and if there was no relief from the gods by the end of the coming day, the young and the old would begin to die, with the healthy not long behind them.

No moon was out, only the dim stars of the late season. The Scorpion held his claws out across the heavens as he always did, passive and uncaring.

I made a sign against evil with my hand against my forehead and closed my eyes. "Great goddess," I said quietly, "give us purity once more."

As I finally approached the bank, my eye caught a glimpse of a small campfire not far away. Curious as to what sane man would be sleeping so near the river in its present state, I rowed my skiff in its direction.

As I drew near, I saw that it was Moses and Aaron sitting across the fire from each other. They were speaking quietly and occasionally taking drinks from two waterskins. I was amazed that their own water had not been contaminated.

I tried to hear what they were saying, but they were just out of my ears' reach. Neither man appeared to be bothered by the smell. I detested them both, but I had to acknowledge that they were courageous, only the two of them in the middle of a land that hated them, surviving only because the king had chosen not to have them killed.

I learned from Moses many years later that, indeed, Yahweh had shielded their nostrils, and their food and water had remained pure.

The next morning I slept late since I had been out all night and I did not have a guard shift in the palace that day. I was in a deep dream as I lay on my pallet. I do not remember everything about the dream, but a creature I had never seen before was swallowing our entire Egypt in its great jaws, emptying the blood-filled Nile down its vast throat, and I was swimming against the rush of blood as hard as I could, crying out for salvation but seeing none. The stench was enough to suffocate me, and as I emerged it seemed only to intensify.

I awoke with my nostrils and throat clogged with the revolting smell of the river. The overnight sacrifices had not worked.

I slowly sat up, my throat parched. I tried to swallow, but it only caused a gag and a biting pain in the back of my throat.

I stumbled my way through the palace to where Pharaoh normally held his audiences, but he was not there. I searched for them for an hour, until finally I caught a glimpse across the gardens of a gathering of people at the riverbank.

There was a small temple on the palace grounds used for the fish sacrifices made weekly to ensure abundant catches, and it appeared as though the nobles and servants were gathered there. I approached quietly, since I had no reason to be there apart from my own curiosity.

The king was sitting on a small wood-and-ivory throne in his full regalia of face paint, robes, and the double crown. Around him, priests stood before various jars with their hands raised, uttering spells over the vases. I leaned in and asked a house servant what was happening.

"The priests have found water from the wells above the cliffs," the servant answered quietly. "Everything below the desert in the valley is contaminated, but the wells above are still clear. They have brought water from those wells before the god-king to demonstrate that they, too, can turn the water to blood."

I saw Moses and Aaron standing on the edge of the courtyard, watching this as well. Pharaoh sat straight up and did not move, impressing the power of the state upon all who viewed him.

With three loud clacks of their black staffs against the smooth courtyard paving stones, the same staffs that had been turned into serpents, the priests held still for a count. No one moved.

One of them moved forward and picked up the middle vase. He held it up before the king and then poured it out.

Blood.

Everyone cheered rapturously, chanting their praise to the god-king for solving the riddle of the demon Hebrews. I was elated as well and waited expectantly for them to change the blood back to water and so rid us of the rotting swamp that had become our river.

Pharaoh appeared to be waiting as well, for he raised his hand for silence from the crowd. Because this temple was just outside the palace grounds, hundreds of commoners and peasants had streamed in from the city upon hearing of what was happening.

Each of the priests apart from Nembit were still smirking to one another about their success in transfiguring the water to blood, but as the crowd quieted down, they appeared to grow uneasy.

"You may proceed with returning our beautiful Nile to its previous purity, and may the gods be blessed," the king said.

Nembit knelt down before the king. Unadulterated hatred was on his face as he glanced at Moses. He bowed low.

"Divine Pharaoh," he said, "we have made every offering known, but we do not know the mystery of blood back into water. The filthy Hebrew has conjured a trick we have not overcome yet." His voice trembled, clearly aware that he could be executed on the spot.

Pharaoh glared at them from behind his white face paint. He stood, turned without a word, and walked down the backs of his slaves until he reached the corridor and disappeared into the palace.

Seven days the river was tainted. Seven evenings I lay down my head and prayed to the gods that water would flow again, and seven mornings I awoke to see that none was forthcoming. Disease started spreading from the putrefaction. We had to clear out the servants and slaves from the palace itself so as not to risk the lives of Pharaoh, his wives, or his children.

For seven nights I climbed the palace wall and looked out over Memphis. It was dark; no one stirred after the sun went down because they had no energy. Many had deserted the Nile Valley and were living above the cliffs. They had little shelter but they had water.

Some finally discovered that if they dug into the mud by the riverbank, there was water to be found there, and many thousands of holes were gouged out, and peasants stuffed their heads directly into the murky water, not caring that they were swallowing just as much silt as water.

Seven days of absolute suffering. The worst we could imagine.

But it would get worse. Far worse.

As the sun set on the seventh day, Moses raised his staff over the waters, and they returned to normal immediately. I did not see it happen, only sensed it when a fresh breeze from the east came in and cleared the air. We had become so accustomed to the stench by then that it was startling to smell sand and palm leaves instead of rotting fish and hippopotamus.

We were overjoyed. I ran down to the bank and dove in, marveling at how crisp and pure and cool it felt, taking great gulping drinks of the water until it made me so full I was sick.

I got in my skiff and saw that it, too, had even been cleaned of the blood from the river. I rowed happily late into the night, working the strength into my shoulders and back that had lain dormant during the suffering.

The stars were dazzling that night. It was as if the river's curse had clouded the sky and dimmed them, but now the dry air had returned and they were on display. The Scorpion twinkled at me, uncaring.

"Hello, old friend!" I cried out to him. "You were not stopped by their god! You hunt the heavens still!"

***

Moses and Aaron appeared before Pharaoh in the receiving hall. I watched from the shadows.

Pharaoh appeared physically well, as did the rest of his house, for he had servants to fetch him well water from the heights during the time that the river was foul. His mood appeared high, for the river flowed pure again.

"Why do you come before me now?" he demanded.

"We have told you," Aaron answered the king. "Yahweh wants his people to be able to leave Egypt and to sacrifice in the desert."

"I will do no such thing," he said steadily. "The Hebrews are mine."

Silence in the great hall. I felt a pang of dread in my soul. The expression on the face of Moses told me that something else was coming. That the river had not been the end of it; that their god might have more than one or two tricks in his powers.

Moses's face was cast half in shadow from the torchlight, giving him a sinister appearance. He nodded at Aaron.

"This is what Yahweh says to you, O king: Let my people go to serve me in the desert. If you refuse to let them go, I will send a plague of frogs upon you."

Pharaoh tilted his head. "Did you say . . . frogs?"

Aaron did not answer.

"How strange," the king said. He grinned. "I suppose I must be terrified at this, but I fear that I am not. Enough! Be gone from my presence."

The priest who served as the Voice of Pharaoh seemed exasperated again at this breach of protocol in the court. Pharaoh speaking! The Divine Voice heard by common men! I knew what they were all thinking, for I was thinking it as well: Perhaps the gods were withholding their helping hand from the king because he had stooped to the level of the Hebrew filth and had actually been speaking to them.

Moses and Aaron turned their backs on the king and left.

I followed them from a distance. They walked through a crowd of Egyptian commoners, who jeered and taunted them. Occasionally a soldier would toss a stone in their direction to make them dodge it. People mocked them, though I noticed it was not as venomous as before. I think they were all starting to become afraid of the power of this unknown new god from the desert, who could turn their river into blood.

Eventually, Moses and Aaron made their way to their camp near the river. No other Hebrews were able to visit them. They were indeed a pitiful delegation to represent the vast numbers of their race.

I watched them pray a while, on their knees with their arms raised, their faces skyward. Their mutterings and groans went into the night in a mournful song of lament.

14

Those Who Remember

Caleb took a long drink from his water pouch and stared into the distance a moment. Othniel held his hand over the parchment, the charcoal stick locked in his hand, anxious to hear more.

"Uncle?"

Caleb blinked. "Yes?"

"You were telling me of the frogs. The second of the plagues."

Caleb sighed. "Do you think it necessary? Our people know what happened then. Moses recorded it. It is read in the tents of meeting and in the tabernacle."

"You are one of the last two who remain who saw it. I wish to record how it was for you."

For the second time that night, and the second time that Othniel could ever recall, Caleb appeared every bit of his eighty-five years in age. He slumped forward, rubbing his eyes. His breathing was labored. He coughed, hard, and spat. He wrapped the blanket around his shoulders. Othniel grew concerned.

"Do not make me relive it, Nephew."

"But Uncle," Othniel said, "it was Yahweh's greatest triumph! The finest hour of our people."

Caleb reached for his water pouch and took another long drink. "Indeed, it was." But he looked at Othniel as though he had been flogged.

"I am confused, Uncle. Can you tell me why you are so saddened by this?"

Caleb nodded slightly, then set aside the water pouch. "I will tell you of the plagues. But I wish that you would let me tell them to you in my own way. They were . . ." He exhaled heavily. "They were the greatest thing I have seen. And the worst."

It appeared to be physically painful for Caleb to say more, so Othniel held off from pushing him. Outside, the watchman came to the flap of the tent and called out the hour. Caleb thanked him. Othniel shifted to a more comfortable position.

Gazing with vacant eyes toward some point in the far distance, Caleb said, "In all the years of battle I have seen, I saw nothing to compare with the horror of what Yahweh struck the Egyptians with. The suffering was . . ."

Othniel could not be sure, but he thought a tear appeared in the corner of Caleb's eye. He was looking older by the breath. Othniel grew genuinely concerned.

"Uncle, I apologize for the strain of bringing it up. I will leave and—"

"No, I will speak of it," Caleb cut him off. "But only once. And I will speak only of the parts I wish to speak of, and leave out the others. Everything that men need to know of this time was written by Moses and his scribes."

Caleb reached up and quickly wiped his eyes. He stared back into nothingness. "You must understand. Many of the people of Egypt were good people. Many were wicked, yes, but many were decent citizens who worked hard, loved their families, and tried to live a quiet life. It was their king who brought this terrible thing upon them. Lost in the telling of our story is the suffering of the people of Egypt for the stubbornness of their pharaoh. Had he simply let Israel go, there would not have been so much death, so much sickness, so much suffering. More suffering than I could write on a thousand scrolls."

Caleb sat up straight and seemed to gain control of himself.

"They were idolaters and pagans, and yet I do not believe that Yahweh *wanted* them all to suffer. He needed to show his might to the Egyptians, for they were a muleheaded people, stubborn to the end. But if Pharaoh had only listened . . ."

Othniel tried to keep his writing steady as he made notes. He was unsure of what to think just yet. Sympathy . . . for the Egyptians? What blasphemy was this? And yet Caleb had been quick to acknowledge that they were heathens and wicked men.

"Two things I must mention before I begin," Caleb said. "The first is that every plague, or *terror* as we called them, had the same thing in common. Darkness. Would you want to relive memories of total darkness and terror? And the other is that regardless of how wicked men may become . . ." His voice then lowered to a whisper, his eyes brimming with pain. "I do not think Yahweh takes any joy in seeing a mother's or father's tears for their dead child."

He took another deep breath and continued.

— 15 —

Infestations

I was sleeping deeply when they came late that night. A creaking sound, dim in my mind. I floated through the darkness of dream, wondering what the strange noise was. Crickets in the tens of millions? What sign was this the gods were giving me?

I rose and made my way to the window of my small barracks room on the palace wall. I pushed aside the curtain and looked out. A full moon shone over the Nile. The city was asleep. Only the occasional watch fire burned, with a few of the poor gathered around them to ward off the night's chill.

Though nothing appeared out of the ordinary, I could still hear that sound. It grew deeper. Less of a whining, more of a crackling. A croaking, even. I peered toward the river.

Something monstrous and black was emerging from the water's surface. A great serpent, I was sure of it, for it writhed and shifted and swirled, a canvas of shadows and darkness that rippled like the current of the river itself, and it was swallowing the city.

I blinked and stared. The noise grew louder. Deeper. Yes, it was croaking, like the croaking of a . . .

The frogs came from the Nile in their tens of millions, hopping on top of one another, smothering each other to make way for the millions hopping fast behind them. They emerged from the waters like clouds rose from a great storm, growing darker and more dense, a black stone wall. So many of them that as I looked left and right, to the north and south as far as the river could be seen, it was as if a god had punched a large fist into the water and sent a wave over the land.

The surge was relentless as the creatures slithered and leaped tightly together, until their wave was twenty, thirty cubits high of solid frogs, dying as they smothered each other. Yet there were ever more that came, painting the city in blackness.

The screaming began as people had their homes covered in frogs. I saw the watch fires snuff out one by one as the awful creatures flung themselves in a mass into the basins of fire and burned themselves to death simply because there was nowhere else for them to go.

Panic-stricken watchmen tried to throw flaming sticks at them in the streets, but it was utterly useless and had no effect on the frogs. They jumped through the flame, many of them heating up and exploding, spraying the men and women who ran for their lives, making popping sounds as they burst. But still the surge of frogs came, overwhelming everything in their path.

I could only stand there and watch and pant. Helpless. Terrified. Then hearing croaking from inside my room, I spun around, startled.

My water basin was filled with frogs. They began leaping out of it, first a few, then a dozen, then a stream of a hundred or more. I am ashamed to admit that I screamed like a woman in pure terror and fled from my room.

In the hall I stepped on several of the frogs, squashing them and falling down hard as my feet slid on their innards. I landed on my shoulder directly on top of another frog, and I was overwhelmed by them as they poured out of every room of the barracks, sending me running to get away. They landed on my face, dug their wet, clawed feet into my eye sockets as they piled themselves up into every corner. I was shaking with fright.

Other soldiers were swinging blades at them as though they were bandits in the desert. I heard a shout behind me.

It was Bakar, my closest friend.

"What . . . what . . . ?" was all he managed to say.

I gagged as a frog found its way onto my face and slid its clawed foot across my tongue. I could not even inhale without a frog leaping for my throat or my nose as if to suck out my very life breath.

"We must protect the king!" Bakar shouted. I nodded at him. We began pushing our way through the mass of frogs, which now rose to our knees. Every time my foot came down, I crushed several frogs.

Shrieks and screams echoed down every corridor, amidst the endless croaking noise the frogs made. All the torches and lamps had been snuffed out, leaving us to have to press forward in total darkness.

We knew the route to the king's quarters by memory or else we would have never found it. We came to his door, which was open, and trudged our way inside. A few torches remained lit in the king's chamber. By their light I saw that Thutmose III, god of Egypt, son of Ra, was standing on his bed, completely naked, using a mallet to knock frogs away from him. Several of his guards were by his side and doing the same.

"Come help us!" he roared when he saw Bakar and me. It was such an absurd sight that I very nearly laughed in spite of myself, but that would have been very dangerous indeed.

It was hopeless. The frogs overwhelmed even the king's bed-chamber, and even though we fought them away all through the night, with the coming of the day we were far worse off than before. As the sun rose and the heat came, the swampy stench and the decay of the frogs' bloating bodies made us vomit until we had nothing left inside of us. Even the king spent his morning leaning over his balcony, retching.

I made my way to the balcony next to him and looked out over the city. Our Great Egypt had turned into a mass of dark green. In countless numbers that man has not reckoned, the hideous frogs covered every bit of ground from horizon to horizon, from canyon rim to city street, from the Nile to the eastern deserts.

Pharaoh ordered us to find the priests and sorcerers and "anyone else who communed with the gods or worked magic." We crawled, stepped, and worked our way out to them in their temples and dens of witchcraft and brought them before Pharaoh.

The king had managed to clear out a spot in his palace free from the frogs. He had ordered the doors shut to his throne room with fifty servants remaining inside with him. The servants worked at trapping frogs and throwing them out the windows until none remained. Every time someone entered the throne room, the servants were there to catch the frogs that hopped in with the visitor.

When we brought the sorcerers before the king, he commanded that they conjure frogs from a basin of water. They did so, and this seemed to satisfy the king, but when he ordered them to cleanse the land of frogs, they could only stare at him, then bow low.

"Great Egypt, we do not know the mysteries of how to remove them," the oldest one admitted. "We can only conjure them." The old man seemed to swallow hard before he added, "Perhaps if you were to beseech the god of Moses—"

"Be gone!" Thutmose yelled, his anger flashing. "What use are you to me if you cannot even overthrow the power of the Hebrew tricksters?"

But the frogs grew worse. Much worse.

Later that night, Bakar and I were summoned to the king's side, and when we entered his chamber, we put our heads on the ground before him. He was standing at the balcony overlooking the city from high above it. His expression was stony.

"Bring Moses and Aaron before me."

Bakar and I made our way through the mass of frogs to the riverbank, where Moses and Aaron had been camping. The two of them were standing at the edge of their fire, fully dressed with staffs in hand, as though they had been expecting us.

When we brought them before the king, he said, "Plead with the Lord to take away the frogs from me and my people, and I will let the people go and sacrifice to the Lord."

The brokenness on the king's face shocked me. This did not appear to be a ruse.

"Tell me when you would like me to plead, so that the frogs are cut away," Moses said carefully.

"Tomorrow," the king said. He was struggling to maintain his bearing and apparently desired to exert whatever control he was offered.

Moses nodded. I would have expected a triumphant look on his face, but there was none. Only resolve.

"Be it as you say, so that you may know that there is no one like Yahweh our God. The frogs will go away from you and your houses and your servants and your people. They shall be left only in the Nile."

The two men left.

The next day, all of the frogs died. Everywhere lay dead and rotting frogs. Your imagination can inform you of how awful that was, Othniel. And yet, true to his form, the king appeared to find his inner strength once the terror had passed.

Not strength, I should say. Stubbornness. Hardheartedness. Strength does not reflect in the suffering of the innocent.

The next plague came. Yahweh was relentless.

On this day, when I was checking the guards, Moses came forward with Aaron to the steps of the palace of the king. Crowds were always passing in front of the grand steps, and now they stopped to see the old, dusty Hebrews.

Under the gaze of the great statues of the king that had been built as columns, Moses touched Aaron on the shoulder.

Aaron raised his staff up high over his head.

We all froze, watching with dread what they would do next. Everyone recognized them as the Hebrew magicians who had struck the land with blood and frogs.

"Spare us!" some of them cried out. "Spare us! Do not afflict the land again!"

I tried to get my muscles to respond, to move myself down the steps to shove them away. But I was mesmerized by Aaron's staff, which glinted in the late afternoon sunlight, hovering above him like a sword that he was about to drop across a neck.

"Behold, great king!" Aaron called so that all could hear him. Total silence was now in the streets.

"Because your heart has become stubborn, Yahweh has decided to smite the very sand and dust of this Egypt, so that you will know that he is the Lord of earth as well as water! Your gods will crumble before him!"

Then Aaron swung the staff down. The top of it thudded into a pile of dirt that had been kicked up by the hooves of donkeys pulling carts through the streets. A puff of dust rose from where the staff had struck, but instead of rising and dispersing as one would think, it seemed to hang there suspended a moment, as though it had been called to attention and would not move unless commanded.

We watched the dust cloud apprehensively, and just when I thought perhaps their god had abandoned them at last, an ear-shattering crash was heard above us in the sky like a strike of lightning, and the dust cloud from the end of Aaron's staff erupted into a column of sand that blew densely skyward, reaching up and growing in size and swirling in fury. It darkened the sun briefly as it cast its shadow.

And then it burst outward, showering us with the thickest, densest cloud we had ever known. I gagged as my lungs filled with the dust . . . but it was not dust.

A crawling sensation began all over my flesh. I looked down at my hands and forearms.

In numbers beyond the calculations of our greatest mathematicians were lice, crawling and swarming on my skin and the skin of those around me. We inhaled them, gagging and coughing. The sky grew dull brown, filled with the swarm.

I swatted at them. I scraped them from my flesh. I tried running and jumping, hoping to shake them off of me, not comprehending it at all. The frogs were awful, but this? Would we survive?

Water!

I staggered toward the nearest fountain but saw it was already full of palace men who had the same idea. Coughing, vomiting, my stomach and lungs retching to get rid of the irritants, I staggered through the porticos of the palace until I reached the lagoon where others sought relief as I did, but there was room for us.

Dimly visible outside the lagoon were thousands of people diving into the Nile, not caring if they were eaten by crocodiles so long as they could get relief from the lice. Many were eaten. I heard their screams of agony as they died with their eyes and mouths full of lice, their legs cut away from their bodies by slashing teeth. Many drowned in a pool of their own blood.

I did not pay them mind, though, because I did not care if I was eaten by a crocodile either. I dove into the water and held my breath for as long as I could. I listened to the gurgling sounds of others who were submerged as well. It finally occurred to me that the lice had slid off my flesh when I submerged, but hearing the thrashing of the Egyptians around me, they could not get the creatures to release their bites.

I suffered, yes. The lice crawled over my skin. They burrowed into my underarms and filled my eyelids. I stood, took a breath between my clenched teeth to prevent them from going into my lungs, felt them cover my head and face, and then submerged once again.

They washed away from my face. At the end of my next held breath, I emerged from the water and decided to hold very still. I kept my eyes and mouth closed. I stuck my fingers in my ears and curled my lip so my nostrils were blocked.

I must have looked absurd, but I knew that the lice could not swarm into any of the openings in my head.

I waited.

The tiny creatures continued to brush against me as they were carried by the wind, but the storm seemed to be subsiding. The breeze began to slow.

I opened my eyes slightly and saw that the air was clearing of them. They had been blasted from the source of Aaron's rod like a windstorm, multiplying endlessly and with impossible speed, sent high into the sky to rain down on us, and now they were settling down. They were flightless insects, carried by the wind, and now that the wind had died they covered the ground in their hordes. Like the frogs, it would be impossible to step anywhere without touching thousands of them. They coated the trees, the Nile, the banks, everything around us.

I submerged once more into the river to wash off any remnants from my body, then came up to gather myself. I looked around the lagoon at the people writhing with itches, scraping flesh with fingernails, rubbing stones against their faces and arms to rid themselves of the tiny insects that had latched on and would not come off.

Shaken, I walked along the lice-covered path back to the palace. Up the steps and into the hallway, I passed dozens of people shrieking in terror at the infestation.

I went to the command post, where the palace guard kept its quarters. The strongest, most robust men in the guard were writhing on the floor or scraping their backs against the stone walls. I saw Bakar tearing at his eyes with his fingers.

"Bakar!" I called. "Bakar, over here!"

But he did not hear me over the wailing of the others. It did not matter, because I saw what I needed to see. He was affected exactly like the others.

I wandered the streets with those who suffered.

A night passed, then the next day. I scratched at my body until my flesh was red and raw. I hid in the shadows of the throne room as Pharaoh, his own body covered with the foul insects, screamed at the magicians. He sat on his throne, berating Nembit in particular.

"Conjure them! Conjure them for me now!"

Nembit bowed low before the king. The ruthless old magician was defeated and carried this on his countenance. He said, "Great Egypt, we cannot conjure the lice. They are of a kind we are unfamiliar with, and our best efforts result in nothing."

"How did you turn the water into blood? How did you create the frogs?"

Nembit appeared unsteady on his feet. "Those were tricks we had learned for the lesser gods. This . . . Yahweh . . . is conquering them."

Soon every head in Egypt was shaved, even the women's. The ultimate humiliation for a woman is to lose her hair. The masses of bald women were hideous; they mixed with the men and looked like a herd of barren and starving lambs being led to slaughter. Their moaning for their lost vanity was insufferable.

We men were disgusted with them and had nothing to do with them.

16

Written by the Hand of Moses

Caleb was quiet for a while. He seemed to be gathering his strength to open his mouth and speak, couldn't manage it, and closed his lips again.

"I know this has worn you out, Uncle. It is more than I ever expected you to tell me in one day," Othniel said.

"I am not worn out," Caleb replied quickly. "I just need a moment to drink a little water and gather my thoughts. I remember many things with precise details. My memory fails me elsewhere. Don't grow old, Othniel. Die valiantly as a young man."

Othniel smiled at the teasing. "I have the record of Moses, copied by the scribes. Would you like me to help your memory by reading it?"

Caleb thought a moment. "That might be best. In truth, it might be best to let the record of Moses tell you of the next few terrors, save the last two. Those I will tell you myself. They are quite vivid to me."

Othniel pulled a scroll out from his pack. "I copied this one myself when we were at Shechem waiting for Joshua's blessing."

"That is good. A man must make every bit of the law known to his mind."

"The law is known," Othniel said, nodding, "but this is the narrative Moses wrote. I believe it is instructive as well."

"It is good that there is a record of what Yahweh did to the Egyptians," Caleb agreed.

Othniel held the scroll to the lamplight and searched the writing.

"How have you kept it dry?" Caleb asked, watching him.

"It is my most sacred possession. I keep it wrapped in oiled cloth so thick that it could fall in a river and not be ruined."

"I have an idea. Read me the parts of the narrative where the other plagues occur. They have what you need to know, but perhaps I can add my part of it."

Othniel held the scroll up and studied it. "You told me of the frogs. The flies came next."

Caleb nodded. "I remember them. Read it for me. I wish to hear it from the hand of Moses, for that is how Yahweh wanted it to be heard."

Othniel cleared his throat. "Then the Lord said to Moses, 'Rise up early in the morning and present yourself to Pharaoh as he goes out to the water and say to him, Thus says the Lord: Let my people go, that they may serve me. Or else, if you will not let my people go, behold, I will send swarms of flies on you and your servants and your people and into your houses. And the houses of the Egyptians shall be filled with swarms of flies, and also the ground on which they stand. But on that day I will set apart the land of Goshen, where my people dwell, so that no swarms of flies shall be there, that you may know that I am the Lord in the midst of the earth. Thus I will put a division between my people and your people. Tomorrow this sign shall happen.'

"And the Lord did so. There came great swarms of flies into the house of Pharaoh and into his servants' houses. Throughout all the land of Egypt the land was ruined by the swarms of flies.

"Afterward, Pharaoh called Moses and Aaron and said, 'Go, sacrifice to your God within the land.' But Moses said, 'It would not be right to do so, for the offerings we shall sacrifice to the Lord our God are an abomination to the Egyptians. If we sacrifice offerings abominable to the Egyptians before their eyes, will they not stone us? We must go three days' journey into the wilderness and sacrifice to the Lord our God as he tells us.'

"Pharaoh said, 'I will let you go to sacrifice to the Lord your God in the wilderness, only you must not go very far away. Plead for me.' Then Moses said, 'Behold, I am going out from you and I will plead with the Lord that the swarms of flies may depart from Pharaoh, from his servants, and from his people, tomorrow. Only let not Pharaoh cheat again by not letting the people go to sacrifice to the Lord.'

"So Moses went out from Pharaoh and prayed to the Lord.

"And the Lord did as Moses asked and removed the swarms of flies from Pharaoh, from his servants, and from his people; not one remained. But Pharaoh hardened his heart this time also and did not let the people go."

Caleb nodded as he listened. "Yes, I remember the flies. It was like the live gnats. So many that a man could hardly breathe. We choked on them. We would wake up from our sleep, whenever we actually had any, and our ears and nostrils would be full of them trying to hatch their offspring."

Othniel winced at this. "Where were you?"

"I had been assigned to the training regiments. The king no longer sent for me, and I requested time away."

"They granted it to you?"

"I wore the Gold of Honor," Caleb said simply.

Othniel looked back down at the scroll. "Next were the livestock."

"Read it to me."

Othniel squinted and read carefully, "Then the Lord said to Moses, 'Go to Pharaoh and say to him, This is what the Lord, the God of the Hebrews, says: Let my people go, so that they may worship me. If you refuse to let them go and continue to hold them back, the hand of the Lord will bring a terrible plague on your livestock in the field, on your horses, donkeys and camels, and on your cattle, sheep and goats. But the Lord will make a distinction between the livestock of Israel and that of Egypt, so that no animal belonging to the Israelites will die.'

"The Lord set a time and said, 'Tomorrow the Lord will do this in the land.' And the next day the Lord did it: All the livestock of the Egyptians died, but not one animal belonging to the Israelites died. Pharaoh investigated and found that not even one of the animals of the Israelites had died. Yet his heart was unyielding and he would not let the people go."

Caleb sighed. He reached over and picked up some of the dried meat near the fire. He held it up for Othniel. "The smell, the lack of fresh meat. I remember those. I will never take fresh meat for granted again."

Othniel waited for anything else, but Caleb did not seem interested in expanding on this. He had a look of apprehension on his face.

"We can be done now," Othniel said again.

And again Caleb refused him. "No, we must press on. Keep reading."

So, clearing his throat, Othniel turned back to the scroll. "Then the Lord said to Moses and Aaron, 'Take handfuls of soot from a furnace and have Moses toss it into the air in the presence of Pharaoh. It will become fine dust over the whole land of Egypt, and festering boils will break out on people and animals throughout the land.'

"So they took soot from a furnace and stood before Pharaoh. Moses tossed it into the air, and festering boils broke out on people and animals. The magicians could not stand before Moses because of the boils that were on them and on all the Egyptians. But the Lord hardened Pharaoh's heart and he would not listen to Moses and Aaron, just as the Lord had said to Moses."

Caleb chuckled. "As you can see, there was a pattern." He raised his arms up close to Othniel. "Do you see these?"

His arms were covered with pockmarks and scars. Othniel nodded. He had seen his uncle's arms before but assumed the scars all came from battle.

"Some are from battle," Caleb said, anticipating his nephew's thoughts, "but most are from those boils."

Othniel recoiled. "Were they all over you?"

"Every speck of flesh. Boils grew on top of boils. They were in our throats. I had one on my right eye, but Yahweh in his mercy allowed it to heal."

"What did they look like?"

Caleb put his thumb on his forearm. "They were about as big as my fingernail, and they grew next to each other until you could barely tell that a person was human. Yahweh be praised, they were awful. I keep saying how painful these experiences were. Perhaps that one was the most miserable for bodily harm."

Othniel waited. Caleb seemed to be finished with describing the boils.

"The fire storm is next, is it not?"

Othniel nodded.

Caleb took a long breath and closed his eyes. He inclined his head, gesturing for Othniel to resume reading.

"Then the Lord said to Moses, 'Get up early in the morning, confront Pharaoh and say to him, This is what the Lord, the God of the Hebrews, says: Let my people go, so that they may worship me, or this time I will send the full force of my plagues against you and against your officials and your people, so you may know that there is no one like me in all the earth. For by now I could have stretched out my hand and struck you and your people with a plague that would have wiped you off the earth. But I have raised you up for this very purpose, that I might show you my power and that my name might be proclaimed in all the earth. You still set yourself against my people and will not let them go. Therefore, at this time tomorrow I will send the worst hailstorm that has ever fallen on Egypt, from the day it was founded till now. Give an order now to bring your livestock and everything you have in the field to a place of shelter, because the hail will fall on every person and animal that has not been brought in and is still out in the field, and they will die.'

"Those officials of Pharaoh who feared the word of the Lord hurried to bring their slaves and their livestock inside. But those who ignored the word of the Lord left their slaves and livestock in the field.

"Then the Lord said to Moses, 'Stretch out your hand toward the sky so that hail will fall all over Egypt, on people and animals and on everything growing in the fields of Egypt.' When Moses stretched out his staff toward the sky, the Lord sent thunder and hail, and lightning flashed down to the ground. So the Lord rained hail on the land of Egypt; hail fell and lightning flashed back and forth. It was the worst storm in all the land of Egypt since it had become a nation. Throughout Egypt hail struck everything in the fields, both people and animals; it beat down everything growing in the fields and stripped every tree. The only place it did not hail was the land of Goshen, where the Israelites were.

"Then Pharaoh summoned Moses and Aaron. 'This time I have sinned,' he said to them. 'The Lord is in the right, and I and my people are in the wrong. Pray to the Lord, for we have had enough thunder and hail. I will let you go; you don't have to stay any longer.'

"Moses replied, 'When I have gone out of the city, I will spread out my hands in prayer to the Lord. The thunder will stop and there will be no more hail, so that you may know that the earth is the Lord's. But I know that you and your officials still do not fear the Lord God.'

"Moses left Pharaoh and went out of the city. He spread out his hands toward the Lord; the thunder and hail stopped, and the rain no longer poured down on the land. When Pharaoh saw that the rain and hail and thunder had stopped, he sinned again: He and his officials hardened their hearts. So Pharaoh's heart was hard and he would not let the Israelites go, just as the Lord had said through Moses."

When Othniel finished, Caleb opened his eyes. "I did not experience pain with that plague. Only fright."

Othniel silently prayed that Caleb would elaborate on this.

As if in answer to this prayer, Caleb sat up and pointed to the sky. "Do you hear how hard this rain has been falling? How savagely it has been pounding against us? Keeping us confined to the camps?"

"It has been terrible, yes."

"It is a baby's whisper compared to that storm. The sky slit open like someone had rent it with a sword. Flames descended. Flames on ice. That does not make any sense. It is impossible. And yet I saw it with these two eyes."

"I do not understand 'flames on ice.'"

"It was hail, but it sparked when it hit the ground, like someone was striking flint. Then the water from it set on fire like oil."

Othniel searched his mind for any hint of understanding as to what that could have looked like.

Caleb was laughing now, which was odd.

"Imagine! The terror on my face! The fright of mighty Caleb, son of Jephunneh, winner of the Gold of Honor as he cowered beneath the stone roof of a cave in the desert! For that is where I fled, Othniel. I fled like a coward out into the desert when I saw the sky open, and I hid in a cave I had known existed." His eyes gleamed.

Othniel smiled at his uncle but still was unsure of what to think at this display of emotion.

Caleb went on, "I walked to the edge of my cave and looked out on the city, and I saw the waterfalls of fire coming from the skies. I sat down and held my knees and screamed. That was how powerless I was." He was panting now. "Continue! Continue!" He laughed again. "See what Yahweh did to them! And to me!"

Othniel tore his eyes away from the old man and blinked at the scroll. "Then the Lord said to Moses, 'Go to Pharaoh, for I have hardened his heart and the heart of his servants, that I may show these signs of mine among them, and that you may tell in the hearing of your son and of your grandson how I have dealt harshly with the Egyptians and what signs I have done among them, that you may know that I am the Lord.'

"So Moses and Aaron went to Pharaoh and said, 'Thus says the Lord, the God of the Hebrews, How long will you refuse to humble yourself before me? Let my people go, that they may serve me. For if you refuse to let my people go, behold, tomorrow I will bring locusts into your country, and they shall cover the face of the land, so that no one can see the land. And they shall eat what is left to you after the hail, and they shall eat every tree of yours that grows in the field, and they shall fill your houses and the houses of all your servants and of all the Egyptians, as neither your fathers nor your grandfathers have seen, from the day they came on earth to this day.' Then they turned and went out from Pharaoh.

"Pharaoh's servants said to him, 'How long shall this man be a snare to us? Let the men go, that they may serve the Lord their God. Do you not yet understand that Egypt is ruined?' So Moses and Aaron were brought back to Pharaoh, and he said to them, 'Go, serve the Lord your God. But which ones are to go?' Moses said, 'We will go with our young and our old. We will go with our sons and daughters and with our flocks and herds, for we must hold a feast to the Lord.' But Pharaoh said to them, 'The Lord be with you, if ever I let you and your little ones go! Look, you have some evil purpose in mind. No! Go, the men among you, and serve the Lord, for that is what you are asking.' And they were driven out from Pharaoh's presence.

"The Lord said to Moses, 'Stretch out your hand over the land of Egypt for the locusts, so that they may come upon the land of Egypt and eat every plant in the land, all that the hail has left.' So Moses stretched out his staff over the land of Egypt, and the Lord brought an east wind upon the land all that day and all that night. When it was morning, the east wind had brought the locusts. The locusts came up over all the land of Egypt and settled on the whole country of Egypt, such a dense swarm of locusts as had never been before, nor ever will be again. They covered the face of the whole land, so that the land was darkened, and they ate all the plants in the land and all the fruit of the trees that the hail had left. Not a green thing remained, neither tree nor plant of the field, through all the land of Egypt.

"Pharaoh hastily called Moses and Aaron and said, 'I have sinned against the Lord your God, and against you. Now therefore forgive my sin, please, only this once, and plead with the Lord your God only to remove this death from me.' They went out from Pharaoh and pleaded with the Lord. And the Lord turned the wind into a very strong west wind, which lifted the locusts and drove them into the Red Sea. Not a single locust was left in all the country of Egypt. But the Lord hardened Pharaoh's heart, and he did not let the people of Israel go."

Caleb hobbled to his feet. His eyes were wild. "Yes, the locusts! Oh, they ate everything! I emerged from my cave in the desert and returned to the palace after the fire storm passed, and it wasn't long before the foulest creatures of all accosted us. They ate our food. They even ate our dead corpses that we had to bury with stomachs full of them, because they were all we had to eat. We had to eat the things that were eating us. Have you ever had locust? Of course you have; it is the food of the war campaign when food is scarce, but it is very different when you have to eat it for days, when everything that was good and life-giving was stripped from us."

Caleb stood still. His panting was deep, his eyes searching in the dark for something.

Othniel reached out and touched the hem of his garment. Caleb blinked, becoming aware of himself again.

"Forgive me, nephew," Caleb said tiredly. His countenance returned to that of a reserved old man. "I told you. These have become the songs of victory for our people. But they came at a cost."

Othniel was unsure how to feel. He was a bit revolted by the display his dignified uncle had just put on. Yet as he thought about it, perhaps he had just been given a glimpse of the madness the people of Egypt must have suffered. If a strong man like Caleb, the strongest of all, had suffered so greatly that his mind went dark after too many memories were brought up, what had been the fate of the common Egyptian?

"We must take a break," Caleb said, sitting down. "It is time for the evening meal. Send for the record keeper."

Othniel went out into the tempestuous weather and wandered from tent to tent until he found the record keeper, the man who kept track of the counts of people and provision. He brought the record keeper back to Caleb, then set out to find food. When he returned, the record keeper had a scroll spread out before Caleb. Othniel brought Caleb his bowl of stewed lamb as Caleb listened to the report.

"We will not have a full count of the women and children until the storm breaks," the record keeper was saying. "It settled on us before we could number them, and many are still trapped in the lowlands. But we know at least three divisions of men are here. Almost forty thousand under arms."

Caleb nodded and tilted the bowl of soup into his mouth. He took a long drink, letting everyone wait for him to finish in silence. "We can take the city with forty thousand," he finally replied, "but we will not be able to feed that many for long unless we can secure the trade road back to the Way of the Sea. Have one division post along the route and serve as our reserve while protecting our Elah and Rephaim passages."

The record keeper stared at him blankly.

Othniel cleared his throat. "Uncle, he is not a general. I don't believe he would know how to . . ."

Caleb squinted at him, looked at Othniel, then back at the record keeper. He started laughing hoarsely. "Maybe it's time for Sheol to take me after all, for my mind is going."

Othniel laughed with him. "If you can recall every detail of what happened forty-five years ago, there is not fear of Sheol coming for you just yet."

Caleb dismissed the record keeper and wrapped himself tighter in his blanket. He picked up his stew again and sipped from it. The old man's thick shoulders and back had not weakened much; Othniel could see muscles that still bulged through the blanket. He was struck again at how odd it was for him to be looking at Caleb, even now. Out of the hundreds of thousands of Israelites that covered the land, only Caleb and Joshua had reached their ninth decade. No one else was even close yet. The rest of their generation had all died in the wilderness before crossing the Jordan.

Othniel had believed that age brought frailty and complaint, an attitude of resigned defeat as the earth stirred beneath one's feet to eventually swallow a man into his grave, and that the man who was being swallowed year by year would be fatally resigned to it, seeking only to bide his time with comfort as his bones moved ever closer to rotting in the soil.

But Joshua and Caleb, the only two old men Othniel had ever seen apart from a few Canaanites who did indeed look like they were waiting for the grave to be opened for them soon, had lost none of their appearance of power and strength. Their knotted strength from years of pulling bowstrings and lifting training rocks and swinging heavy bronze weapons had not left them. Perhaps they moved slower and walked with a staff once in a while, but they had not given way to frailty whatsoever.

"You wish for me to read what came next?" Othniel prodded after a while. "What Yahweh did to the Egyptians next."

Caleb set down his bowl of stew and nodded his thanks, then stared quietly at the fire. "No. I will tell you of those myself. I remember them very well. Two more terrors Yahweh sent to the Egyptians. Two more gods to destroy and humiliate."

"Which gods?"

"The sun god Ra . . . and Pharaoh himself."

Othniel realized what was coming and drew a short breath. Were they at this point already?

"This will be the last time I ever speak of these events," Caleb said, emphasizing the point once more. "I will happily tell you of what came later, after we left Egypt, but I wish to be done with this part of my life for good. When I have concluded, do not ever ask me about the plagues again. I wish them to be recorded and remembered, yes. I wish for our people to know the power of our God and remember it. But do not ask me to relive it again."

"I will not ask you again, Uncle," Othniel reaffirmed.

Caleb nodded and then continued.

— 17 —

The Endless Black

By now, yes, I recognized that these were the events of my nightmare on the river of blood that I had dreamed for so many years. As they came, I knew them. But the remaining terrors in my dream were still unfathomable to me.

With the last of the locusts gone, I thought perhaps Pharaoh would finally relent and allow the Israelites to go. What else could be sent to us? Our land was nothing but waste now, burned by fire and bitten by insect. What else would our god-king need to see to realize he was dealing with a power utterly foreign to us, a wild desert god of endless power that was intent on destroying our beautiful valley? My very soul ached.

A man needs an allegiance. He must have a cause and an identity that lays claim over him and compels him to pick up a plow to cultivate it or a sword to defend it.

The morning after the locusts had been swept away by the wind, as I sat in my quarters and watched the thick, hazy sunrise that would bring another suffocating day, wondering what would befall us next, I realized that I no longer had such an allegiance.

My eyes wandered to the Gold of Honor that hung near my door, ready to be donned every time I left my room and sought the praise of men. It was the symbol of my earthly pleasure, the token of everything I had ever wanted or known.

When I wore it, men and women in the streets would part the way before me, speak respectfully to me, and offer me opportunities for commerce or pleasure that no one else in the kingdom could hope to have in a lifetime.

Now it glowed dully in the morning light, and it had no power to drive away a locust or heal a boil. It could not grant me passage in the afterlife, not when a god such as the Hebrews had prowled the earth.

And I thought of Maia and my boy, and I was heavy with grief for them, but grateful they had not been alive to suffer the terrors.

I finally rose from my bed and washed my face in the water basin, remembering when it had produced frogs from nowhere. I wrapped on my white linen kilt and slipped into my sandals, then walked back to the window and looked out again.

Burned ships crumbled at the docks on the river, while emaciated men were still checking nets for snags so that they would be ready for casting, as though any fish were actually left in the water. Vendors pulled burned carts through the soot and ash-filled streets and set up whatever goods that remained to sell. Tradesmen wandered about the streets below with their tools, going to work sites that may or may not be open anymore, much less have the food to provide them their midday meal.

All were aimless and wandering, their worlds upheaved. They waited numbly for the hours to pass. The very air was pregnant with dread as we waited for the two Hebrew monsters to appear to smite us again, now fully convinced that our god-king could do nothing whatsoever to stop them apart from giving them what they wanted.

I tucked my short sword into my belt and draped the Gold of Honor around my neck. Did it mean anything to me anymore?

It did, I suppose. It was all I had left, my last idol that had not been taken from me, and I had to hold fast to it.

I left the barracks and walked through the market. In better days it would have been bustling with the exotic smells and sights befitting the center of the universe, where goods and pleasures from all realms were only an exchange of coins away.

Now it was half filled with silent, living corpses who had only their routines to rely upon, while their fates were determined echelons of power above their heads, behind the walls of the palace that had once gleamed white but were now charred black from the fire storm. Many were still shoveling the rotting, putrid intestines of the dead livestock into oxcarts to be removed.

"Did you hear?" a cracked voice called out. I turned around and saw an old man with his hand cupped around his mouth, trying to get the attention of the silent mass of people. "The Hebrews are before the palace again!"

I felt my stomach tighten with terror. Whatever was coming, I did not want to be in the city for it.

I quickly purchased a goatskin water pouch from a vendor, who did not even acknowledge my Gold of Honor. I did not bother to correct his disrespect but hurried through the streets until I came to the well. After I shoved aside others who were clamoring for the water the same as I was, I filled my pouch and ran immediately toward the edge of town.

I was going to climb the bluffs that overlooked Memphis

and wait out what was coming in the emptiness of the desert, but then a thought occurred to me. Goshen was only a day's journey to the north if I moved quickly.

Rumors had persisted that the Hebrews themselves had been untouched by any of the plagues except the first two, the two that Nembit and the other Egyptian magicians were able to conjure themselves. But it was widely spread on the streets of Memphis that the lice gnats had not come to them, and neither had the fire storm or the boils or the other horrors that had laid us so low.

I was now running for the training pitch to secure a chariot to take to Goshen to find out for myself. I had witnessed impossibilities since Moses and his brother had emerged from the desert, but I needed to know what their god was allowing to happen to his own people. Was he vindictive against them as he was against Egyptians? When they failed him, did he lash out at them with violent destruction?

The chariot master recognized me as I approached him at the pitch.

"Caleb. It has been a long time."

We embraced.

"It is good to see you, Amnon."

"The palace has made your muscles soft," he said, squeezing my shoulders tight. "Come back to the wheel regiments and we'll harden you again."

A quick glance around told me the chariot pitch had been spared none of the Hebrew god's wrath.

"It has been no better in the palace than out here, Amnon," I said.

"I've heard. Pharaoh himself had the boils?"

"He did."

Amnon shook his head. He was older than I, a rough veteran who was disturbed by very little. His face, like everyone else's, was covered with the gruesome remnants of the past months. Scars and scabs, especially the effects of the boils.

He did not appear to notice. "We had no horses left, you may have assumed," he said cheerily, guessing my intent. "Then another herd arrived from Canaan to replace the ones killed in the . . . sickness. But then I lost most of those in the fire storm. The locusts took most of my remaining hay. Another caravan with hay is supposed to arrive any day, but *kham sur*! How wonderful it is to be utterly dependent on outside nations for our supplies! Mighty Egypt, begging from the barbarians! A few horses remain, but I expect those will soon be consumed when every grain of sand in the western desert turns into a lion and we are devoured by them."

I smiled, appreciative of his good humor. Soldiers were always the first to complain but also the first to tease.

"I need a rig, my friend," I said.

Amnon scoffed. "You and the entire army. Everyone wants to flee our land. I'd do it myself if I had the gold. The first place I would head is Nubia. The girls there are marvelous; they'll do anything you—"

"I am sorry, Amnon, but I am in a terrible rush," I interrupted, holding up the heavy chain of the Gold of Honor from around my neck.

I tried not to appear too eager, merely decisive. I could not help but glance at the horizon toward Memphis.

He eyed the chain, then bowed his head slightly. "I acknowledge the Gold of Honor. But it was not needed." His eyes were now full of curiosity and inwardly I scolded myself for not trying to merely persuade him more.

He led me to the stables. As we walked, I tried to think of something to ease the suspicious mood I had likely put him in. I was not acting under official orders, and he might report me to a superior.

"I am to survey the northern territory to evaluate what remains of our posts on the Way of the Sea," I lied.

Amnon grunted. "I will tell you what remains. Piles of ash and bones. Let me know if monsters crawl out of the Great Sea when you are there. I wagered fifty to Horemheb in the archer regiments, do you remember him? Ugly, lost an ear? I wagered fifty that the next one from that Hebrew would come from the sea, and he . . ."

Amnon chattered uninterrupted as he led me to the stables. I picked out two fine brown-and-white animals with sturdy necks and strong flanks. My trained eye told me they would not have been the fastest in a sprint, so I would not have taken them against foot soldiers and archers, but they would hold their pace longer than the others.

I helped Amnon harness the horses and attach the chariot. The old movements were mechanical and felt like coming home after a long sojourn. The hours I had spent doing this very mundane task! My fingers still flew with ease over every buckle and strap.

Amnon loaded up the chariot with water pouches and filled the quiver with arrows. "Why didn't you bring your bow?" he asked.

I thought quickly. "They told me you had extras in the armory. I just strung mine again and don't want to put it through a journey."

This seemed to suffice. Amnon knew well that a newly strung and waxed bow was cherished by charioteers and only reluctantly used.

"So you just assumed you would use one of mine?" he said in a mocking tone.

"I knew you had nothing to do anymore but string bows. We aren't invading anyone anytime soon."

I mounted through the back of the chariot and gripped the rail. I was in a hurry, yet the familiarity of standing behind a loaded team, the equine smell, the fresh fletching on the arrows made me pause.

Amnon smiled. "You've been too long in the palace. Palaces aren't where men are supposed to live."

I nodded. "I'll have it back within the week."

I cracked the straps against the flanks of the animals, and they lurched forward. My left foot slid back against the bar brace, with the weight of my body slipping instantly into its old balance.

I cracked the straps again, and the horses moved to a trot, then again and into a run. I would not run them for long, but I was overcome with the desire to feel the wind rushing against my face again, the sensation of the distance I could cover, and the terror I could strike into even the hardest of soldiers.

How I loved the chariot! How I loved angling in on a rank of troops while my weapons mate wielded a javelin, or riding as a passenger and sending arrows whipping through the air into throats and bellies.

The horses snorted and kicked up the sand, and I laughed. They were testing me, and I them. I guided them down the bluffs toward the river, only slowing enough to ensure I would not be thrown in a fit of their fright, then when we reached the open silt-covered river plain I spurred them again.

For a moment I forgot all that had befallen us. I did not notice the burned and ruined land around me, locust-eaten and hail-crushed. I knew only the speed of the chariot and the wild freedom that a desert gazelle must know when it is in full flight.

Finally I slowed the team to a slow trot again. I had had my fun and now I needed to spare them for the journey to Goshen.

When I first came to Egypt along this very route, it had been a vibrant, lush land of fat cattle and swollen fields of dense grass. The Egypt I passed now was unrecognizable.

A fine dust cloud rose from the horses' hooves and chariot wheels. An endless skeleton forest of dried-out stalks poked up from the earth from when the locusts had passed through. It occurred to me that I had no way of knowing whether there would be anything for my horses to eat; I had just assumed that, as always, I could easily find a patch of river grass to feed them.

Few farms had anything resembling crops. I shuddered as I thought about the famine that could be coming once the land had gone through its grain stores. There was of course no harvest this year of any kind.

Brush fires, more than could be counted, had spread along the river from the fire storm. The pattern appeared to have been a strike of lightning and sparks of hail igniting a patch of ground, burning for an hour or more, then snuffing out once the drenching rain had washed over it.

I saw people occasionally. They looked as though they were ready for the embalmers. It occurred to me that they would have little idea of what had been transpiring in the cities, or what had even been causing these calamities besides the unknowable wrath of the gods.

Did they know that the two ragged-looking old men who came and went along this road were responsible? Did they know that the desert god Yahweh had overrun their sky and earth, driving out the weak and womanly gods of Egypt? Did they comprehend that they were mere ash and dust in his hand? Did I, truly?

I know of no other way to describe it, Othniel. It was an endless scene of horror and suffering, very much the embodiment of desolation. The deserts of our wandering would be sparser in coming years, but the tragedy of that once-beautiful land going to ruin was more than I could bear.

The farther north I went, the more I found myself looking over my shoulder with increasing frequency, ever since Amnon had mentioned the sand turning into hungry lions.

I rode all day as fast as I dared, not knowing when grass would appear for my horses. The road along the river had always been filled with travelers and their mules or oxen; today it was rare to see a single person.

Dusk was approaching when I pulled the horses up to a small inlet in the river. I let the animals drink and stretched my legs.

Standing up, I saw a flicker of movement in the barren trees nearby. I did not wait to see what it was but darted for the back of the chariot, shouting "Yah! Go, yah!" to the horses and yanking backward on their reins. They snorted and whinnied, protesting that I had interrupted their drinking. I cursed myself for my tactical error, being lazy and not pulling them into a place where they could quickly withdraw.

"Yah!" I shouted louder, pulling desperately on the reins. I sensed something rushing toward me and ducked.

A loud *twang* as an arrow punched through the chariot wall near my head.

"Go! Go!"

The horses were finally pulling back, handbreadth by handbreadth, but they would not be able to turn and run forward in time. I stayed crouched behind the chariot wall and pulled the bronze short sword out of its sheath near the front.

Another arrow whistled overhead. Then another came that struck the opposite rim and clattered onto my lap. I had just been wondering who my attackers were when I recognized the fletching and blade of an Egyptian military arrow.

Deserters.

Driven by hunger or greed, these well-trained fighters were no ordinary bandits. Deserters from the armies, and like their namesake predatory bats that hunted the deserts, they prowled the trade routes and used their weaponry skills to plunder caravans, but they had never been seen in our very land itself.

Where there is a dying carcass, the vultures soon gather.

I drew a long, steady breath. Another arrow overhead, followed by another.

"Kah! Go!" I shouted again, pulling hard on the reins while keeping my head as low as possible.

I kept my head turned back, waiting for the first sign of a body to appear in the entry gap. They would be too smart to rush me, not wanting to risk a blade or an arrow over a simple robbery. They would recognize the chariot as one of the king's, though, and might take extra risks to capture it.

"Kah!" I shouted. Finally the horses had pulled back enough from the water to allow me to crack the right side twice, signaling a fast right turn and sprint. They responded instantly and lurched to the right. I did not have the time to brace myself and I crashed against the opposite side.

I had to risk peering over the rim to see where I was going and quickly did so. The horses had found a narrow path back to the main road that they were charging along, and then another arrow struck me in the shoulder and I felt the deep, intense burn of the metal searing its way through my sinews.

I cried out and fell back down. I managed to hold on to the reins and cracked them hard twice to remind the horses to keep going as fast as they could.

A man appeared overhead. He had leaped onto the chariot despite its speed. His sword was immediately stabbing downward toward my chest, but I rolled my shoulder over in time and it missed. I kicked at him clumsily, my angle far off. He avoided my foot and stabbed again, this time getting me in the hip, yet my leather sheath turned the tip aside.

I threw myself sideways against the flat of the blade to pin it against the wall, and the chariot suddenly hit a bump and sent both of us into the air, spinning, landing in the ash-covered ground as the chariot careened away.

I hit the dirt hard. Instantly the breath was forced from my lungs. No time to catch it, as I was being rushed by three others, maybe a fourth, five total, including the man who had leaped onto my chariot, and he was now back on his feet and charging me again with his sword.

I had no strength in my fighting arm, felt very tired all of a sudden, but then it surged back into me and I was able to roll out of the way of the first sword strike and gain my feet. I ran in the direction of my chariot.

I was the fastest man in the armies. It had been decided many times, and I knew that no matter how fast these men were I could outrun them. Only a fool chooses to fight when outnumbered if escape is both available and honorable.

That did not mean I would not send them to the underworld if given the chance, and I did so to my first pursuer, whom I had allowed to gain on me and then I stopped, cut to my left, and jumped backward before he could react. He tried to stop himself, but I was right behind him, my footwork as quick as it always had been.

I snaked my arm around his neck, pulled hard, feeling his windpipe crush in my elbow, the panic and surge of fright I had felt turning to anger that he and the others would *dare* assault me, Caleb, bearer of the Gold of Honor and the rank of Scorpion of Egypt.

I wrenched his neck until I broke it, then dropped the corpse.

I took off running down the path again, this time giving my legs full strength to fly. I glanced over my shoulder and saw one of my pursuers stopping to notch an arrow.

I looked back ahead, believing that around the next bend in the burned forest I would see the chariot horses waiting for me. They were trained to sense the loss of weight when their master had fallen from the rig and stop.

My ears caught the sound of the twang of an arrow being loosed, and I darted to the right, avoiding the arrow, then back to the path when I saw it land.

There, ahead, the chariot and the horses waited patiently for me.

"Well done, Amnon, you prickly old oaf. You have kept our discipline alive!" I said as I ran. I reached the chariot and leaped into the back. Grabbing the reins, I gave them a solid two cracks, and the horses lunged forward.

I turned around and saw the remaining pursuers stop and put their hands on their knees to catch their breath. I had not noticed it before, but now that I was safely away, I could see the skeletal outlines of theirs ribs and bony shoulders. They looked emaciated.

It was a wonder that I had been able to evade them so easily, I with my fattening diet in the palace. As struck as we had been, the king was always able to dine on the best of whatever remained, and the palace kitchens were stocked.

The famine had not even begun yet and people were already trying to attack each other over food.

I rode all that evening and through the night. When it was fully dark, I found another place to water the horses and un-hitched the rigging this time, leading them to the edge of the river and listening as they lapped at it eagerly. I bent over and drew my own handfuls of water, also replenishing my pouch.

I slept for an hour while the horses were tied to one of the few remaining living stands of trees that I had seen. The un-dergrowth was still growing as well, providing concealment.

I awoke and hitched up the chariot again, a very difficult task for only one man, but you will excuse me if I say that I was no ordinary charioteer.

As I rode out in the early morning darkness, I hummed various songs that I knew so as to pass the time. I saw no other people; it was likely that they had fled to the cities for the grain stores. Once verdant farmland now lay barren and scarred. Rotting cattle carcasses were everywhere still. The stench had become so prevalent that I only noticed it when the air cleared every few hours and it was missing.

Dawn broke as I guided the chariot up a small bluff to get a better view of my progress. When I reached the top I almost fell out the back again. I was in the northern territories of the Lower Kingdom, where the Nile began to divert into thousands of smaller channels as it reached its delta. To my right, the east, was the land we called Goshen. Ahead and to my left was the Nile Delta region known as Avaris.

Avaris looked as the rest of Egypt had looked throughout

my journey: a scorched, barren, scarred, rotting, fly-infested underworld.

But . . . Goshen.

Goshen was so green and lush that it may have been a woven and dyed linen tablecloth that had been draped over everything. Dense tree canopies hung heavy with fruit-filled boughs. Water gleamed and sparkled from a thousand small waterfalls and dribbles of irrigation ditches.

I turned and looked behind me, and then gazed back toward Goshen. Then I did it again to make sure I was not seeing a false hope, so common in the desert.

All of Egypt that I could see, except for Goshen, was a waste of a land, rotting and putrid. Goshen was a swollen garden. A very clear line of green was visible at what I could only assume was the border. The hand of their god had spared them Egypt's fate.

My only thought was, *Inconceivable power.*

What kind of God was able to do that? Destroy utterly an entire kingdom, but cover a tiny portion of it with his hand?

It was a while before I could goad the horses back onto the trail to finish the journey. I guessed that there was another hour of the journey until I made it to the green line I had seen in the distance.

But there was no reason in it. No purpose. I had no home in the land of Goshen. So I turned the chariot away and made my route back toward the south.

All that night I rode, taking an overland route near where the Amalekites had been to avoid them. By dawn I had reached the river again close to Memphis.

The sunrise was spectacular that morning. I remember it so brilliantly because of what came next.

I did not see it at first. Maybe because it was below the horizon where I could not see it approaching, but I sensed that

I needed to look up again, that whatever I was running from was coming.

Then I saw it.

A wall of black, growing taller even as I watched it, climbing higher and erasing the blue sky from existence.

I squinted, trying to make sense of it, but I could not, even when I heard the distant roar of what sounded like the wind.

Perhaps it was another storm, like the nightmare of hail and fire we had before? It resembled a storm in its approach, yet the blackness was too full and complete. It was not the angry purple-and-blue hue of clouds that signaled a storm; it was nothing at all that could be seen but only a wall of pure black nothingness that extended from my left all the way to my right and was growing taller and faster every second that passed.

The palm trees nearby, their fronds stripped bare by the locusts, suddenly bent over under a great wind, and I only had time to jump from my chariot and roll to the ground as the wave of shock and pressure picked me up and threw me dozens of cubits into the dust.

Trees snapped. My chariot was tossed like a straw toy into the air, the horses with it, and I felt a stab of sorrow in spite of myself to hear their cries as they were hurled to certain death. I was pinned down, clinging to the earth with my fingers, trying with all my strength to keep my grip, grasping at roots in the soil for any kind of purchase to prevent my body from being picked up again.

The sucking, all-powerful wind seemed to speed up time itself, then stop it, speed it up again, and then the wall of black was upon me.

My world was nothing but darkness. Every thought, every sense brought darkness. I could taste it, feel it crawling on my skin. It was as if someone had thrown a soaked, heavy wool blanket on top of me, and I had to take panicked, small breaths through the fibers of that blanket in order to get the air I needed because it was too thick to allow me to take a full breath.

The air had died around me. No sound, no puff of breeze, where just a moment before had been a gale so strong that it picked up my entire chariot and team and thrown it.

I sat up. Opened my eyelids as widely as possible. Nothing.

I waved my hand in front of my face to try to at least see the movement. Still nothing.

I opened my mouth to cry out, by my throat was filled with the darkness as well, so potent that its tendrils snaked down into my lungs. I gagged and coughed like I never had in my life, even after the lice and the flies and everything that had come before.

Suffocation was all I could think about. All I could fear.

So this was the next terror. A plague of darkness.

Ra, the sun god, the one that Great Egypt's greatest sorcerers and magicians and priests and even Pharaoh himself believed would finally answer power with power, had been swallowed by Yahweh.

The silence was pierced at last by an unearthly screaming. Not made by the lungs of man, for the sound was too loud. I listened as best I could, for the darkness had clogged my ears too.

It was my horses, singing their death song. It was not a noble sound.

I listened to the powerful team of army horses paw at each other and whinny in terror and pain. They were either suffering from shattered legs or had been impaled when they were thrown, and now they knew the same darkness I did and could not contain their fright.

What should I do? I could not even see to the end of my nose.

I decided to crawl. Kneeling down, I felt along the ground in the direction that I thought the road had been, searching for the grooves in the dirt cut by carts. I found them and turned to my right, which was my best guess for south.

Hours and hours I crawled. My only companion was the sound of the horses shrieking while they died in the blackness.

It was the most bizarre form of suffering I had yet known. There was no pain, nothing that directly harmed me. Imagine having to fight for breath while trapped underwater, and you are allowed to expose your lips and nostrils for one count to suck in a quick breath before you are pulled under again, and then repeating that for hours upon hours. For that was some of the panic we knew.

It seemed as though I could wipe the black mist from my face, so I kept swiping at my eyes and forehead. But nothing helped. I knew only darkness, felt only darkness.

Despair finally overwhelmed me. I could not move another handbreadth. My muscles locked into place. I could only press my face to the ground and hold still. The deepest terror of a nightmare, that's what it was. And soon I was asleep and the nightmare came back to me.

I was on the ship draped in black, sailing through murky water. Was it a vision I had been given, those many years before? When I was strong and brave and invincible? When I worshiped the strength of my arm and the adulation of the masses? Had the Hebrew god sent me the vision to warn me of what was to come, and then when it arrived, show how utterly helpless I was before him?

There I was, curled up like a baby in its birth cloths. The darkness hung on me, pressing down on my back. I drifted in and out of a fretful sleep. Every time I succumbed I was on the ship, and another one of the terrors was in front of me. The frogs. The lice gnats. The fire hail.

I do not know how long I lay there. Hours? A day or two? But I, brave Caleb the Kenazzite, winner of the Gold of Honor, who thought himself among the greatest warriors of Egypt, was curled up in the darkness and unable to do anything but whimper.

What do you think of me now, Othniel? Is it not more frequently that I describe my cowardice than my heroism? Every man has cowardice in him. Yahweh exposed mine.

May it be a lesson. A man can be brave and accomplish much, but his fate is only ever in the hand of Yahweh.

Finally, when I was close to going mad from the despair, I heard a shuffling of footsteps behind me. I looked around wildly but saw only darkness. Yet I could still hear them. Footsteps.

Dimly, as though an ember had suddenly breathed back to life with an unexpected gust of wind, I saw the orange glow of a lantern emerge from the darkness. It cast a ring of light as wide as the road. Two men approached, carrying staffs. I knew the staffs. I certainly knew the men.

Moses and Aaron.

I tensed myself. The light had sparked in me my last desire to fight, to do *something* about my fate besides lie in the dirt.

The ring of light halted as soon as it hit my prostrate form.

Aaron held the lantern out and squinted at me. Moses tilted his head. "You," he said, and I realized it was the first time I had heard him speak.

"What . . . ?" was the only thing I could muster to say. It

must have been ridiculous to them, but in my hungry, paranoid condition I could say nothing else yet.

"Have you been in this spot since the darkness came?" Moses asked.

I nodded weakly.

"What is the personal guard of Pharaoh doing this far away from his master?"

I searched for a response. "I . . . do not know if he is my master anymore."

"You are an Egyptian."

I shook my head. "No. I am from the Kenaz."

Moses glanced at Aaron, then back at me. "That is on the way to where we seek. Yahweh has promised it to us."

I nodded. "It does appear that Yahweh is intent on helping you leave."

Their eyes wrinkled up. They were old men, and I could not tell if they were laughing at my comment or annoyed with it. But Moses's voice was lighthearted when he said, "Come with us when we leave, Kenazzite."

I ignored this. "I wanted to see for myself whether it was true. Whether your god spared Goshen and his people our sufferings."

Moses nodded. "He spares any who fear him. Aaron and I can see by the light of this lamp, but every flame in Egypt is useless. Fire burns but it casts no light. There is great suffering."

"There has been great suffering for a long time, and yet your god does not relent."

"Your king has chosen an unwise path."

I had no reply to that. It was true. But I did not want him to have the pleasure of hearing me say it.

"What is your name?" Moses asked.

"Caleb, the son of Jephunneh."

"How long have you been a soldier here?"

"Seventeen years."

"Do you have any other skills?"

"I . . . carve. And draw."

Moses frowned. "That is useless to me. But a soldier will be of help on the frontier."

"You assume I would go with you," I said.

"You may stay here," Moses said, gesturing around. "But I do not advise it."

He was a mystery, this man. There was sorrow in his eyes, but also laughter. I had many questions for him, and naturally I could not think of a single one in that moment. I did ask him, "How long will this one last?"

"Three days," Moses said. "Then Pharaoh will beg us to remove it."

"You know what he will do?"

Moses smiled. "The Lord our God controls even Pharaoh's heart. Not just his light or his cattle."

They sat down and began building up their fire for the night. Aaron unwrapped several date and fig cakes and offered me one.

I realized I was at the place where they had been camping along the river. Was I truly so close to the city? Why could I hear nothing at all of people crying out for help? The blackness had even muffled all sound.

"Is the darkness in Goshen?" I asked.

Moses nodded. "It is. But our people have light. Their flames work."

"What is the meaning of this plague?" I asked, even though I knew the answer.

"Yahweh detests the sun god of the Egyptians," Moses answered patiently. "So he has struck him down with his fist."

We talked into the night. I had many conversations over the years with Moses, but that first one remained my favorite. He explained for me what he knew of Yahweh. He told me that when he had fled Egypt he had served as a herdsman in Midian, a desolate place I was not aware had been inhabited by anyone but snakes. He told me of the bush that burned, which you know of. All of our people know those parts of his story, so I will not belabor them here.

But I was hearing them for the first time, so when he told me that the voice of Yahweh had first come to him from a bush that burned, I stopped him.

"What do you mean, *burned*? A voice? No idol carved? No offerings given?"

Moses shook his head. His features wrinkled and he grew thoughtful. "It was a flame so intense that I knew I would die just by looking at it, and yet I could approach. Then he spoke to me."

"What did his voice sound like?" I asked, leaning forward.

Moses looked up from the fire and stared at me. "Like the raging of thunder and lightning. Like the roaring of the cataracts of the Nile. Like the gentle cooing of a dove searching for its young. Like the whisper of an eastern breeze when you stand on a mountain. All of those things. All at once."

"Were you afraid?"

"Terrified. I was even more frightened than when Yahweh told me to come to Egypt, the land of my dark past I had hoped to forget, and proclaim freedom for those in bondage to Pharaoh."

We went on like this for a while, until it had grown late and the old men expressed their weariness. They invited me to stay at their fire, and as they drifted off I could only lie on my side and watch the flames grow dimmer, fading to glowing coals, the warmth receding until there was only darkness again.

Three days. That was how long the darkness lasted. I stayed with the two of them for the duration. I asked them every question I could think of. What amazed me was how little they actually knew of Yahweh. They knew his name, knew that he was the god of their ancestors, and knew that he would be relentless in his wrath until the king released his people.

But that was all.

I returned with them to the palace at the end of the third day. We stood before Pharaoh, who begged them to drive away the darkness. It was the most pathetic I had seen him yet. How long ago was that day in the Ring of Horus! When our proud young ruler had tasted his first battle and emerged triumphant.

Thutmose said that the Hebrews could leave, but they must depart without their livestock. Moses refused.

With the fury that I had come to know well, Pharaoh shouted at Moses, "Be gone from my presence! If you come before me again, I will have you executed!"

Moses and Aaron, even the rest of us, sensed that this was the last time they would appear before him. They nodded respectfully, for what purpose I do not know, and then departed.

As he left the palace for the last time, Moses raised his staff, and as quickly as it had arrived, a strong west wind pushed the black air away from our land, the sun emerged high above us like the rising of a dead man, and the people rejoiced that the Hebrew god had relented.

And once again, despite his promises and pleading, our proud pharaoh refused to let the Hebrews go.

—— 18 ——

The Destroyer

I have come to the end of the terrors, Othniel. The worst was the last one.

A blood sun had set in the west, as it had so often over the past months. I was on duty in the palace, walking along the rooftop and enjoying the evening breeze that was finally blowing down the Nile after many days of hot, pregnant air. I tried to find some joy in the moment. I failed.

I had no knowledge of what the final plague would be, the one Moses said would release the Hebrews at last. After the nine that had come before, I couldn't imagine anything could possibly be conjured that would change the mind of the king if nothing else had worked. Our land was devastated in every way, our gods humiliated and defeated, our proud people reduced to begging and searching for scraps.

I replaced the guard for the coming second watch and returned to my quarters. Sleep came to me quickly.

I dreamed the nightmare again, the very night the last plague came. I was on the boat again. The sails were black. Black was draped across it everywhere, as it always was.

But this time a man stood on the bow of the ship. He had immensely broad shoulders, the build of a warrior, and his face was hidden in shadow.

I wanted to approach him to see what his purpose was, for I knew even while I slept that the dream was different from what came before it. I sensed he was looking at me, though I could not see his eyes.

"Who are you?" I heard myself asking.

He said nothing. Did nothing. Only stood there. The water passed silently all around us as we sailed beneath the river.

Cold, deep fear crept into my soul. The figure did not move, did not say anything, but his presence made me feel such dread as nothing in my life to that point had ever made me feel.

He was death. He was the Destroyer.

I awoke, shivering. Puzzled.

The night was brilliant, I remember. I rose from my mat and looked out the window. It was the clearest night in a long time. The dream had disturbed me deeply. The silence of it. The menace of the man I had seen in shadow.

I went on the roof to cool off from my night sweat. I remember taking a pitcher of water with me as a refreshment while I watched the city twinkle in the night and tried to calm my nerves.

I took a long drink and then put the pitcher down. It was midnight. I could tell by the stars and the moon.

And then the moon disappeared, like someone had suddenly doused it as though it were a campfire. I squinted at the place where it had been. The stars still shone brightly, but the moon was gone.

No, I then realized, feeling my flesh shiver. Something was blocking it.

An outline emerged in the sky, a spreading mass of darkness. At first I thought another darkness plague was coming, but that did not make any sense.

Yet the darkness grew in the sky. Rather than swallow everything as before, the darkness instead stopped its spreading and took on a specific outline I had trouble recognizing at first. But when I did, I felt the last remaining fleck of courage I had after all that had befallen us shrivel away.

It was the outline of the man I had seen, the broad-shouldered warrior. He was as vast as the heavens and was moving toward us. The figure was so impossibly large, Othniel, that it could have picked up the palace itself and tossed it over the hills like a mere stone. And then I saw the outline of the sword of the ages, a sword greater than the mightiest storm that had ever rolled in from the east. The sword rose higher and higher, the Destroyer's wrath growing eternally.

I recoiled as though the blade's edge was about to come down on me, and indeed it did, all in a blinding rush. The sky became completely black. Wind erupted from every direction. Fire in the heavens, smoke, fury, wrath, sand stinging my face, the building shaking beneath me.

What was happening? *What was happening?*

Then all went still.

The moon reappeared. The stars resumed their watch, as if nothing had occurred at all.

Later, when we had the time to discuss our experiences, once we were gone from Egypt, I found out what had happened that night. Moses had told the Hebrews in Goshen to take the blood of the lamb and mark their doors, to prepare the meal with haste and to bake without leaven, and if they did these things, the Destroyer would pass over them.

These things you know. But I, in Memphis among the Egyptians, knew none of it. I stood on the roof of the palace and tried to grasp what had just happened and whether I had gone mad at last.

The night was perfectly quiet. And then it was not.

The rush of wind and fire, instant though it had been, had woken up the city. I listened to the masses stirring. I listened to the first cries of shock, then more, then more after that, then even more until there were wails of agony that cannot be imagined and that I must fail to describe adequately, for it was the sound of suffering most profound, Othniel, the sound I had heard in the nightmare, but far, far worse.

Women screaming.

And screaming.

And screaming.

My ears hurt, it was so loud. I was bewildered by it all. What had happened?

Inside the palace below and behind me I heard even more of it. Men were joining the cries. Weeping and panic-stricken wailing. What were they seeing?

I finally roused myself enough to run into the halls. I searched around for an hour and realized there were dead bodies everywhere. Children, adults, many bodies scattered around. Who had died? Why?

I finally made it to the king's chambers.

He was there, bare-chested and covered in sweat, pacing back and forth, holding a limp form in his arms, the deepest tears of sorrow streaming down his face.

"My son! My son! My firstborn!"

I will confess to you now that much of that night is lost to me. I have closed it away. To pry into the depths of such despair and heartache does no man any good.

But you can know that Moses and Aaron were summoned that very night, and when they appeared before Pharaoh, the mighty Thutmose III, ruler of Egypt, they saw that the king's eyes were filled with tears. "Go," Thutmose choked out.

I found myself standing at the edge of the palace lagoon the morning after the Destroyer came. The king was swimming back and forth across it for his daily exercise. I noticed his stroke was more frenzied than normal. All of his movements were so.

Eventually, he exited the water and let the slaves dry him off.

"Was it the Hebrew god who came?"

I looked up and realized he was talking to me.

"I do not know, my king. Forgive me."

The agony of the loss of his child hung on the king's face. He had none of the proud air I'd known so well. His immortal life was in danger, for he had no other male heirs to inherit his line yet. When he was fully clothed again he gestured for me to follow him.

We walked along the corridors. The bodies of the royal household had been removed and were being embalmed in the temple.

Every firstborn child. That was the curse. The end of male lines all over the kingdom. The assurance that Seth would triumph and few would make it through the Duat.

As though hearing these thoughts, Pharaoh said, "This Yahweh has halted my line." His voice was weak and broken. I could not help but think of the man I had once fought next to and how he no longer resembled him.

"He has shown power, my king" was the only thing I could think to say.

"I have ordered the Hebrews to leave. You will oversee their departure and report to me when they are gone."

"Yes, great king."

"And then perhaps we could go for a ride again when you return. Like the old days."

He looked at me with a somber expression. I smiled slightly and bowed. "Of course, great king."

He nodded, and I retreated away. If I had known that this was the last time we would ever speak together, perhaps I would have said something more meaningful. I did think to turn around, however, when I reached the end of the corridor.

The king was staring out over the ruined gardens of his palace, out over the Nile. Perhaps he was looking toward the old training grounds of our Red Scorpions, and thinking of that day of magnificent battle we had known together.

May the Lord forgive me, but I had sympathy for him in that moment.

But only a moment.

I went north to the land of Goshen where I encountered the hordes of Hebrews, going through the Egyptian homes and taking everything with them. All of the gold and anything else to plunder was gathered.

I had not spent time among them in their masses, but here was the most clamorous of sights.

You will know of most of this because it was written down by the scribes of Moses. I will not improve upon their account.

But it was this river of people, spread in every direction in their hundreds of thousands, like a herd of cattle that had been allowed to wander, that bade me to follow them. They ambled their way from the lush green land they had been dwelling in toward the vastness of the eastern deserts.

I trailed them for a while, and then I knew. I just understood. My destiny was to go with them. It was no longer behind me in the golden land.

Their god had captivated me. A powerful god was nothing new to us, but a powerful god with compassion? A god who would destroy and destroy again everything in the empire of the ages, just to protect the laughing little girl next to me, tugging a goat along? To bring her and her family out of bondage?

I had to know more. Was it true what Moses had said? Did this god accept others?

Whatever he was, and whatever he would do, I could no longer dwell in Egypt. Startled at how quickly I had come to this knowledge, I reined in the horses and took a moment to gaze behind me, toward the west. My last Egyptian sunset.

It was not Ra. Ra had been swallowed. This sun was a remnant, a mere process of light.

The gods I had known were no more.

— 19 —

The Outstretched Hand

Othniel rose to light another lamp. The storm outside blew steadily on. They hardly noticed it anymore.

"I am exhausted, Othniel."

"I will leave you now, Uncle."

"No, I wish to hear of our deliverance."

Othniel looked at him, confused. "You have been telling me of your deliverance. It has been compelling. Life-changing for me."

"No," Caleb said quietly. "I wish to hear it from the hand of Moses. I wish to worship the Lord as I hear the tale of his delivering us. I will tell you of the wilderness years tomorrow. Tonight, I want to hear about the end of our bondage." He closed his eyes and settled back with a smile on his face.

Othniel smiled in return. He sat down and pulled out the scroll. As the storm raged and the lightning flashed and the wind and rain ground through the mountains, he read the story of Yahweh's deliverance.

"Now when Pharaoh had let the people go, God did not lead

them by the way of the land of the Philistines, even though it was near; for God said, 'The people might change their minds when they see war, and return to Egypt.' Hence God led the people around by the way of the wilderness to the Red Sea; and the sons of Israel went up in martial array from the land of Egypt.

"Moses took the bones of Joseph with him, for he had made the sons of Israel solemnly swear, saying, 'God will surely take care of you, and you shall carry my bones from here with you.' Then they set out from Succoth and camped in Etham on the edge of the wilderness.

"The Lord was going before them in a pillar of cloud by day to lead them on the way, and in a pillar of fire by night to give them light, that they might travel by day and by night. He did not take away the pillar of cloud by day, nor the pillar of fire by night, from before the people.

"Now the Lord spoke to Moses, saying, 'Tell the sons of Israel to turn back and camp before Pi-hahiroth, between Migdol and the sea; you shall camp in front of Baal-zephon, opposite it, by the sea. For Pharaoh will say of the sons of Israel, They are wandering aimlessly in the land; the wilderness has shut them in. Thus I will harden Pharaoh's heart, and he will chase after them; and I will be honored through Pharaoh and all his army, and the Egyptians will know that I am the Lord.' And they did so.

"When the king of Egypt was told that the people had fled, Pharaoh and his servants had a change of heart toward the people, and they said, 'What is this we have done, that we have let Israel go from serving us?' So he made his chariot ready and took his people with him; and he took six hundred select chariots, and all the other chariots of Egypt with officers over all of them.

"The Lord hardened the heart of Pharaoh, king of Egypt, and he chased after the sons of Israel as the sons of Israel were going out boldly. Then the Egyptians chased after them with all the horses and chariots of Pharaoh, his horsemen and his army, and they overtook them camping by the sea, beside Pi-hahiroth, in front of Baal-zephon.

"As Pharaoh drew near, the sons of Israel looked, and behold, the Egyptians were marching after them, and they became very frightened; so the sons of Israel cried out to the Lord. Then they said to Moses, 'Is it because there were no graves in Egypt that you have taken us away to die in the wilderness? Why have you dealt with us in this way, bringing us out of Egypt? Is this not the word that we spoke to you in Egypt, saying, Leave us alone that we may serve the Egyptians? For it would have been better for us to serve the Egyptians than to die in the wilderness.'

"But Moses said to the people, 'Do not fear! Stand by and see the salvation of the Lord which He will accomplish for you today; for the Egyptians whom you have seen today, you will never see them again forever. The Lord will fight for you while you keep silent.'

"Then the Lord said to Moses, 'Why are you crying out to Me? Tell the sons of Israel to go forward. As for you, lift up your staff and stretch out your hand over the sea and divide it, and the sons of Israel shall go through the midst of the sea on dry land. As for Me, behold, I will harden the hearts of the Egyptians so that they will go in after them; and I will be honored through Pharaoh and all his army, through his chariots and his horsemen. Then the Egyptians will know that I am the Lord, when I am honored through Pharaoh, through his chariots and his horsemen.'

"The angel of God, who had been going before the camp of

Israel, moved and went behind them; and the pillar of cloud moved from before them and stood behind them. So it came between the camp of Egypt and the camp of Israel; and there was the cloud along with the darkness, yet it gave light at night. Thus the one did not come near the other all night.

"Then Moses stretched out his hand over the sea; and the Lord swept the sea *back* by a strong east wind all night and turned the sea into dry land, so the waters were divided. The sons of Israel went through the midst of the sea on the dry land, and the waters *were like* a wall to them on their right hand and on their left. Then the Egyptians took up the pursuit, and all Pharaoh's horses, his chariots and his horsemen went in after them into the midst of the sea.

"At the morning watch, the Lord looked down on the army of the Egyptians through the pillar of fire and cloud and brought the army of the Egyptians into confusion. He caused their chariot wheels to swerve, and He made them drive with difficulty; so the Egyptians said, 'Let us flee from Israel, for the Lord is fighting for them against the Egyptians.'

"Then the Lord said to Moses, 'Stretch out your hand over the sea so that the waters may come back over the Egyptians, over their chariots and their horsemen.' So Moses stretched out his hand over the sea, and the sea returned to its normal state at daybreak, while the Egyptians were fleeing right into it; then the Lord overthrew the Egyptians in the midst of the sea.

"The waters returned and covered the chariots and the horsemen, even Pharaoh's entire army that had gone into the sea after them; not even one of them remained. But the sons of Israel walked on dry land through the midst of the sea, and the waters *were like* a wall to them on their right hand and on their left.

"Thus the Lord saved Israel that day from the hand of the Egyptians, and Israel saw the Egyptians dead on the seashore.

"When Israel saw the great power which the Lord had used against the Egyptians, the people feared the Lord, and they believed in the Lord and in His servant Moses."

Othniel looked up from his reading because he heard something.

Caleb was singing.

Othniel smiled, trying to make out the tune.

The old man, his face radiant, let his lips part, and the words came out in a robust song, his lungs filling.

> "I will sing to the Lord, for he has triumphed gloriously!
> The horse and his rider he has thrown into the sea!
> The Lord is my strength and song, and he has become my salvation;
> He is my God, and I will praise him; my father's God, and I will exalt him.
> The Lord is a man of war; the Lord is his name."

The old man sang louder, and he did not care who heard him or how he sounded to anyone but the Lord his God. It was not the mere song of a war regiment. It was the song of victory.

> "Pharaoh's chariots and his army he has cast into the sea;
> His chosen captains also are drowned in the Red Sea.
> The depths have covered them; they sank to the bottom like a stone.
> Your right hand, O Lord, has become glorious in power;

Your right hand, O Lord, has dashed the enemy in
   pieces.
And in the greatness of your excellence
You have overthrown those who rose against you. . . ."

Caleb's voice rasped by the end of the song. He fell silent, but his eyes gazed heavenward.

Not for the first time that night, Othniel had no idea how to respond.

A man mighty in war, mighty in deed, mighty in worship.

After he thought enough time had passed, Othniel asked, "Could I at least hear you describe the sea parting?"

Caleb glanced over at him. He appeared to remember where he was.

"When the chariots came, I was near the water's edge. Moses raised up his staff, and the great wind came over us. It knocked me down. It knocked everyone down. And then . . ." Caleb sighed in wonder. "As the song describes, the seas parted. As though Yahweh's hand came down with a mighty rush and split it."

Othniel shook his head. "And the pillar of cloud?"

"It was like fire," Caleb answered. "Like a swirling column of fire and cloud and dust and light. And darkness. But light." He threw up his hands. "I have nothing further for you that Moses did not write himself."

Othniel looked back down at the scroll. His uncle had a gift for storytelling, but perhaps these sights were beyond what he could describe.

"I lost many brothers when the waters closed in," Caleb added.

This was the first time he had sounded somber since Othniel had read the narrative. It did not last long.

"But they were not my real brothers. I had found my real brothers." He sat forward eagerly. "You must let me tell you a little more. It is important."

"You said you were exhausted, Uncle."

"Yes, yes, I said it. But I changed my mind. Hearing of Yahweh's deliverance has revived me. You must let me tell you this part myself."

— 20 —

War Brother

A final roll of the waves slid up the sand, steadily gaining distance but slowing, finally dissipating and then lapping at the soles of my sandals in a gentle nudge.

The sea was calming again. The surface smoothed over and became very still.

I fell to my knees. My astonishment at the act of Yahweh was there, yes, and yet I also grieved all of those men lost.

But where I was grieving, the people behind me sent up a tremendous cheer, their voices raised as one, shouting so loudly that I had to cover my ears. Tambourines banged together, hands clapped, the women trilled, and this sound was magnified by the thousands and thousands, so loud that I thought the water might part again.

Camp that night was on the seashore. In all the years to come, the long, brutal years in the Sinai, where so much heartache and sorrow had been endured, I never saw a happier sight.

I was lying on my side near the shore, alone. Not far away

was a young family, sitting up late around their fire. The sky was clear and sparkled above us. The smell of the driftwood smoke was sweet.

The father was holding his hands up and gesturing wildly. I could not hear what he was saying, but it was clear he was enacting the events of the day. Two young children stared at him with wide eyes and wider smiles. The wife went about cleaning up after their meal, her own face full of contentment.

I watched them late into the night, eventually pulling out a sheet of papyrus and my sketching sticks and drawing the scene.

It soothed my mind, so I turned the papyrus over and sketched another image. I took careful time with it. It was the symbol of a journey. The conclusion of my old life. The symbols of who I had been.

The sketch was my Egyptian clothing and armor being left in the sand as I had left it that afternoon. With them, for it had no use to me anymore, was my Gold of Honor. My footprints led away from these objects, wandering into the wild and unknown lands.

The next morning we broke camp. It was simple enough for me, because I only had what I could carry. I noticed that was true for the others too. At the most, people had mule carts or handcarts. I made my way over to the father of the family I had seen the night before as he prepared his family to depart with the others who were streaming off in a line through the rocky hills.

He eyed me warily as I approached, so I held my hands up in a gesture of submission. "Please, I long to go with you and only wish to ask you some things."

The man's eyes grew cold. "Egyptians cannot come with us."

"That is not what I heard. I heard that your god allows others to come if they desire."

"You heard wrongly."

"Moses himself told me this."

"Nonsense!" the man scoffed. "No one speaks to Moses who is not an elder!"

By this time the wife had finished packing up their belongings and was standing behind her husband, watching us. Their children stopped playing and watched as well.

I could not be angry at the man for treating me this way. His face and arms bore terrible scars from his lifetime of bondage, as did his wife's and children's. They had been fed to be kept alive, but that was the extent of any luxury they had known.

I bowed my head. "I will leave you alone. I only had some questions that I pray you would answer for me. And . . ." I let this draw out a moment. "I am not an Egyptian. Not anymore."

The wife had moved up close to her husband and, shockingly, placed her hand on his elbow while he was still engaging with me.

He turned on her, too surprised to be angry. She leaned in and whispered in his ear, then bowed respectfully.

He looked back at me, his face less hostile. "My wife tells me that she has seen you before. With Moses. Now that I look at you longer, I recognize you as well. How do you know him?"

"May I have the honor of knowing your name, and that of your father?"

The man glared at me. "No Egyptian has ever cared to know my name."

"As I said, I am not an Egyptian. And I do care. I have no friends in this new land."

"Perhaps I will share it later. You will soon learn among

my people that a name is all a man has to offer. How do you know Moses?"

"I was in the palace guard of the king of Egypt. I saw them perform your god's wonders. And I met them on the road from Goshen when the curse of darkness came. They were kind to me."

The man appeared to be at a loss as to what to make of me. I was not posturing arrogantly like an Egyptian is prone to do, and yet I was dressed like one. I was being courteous to him, and it appeared to help him relax.

"What are your questions?"

Grateful, I asked, "Why does everyone pack so lightly for such an unknown journey?"

"We were told to pack lightly the night the Destroyer came. We painted the doorposts of our homes with lamb's blood to make him pass over us. We had a meal made with unleavened bread, because we were told that the Lord required it of us to be able to leave to symbolize how he had delivered us. We were told to pack only what we could carry."

I did not understand what he meant by any of that, of course, but this made me think about the night of the final terror and how the shadow seemed to have come from the north. From Goshen. As though the figure I saw devouring the moon and stars had indeed come for Egypt like a rampaging lion.

"How will you . . . how will we survive out there? I have been a soldier on the frontier. There is nothing that could possibly sustain us."

For the first time, the man smiled. "After all you witnessed, after all of the signs and wonders, you ask how Yahweh could provide something as simple as water and bread?"

"Perhaps we could pitch our fire together," I said.

The man tilted his head. "Do you have a woman?"

"None. Not anymore."

His eyes flickered down at my chest. I realized I still wore the Gold of Honor.

"You say you were a warrior."

"I said I was a soldier. The two are different."

He pointed at my neck. "I know that chain. It is the Gold of Honor. It tells me you were more than a mere soldier."

I nodded, convinced now that an Egyptian soldier would never be welcomed in these ranks. I started to turn away from him.

But I was wrong.

"We will have need of warriors in the days ahead. You have shown humility. Far more than a winner of the Gold of Honor could be expected to show. We have nothing promised to us but our inheritance. We must go and fight for it. Are you prepared?"

I began to notice more things about this man. He had a firm confidence, a quality great leaders carried that could not be taught or explained well. Men were simply drawn to such leaders, prepared to follow them wherever they might go. The wife looked at him with eagerness and admiration, not fear. His children crawled around on his legs, and he did not swat them away as most other fathers would have.

"I am prepared," I answered. "I will fight for whatever life your god delivers to me."

The man smiled. It was his true self, I could tell immediately.

"If you are to win victories, he must become your God as well."

I had nothing else to say. I waited patiently for his decision. If he said no, that I could not pitch my fire with him, then I would move on alone. But I did not wish for that.

"You may pitch your tent with us," he said finally. "I will

take you to Moses and Aaron once we have left the sea behind us. Perhaps they can appoint you to some needed task. Forgive me for being rude earlier."

"No forgiveness is necessary. You have every right to be suspicious of my kind."

I walked back to retrieve my pack and sword, which were lying in the sand. The man's family was already heading toward the mass of others, hundreds of thousands slowly shifting away from the shoreline, forming a long line as they walked through a craggy pass leading to the east.

"Wait," I called out. The man turned and looked at me curiously.

I hurried back to the edge of the water. Lifting the Gold of Honor from my neck, I looked at it one more time. All-powerful where I had been. Powerless where I was going. I threw it as far as I could and watched it splash way out into the sea, where it sank to the depths and was beyond my reach forever. It would remain buried there, along with my lost comrades.

I watched the waves a moment more before returning to where the man stood waiting for me. He studied me as I approached, respect and slight amusement on his face.

We were not friends yet, but as we turned and followed the others into the desert, the beginning of a long exile of difficulty and war and suffering we could not possibly grasp at the time, I sensed that we would be.

Indeed, this man became my truest war brother.

I would shed blood for him, and he for me. We would grow old together, sharply disputing at times, as two strong-willed men are prone to do, but sharing a brotherhood that would never be broken. We would grow old and gray together and spend our lives threatening the enemy.

I heard a song, a chant rising up from the crowd. Countless voices took it up. The melody was difficult to place, and the people were too overjoyed to sing the right notes, but I had the feeling the song had been made up in this very moment. I listened for the words.

"Yahweh is a warrior; Yahweh is his name!"

"Yahweh is a warrior; Yahweh is his name!"

Yes, I thought to myself. This Yahweh is indeed a warrior. I now know his name.

I fell into step next to the man I had been conversing with, my new companion.

"Would you do me the honor of sharing your name?" I asked again as we were swallowed up by the desert, the distant pillar of fire guiding us on.

"Joshua," he replied, "the son of my father Nun."

— 21 —

Sorrow and Might

It was dark in the tent now. The oil lamp had flickered and snuffed out during the last hour, but Othniel was so enraptured that he could not bring himself to strike another flame to a new one.

Othniel inhaled the dank, musty air inside the wet tent and tried to rouse himself. "Then the wandering began," he said quietly.

"Then the wandering began." Caleb sighed. "And as difficult as those months were when Pharaoh kept refusing to let us leave, they were nothing compared to the wilderness."

"We need to be finished for the night, Uncle. You must rest now."

"No. I do not need to rest, not yet."

Othniel smiled. "Then I need to rest." He stood up to leave. His joints and muscles felt tight from sitting in the cold for so long; he couldn't imagine how the old man was feeling. "Do you want me to send for a maid to lie with you for warmth?"

"I would be lying if I said that was not tempting. But no."

"Is there anything else I can get for you?"

"I will go and fetch a hot drink from the watch fire. Often-times the watchmen keep a pot boiling over the flames on nights like this."

"I can fetch it for you, Uncle."

"I want to stretch my legs some more before going to sleep."

"Please do not go out on the watch tonight. It has been a long day. We need you to have a fresh mind."

"The day I do not take my turn on the watch is the day I am buried. And even then, I will take the first watch in Sheol."

Othniel smiled and shook his head. It was no use arguing with his uncle. Before leaving, he sparked a fresh lamp for Caleb to have in his tent. He set it on the small table at the entrance.

"I look forward to hearing about how Yahweh sustained you in the wilderness, Uncle. No one remains who can tell us of these things."

Caleb nodded. "I will tell it to you."

"We must always remember how he saved your generation from the Egyptians," Othniel said, more to himself than to Caleb. Then he left.

Caleb used his walking stick to help himself to his feet. He stretched as best he could. Pain. Constant, eternally deep pain, from the back of his neck all the way down to the toes of his feet. The prickling sensation felt like a hundred weavers' needles pressing into his elbows, knees, and feet.

"Must get moving to loosen up," Caleb mumbled to himself as he made his way to the flap of the tent and stepped outside.

It was late evening now. He could see the watch fire being stoked with more wood as the first watch of the night prepared to go to their positions on the perimeter. Troops stood around the fire warming up before heading to their shift.

It made him forget the pain for a moment. Such a wonderful sight. Troops encamped in the woods. No arrows flying yet. No death to grieve. No mothers or wives to give the sackcloth of mourning to. The night before the first battle felt like the thrill of a great hunting expedition and not the last night many of them would see before Sheol devoured them.

He poked his walking staff along the trail toward the fire. He thought about letting them see him smile, but waved the thought off. He would smile for them when the Baal worshipers were all dead.

Thunder rumbled long and steady. He noticed it because it had been many hours since he had heard any, despite the constant rain. Lightning flickered high above in the same casual pace as the thunder.

Movement. To his left.

He crouched and turned to face it, but the night was too dark to see anything clearly. But there was movement, he was sure of it. Unusual movement.

Wiping the rain from his eyes, he stared at the black forest. Squinted. Held absolutely still. "Yahweh, please illuminate the sky for me once again," he whispered.

And Yahweh did so. The sky lit up with lightning, and the movement he had seen was now bearing down on him. Massive, mountainous shapes running toward him.

Anakim.

They must have smashed through the perimeter, and the sentries' shouts had been drowned out by the storm. He did not have time to think of anything else, for the nearest monster was almost upon him.

Anakim were all at least two heads taller than any other man, and as their dark forms drew closer he could see their immense, bare, mud-covered torsos.

Caleb quickly realized they were wearing only loincloths, no armor, probably to be able to sneak up noiselessly on them. He strengthened his grip on his staff, his only weapon, and held absolutely still.

Do not shout for the others yet. Kill the first one through surprise, disorient their attack.

The first of them was three strides away, and the giant had his face turned toward the watch fire and the men around it. They would strike the camp, kill as many as possible while they fought their way through, then disappear back to their city with a few captive women.

A heathen raid just like every other heathen raid, be it Amalekites or Philistines or any of them, and Caleb's anger flared hotter than the sun. He yearned to slaughter them and feel their hot blood on his face. His muscles tightened.

I have killed you before in your dozens, and I will kill you in your hundreds and thousands if I must.

Caleb watched the giant's waist rise, then fall in stride, then rise again, and that was when he attacked, emerging from the shadows and sliding his staff into the gap between the giant's legs, which were so thick and he was running with such force that it jerked the staff out of Caleb's hand.

But the attack worked. The giant tripped and hit the ground with a heavy thud. Caleb scrambled to find his staff, probing his fingers into the undergrowth where he thought he saw it land. He had only seconds before he lost the advantage. He pushed his hands through the mud again, again . . . there!

As soon as he had it he staggered to where the Anakite had

fallen, glancing to his left and right to see the others descending on the camp. He yelled, "Ambush! To arms!" but that was all he had time for, because the giant had gained his hands and knees and was spinning toward him.

Caleb darted around his enemy's blind side and leaped on top of his back, putting the staff against the thick neck and pulling with all his strength to cut off the man's windpipe.

But he was not strong enough to hold it. Not anymore.

The Anakite lurched back against him, flopping like a fish on land, and Caleb winced as the great bulk pinned him backward onto the ground, trapping a sharp rock against his spine. His mind became foggy from the pain, then cleared. Then he realized he needed to release the staff and grab for the rock, yet he was too late. The giant twisted, and a massive fist swung around and struck Caleb on the side of the head, hurling him back to the wet earth.

"To arms!" Caleb cried again, though weaker now and with bursts of light in his vision. He still had the rock. Still had the rock. What to do with it? He had a plan, could not remember it.

The Anakite was standing above him, holding a blade high, about to drive it down into his gut and send him to Sheol.

The rock.

What about the rock? Fog. More bursts of light. He could not think. Wished he was a younger man.

Something in his instincts triggered, and he managed to roll to the side just as the sword of the giant slid deep into the mud where he had been.

The rock!

He screamed and threw the rock as hard as he could directly into the giant's face, which was so close he could smell the foul breath. The Anakite recoiled in shock, his face shattered.

Caleb's fury raged hotter as he regained clarity. Exchanging blows with this enemy would not work. He saw the sword. Dove for it.

He pulled the sword out of the mud and begged for just a little more strength from his old, tired muscles.

The Anakite was rising. Caleb thought, as he stabbed the tip of the bronze sword forward, that they had been fools not to wear armor coming against him.

The blade's aim was perfect. It cut through the flesh of the giant's torso and slid out the other side with little resistance. Caleb did not stop to examine the result of the wound, for he knew it was fatal. Instead he started running back to his tent, to where his own weapons were. The death scream of the Anakite rose up as he pulled at the sword that had run him through.

Caleb saw nothing in the darkness. The Anakites had doused the flames, as he knew they would, for they wanted terror and confusion, wanted to kill as many of Caleb's people as possible in one swift pass through the camp and then disappear back into the woods.

"God of my people," Caleb shouted hoarsely as he approached his tent, "give me battle this night! Look with favor on me and strengthen me to kill your enemies!"

Just before he reached the tent, he felt it coming across him. The warmth in the back of his neck. The sensation of a hot breath blowing through his blood. His eyes flaring wide. Muscles surging and twitching.

He did not know what it was, but it had come to him in desperate times, from the days he had killed Amalekites for Moses until this very night.

"Yes, Yahweh! I receive!" he shouted.

He tore into his tent and found his sword and his battle-axe.

Both forged from new copper. Both yet unstained with the blood of enemies. That would change.

Back out in the camp, running fast, his blood heating up, Caleb saw the figure of one of the giants tearing into a tent. The screams of a woman from inside. Caleb rushed forward in that direction.

Men were emerging from tents at the commotion. "Rally on me! Rally on me!" he called out.

Caleb entered the tent. An oil lamp was casting just enough light to show the Anakite pulling one of the cooking women toward the entrance by her neck.

Caleb locked eyes with the man for an instant. The giant nearly filled the tent with his bulk. His eyes flickered between Caleb and the woman, and Caleb knew what he was about to do if he could not capture her alive.

"Stop!" was all he could cry out as he lashed forward with the blade, but the giant already had his elbow crooked around her neck, and it was easy for him to snap it, killing her instantly, just before Caleb's sword slid through the Anakite's ribs and was buried to the hilt. Tears burned in Caleb's eyes as he wrenched the sword around, trying to slice the giant's insides into ribbons before pulling it out with a firm yank.

The giant screamed at him through a mouthful of blood. Caleb dodged the swipe from his hand and swung the tip of the blade across the man's neck, opening up a wound that would be fatal. Caleb turned away from him to rush out of the tent. No time to weep for the dead woman; they were killing more of them all across the camp.

Pagan filth, attacking our women! Cowards!

He ran into several of his men as they tried to enter the tent and knocked them backward out of the entrance with his force.

Outside, he tore his cloak in grief and stripped it away, baring his chest, until he stood in the rain wearing only a loincloth. His skin was wrinkled with age, but in this moment his muscles were taut and strong.

"May the Lord strike me down if I do not kill every one of them!" he cried out. He whirled around and saw Othniel.

"Come with me and bring fifty men. Where is Abnedeb?"

"Here, my lord," the commander of one of his divisions shouted while pushing his way from the back.

Caleb ran to the nearby watch fire and knelt down, using a stick to draw out his plan. Screams and cries were heard all down the ridge.

"General! They are killing our people!" someone said.

Caleb did not look up. "They will kill even more if we attack them without a strategy. Abnedeb!"

"Here, my lord."

Caleb pointed to a route on his rough map that led down the ridge and ended below the walls of Hebron. "Take your men down this way and cut off their retreat. We will chase them along the ridgetop. They are only here to kill our women, so they will not want to engage too many of our soldiers."

"But, lord, they are enormous," Abnedeb said, his voice shaking.

Caleb glared up at him, and then he saw the same fear in everyone else's eyes. His temper flared, but he forced himself to speak calmly. "Yes, they are enormous. But I have killed two of them by myself this very night, and I will kill many more, and so will you. The Lord is our strength and salvation, and he will deliver them into our hands." He looked back down at his map. "Abnedeb, do you know what you are to do?"

The general swallowed hard. "I . . . I am to take my men down this ridge and stop their retreat."

Caleb looked up at him. He stared hard into his eyes. "Get moving then."

Abnedeb departed. Caleb was back on his feet instantly. "Kill all of them," he said to the group, and they all rushed into the night to their tasks.

Othniel fell in behind Caleb as they ran through the tangled undergrowth in the direction of the rampaging Anakites. Caleb stopped to listen for the screams and, hearing them, adjusted his direction. Soon the attackers would be reaching the other side of the camp and bursting through the perimeter with their captives under arm.

Tents appeared everywhere around them. This was the encampment, deep inside the lines where it was thought to be safe to have serving women, but the shrieks and cries Caleb heard echoing through the night proved that thinking had been futile.

"Go left!" Caleb shouted to Othniel, and his nephew gestured for the men with him to bank left through the tents while another squad followed Caleb.

Caleb caught a glimpse of the fleeing forms of the Anakites as they sought the concealment of the woods. The Israelite archers had finally found their nerve. Caleb raced past the arrow-riddled corpse of one giant, who had been brought down by them, and sent the others into flight with deadly, consistent releases. *Regardless of how big a man is*, Caleb thought, *he is not too big for our barbed arrows.*

He still could not understand their numbers, had no idea how many were cutting through his perimeter, vowed to deal harshly with the commander of the night's watch.

Shouts, clashes on the right. He slowed, holding his hand up to stop the men behind him. What was it? Where were they? He strained his eyes and ears.

Only the rain. A rumble of thunder. Clanking, clashing to his left.

There. Fifty paces away. An Anakite fighting with Othniel's men. At least that was what he thought he saw, but it was dark and confusing. Where were his men? Abnedeb, where was he? Cutting off the retreat, he remembered.

What are we supposed to be doing? Caleb asked himself. Abnedeb sent to the flank . . . but what was his own assignment?

He wiped his face, cursing the confusion of battle. Attack the Anakite with Othniel now?

No, keep pursuing.

"On me!" he shouted, and ran forward again, leaving Othniel to handle the straggler.

"Lord God of the heavens, great Yahweh who delivered us from the Egyptians, please hear my prayer," Caleb said as he stumbled in the direction the Anakites might have gone. He cursed them bitterly again. Attackers had every advantage. They had the plan, had knowledge of their objectives.

Caleb and his men passed several wounded and dead, a few more women, some of them elderly. They had been hacked or clubbed to death, their bodies twisted and contorted from the power of the blows. A fleeting thought, gone as soon as it came, that perhaps his army was doomed if it was facing an entire city of these monsters.

They passed where he knew the perimeter line had been, and he saw the dead body of a sentry, vowing again to punish the commander of the watch. From behind, more men in the camp were running after them, terrified and desperate for vengeance at the same time.

Over the rain they could hear more screams. Lightning flared. Ahead through the woods, Caleb saw six great figures illuminated.

"How many did you see?" he shouted over his shoulder.

"Five," answered his shield bearer.

"Four," answered another warrior.

"Six," the shield bearer said, changing his mind.

"I saw six," Caleb confirmed. "Stay concentrated together! We have to take them down one at a time!"

The Anakites were tall and massive, and they were carrying captives, making it hard for them to navigate through the thickets of the hillside. Caleb and his men were able to gain ground on them quickly. The one in the back of the group, carrying a screaming young woman in each arm, looked back and saw them pursuing. He soon realized he could not outrun them, so he threw the two women to the ground and turned to face them.

By this time Caleb's men had shed their rain-sodden cloaks and were down to loincloths. Caleb called for a wedge, and they closed on the Anakite in the formation with their swords up. Caleb's shield bearer held a long spear up, ready to jab with it when the giant was off-balance after an attack at them.

The Anakite had a tangled mass of long hair tied in braids that flowed down his back. The muscles in his shoulders and chest were impossibly large, and he attacked silently, fast and with skill, and Caleb moved aside as the Anakite pulled the sword from his belt and lunged at him.

Caleb parried the blow but only slightly. The force would have knocked him over with direct contact. As he did, the shield bearer moved in with a spear jab, which the giant saw coming but was too slow to avoid. The spear tip hit the arm and bit deep. The giant howled and wrenched his arm away, and Caleb and his shield bearer crouched side by side for the next attack.

The giant glared at them, saying something in the tongue of his race.

"I do not understand the language of dung," Caleb spat at him.

"You have fought my kind before," the giant said in the Canaanite tongue, which Caleb did understand.

"I have killed many of your brothers, yes. I will not go down to Sheol until I have brought you all with me. Now hurry up and attack so that I may take your head off and then run down the others."

The other Hebrews had circled the Anakite, weapons raised. The giant realized he would not make it past fifty men alive, with more rushing down the hillside from the camp, and he decided to attack through them to kill as many as possible in the hope that he could penetrate the circle.

The giant whirled to his left and lowered his head to charge the ranks. He knocked down three men with his rush and absorbed the full strikes of three clubs without effect. He cut his blade across the bare chests of two men, nearly cleaving them in half.

"Remember your training! Fight them in teams! No clubs!" Caleb shouted, angry that his men had so quickly forgotten all that he had taught them about this race. But he did not have time to think anything else because the Anakite had turned on him, knowing that he was their leader, and if he was killed, the others would likely scatter. Caleb cursed the ground again, because the giant knew that these men had no experience battling his kind.

The Anakite rushed him, but Caleb's shield bearer feinted an attack low, giving the temptation to strike him first. The giant took it, kicking at the shield bearer, allowing Caleb time to make one stab with his blade. But the Anakite had anticipated him, set his own trap for them. His fist swatted the blade aside, and he kicked the shield bearer full in the chest, sending the young man sprawling into the mud.

"Attack him! Attack him!" Caleb shouted at the others, but the Hebrews only crouched and watched, waiting for an opportunity to strike that would never come.

"Attack from behind while he is facing us!" Caleb ordered. "Do it now or you all are dead men!"

Finally one of the Hebrews ran forward in spite of his terror and tried to cut the back of the Anakite's legs, but the giant saw him coming in his peripheral vision and swatted his blade away as well.

"You cannot cut! You have to stab! Get the point buried into his flesh!"

Every lesson he had taught them, forgotten! Caleb's fury was unending. He would replace all of the training masters, make them all carry rocks up the mountain until they . . .

The giant moved to face him again, then rushed forward. Caleb was bending low to counter the attack when his knee gave out, biting sharply in pain as he forced himself into a crouch. He pleaded for Yahweh to strengthen his wretched body.

The giant drew closer, raising his arms over his head. Caleb held the sword up, desperate to get enough of an angle to intercept the blow.

The shield bearer had gained his feet and dove at the giant's legs with enough force to cause the Anakite to buckle. The giant caught himself, threw enough into his next punch to crush the Hebrew's ribs and send the man flying once more.

"Attack him, you fools! Attack!" Caleb shouted, and finally another Hebrew found his nerve and ran a spear into the giant's thigh, which made him cry out in pain.

The Anakite seized the spear shaft and pulled the broadhead

out, then spotting a gap in the lines, decided that he would eventually die if he remained where he was. He ran for the gap, using the spear he pulled out of his leg to pierce the skull of a Hebrew soldier who was scrambling to get out of his way.

Caleb gained his feet, his eyes burning with tears at the foolish loss of life, the deaths caused by green troops, cursing himself louder than any of them. "Yahweh, if there is any favor left for me in your great heart, give me the strength to run this man down!"

The blood in his veins grew hot, the pain dimmed, and he felt himself flying through the rain, through the brush, closing in on the fleeing giant, who looked behind him just in time to see Caleb leaping up with his bronze sword and aiming the blow between the shoulder blades.

The Anakite tried to dodge it, but his foot caught in the bramble, causing him to stumble. Caleb landed with his full weight against the blade and drove it between the shoulder blades, severing the spine of the giant. They crashed together to the ground, then Caleb had to duck another wild swing. The giant was paralyzed below the waist and would be dead soon, but his arms still flailed, and he hit Caleb so hard that he nearly passed out, feeling something crack in his ribs. Immediately his lungs began to burn.

Move . . . the . . . weapon . . .

He lurched. The sword arced up and over and down on the giant's neck, but the giant caught it and pulled it away, grabbed Caleb's throat with one of his hands and started choking him.

Caleb gagged, bile rising in his gut as he lost his breath. He flailed at the giant's head, his face bent skyward as he was being strangled. Water flooded his eyes so that he could not see anything.

Eyes . . .

His fingers groped along the giant's face until they found the soft bulbs of flesh, and he pressed as hard as he could.

The Anakite yelled and tried to bite his fingers, succeeding in getting one of Caleb's fingers in his teeth. He bit down hard and tore away at Caleb's skin.

They were locked together, Caleb's fingers in the Anakite's eyes, the paralyzed Anakite choking Caleb with both hands and tearing his finger to shreds with his teeth.

Press . . . harder . . .

Caleb extended the tips of his fingers deeper into the sockets, praying the pain would be so great that the Anakite would finally yield.

What finally ended it was the blade, which had been buried deep between the giant's shoulders. Caleb felt the struggle from the giant start to ebb as he bled out from his heart getting slashed to pieces by the blade, his damaged lungs collapsing.

Moment by moment the giant weakened, though his jaw remained locked tight on Caleb's finger. The chokehold on Caleb's neck loosened enough to allow Caleb to break free, and he used the opportunity to seize the hilt of the sword and jerk it back and forth inside the giant's chest.

The Anakite gave one more death shudder, then fell still. Caleb gasped for air, realized that the jaws were still clamped shut on the tip of his little finger. He rolled away and tried to tug the finger free, but it would not budge. The jaw muscles had locked in their death struggle.

His men gathered around. He gestured for them to help him, and they tried to pull the finger loose.

Caleb cried out in agony. "Cut it off! They are getting away! Cut it off!"

It was Othniel whose face appeared above him. "Uncle, I am sorry we are so late. The Anakite killed five of my men before we could bring him down."

Caleb nodded, then closed his eyes and said more quietly, "Cut the tip off. He only bit the tip. I don't need it. It's not my weapon hand. Cut it off. They are getting away!"

Othniel hesitated only a moment before he motioned for one of his men to bring him a war axe, which he lined up and swung down on Caleb's finger. Caleb felt a pierce of pain, and then it was only a dull ache. He glanced at the bloody stub of his finger, grateful that it was less than he thought. Only the top joint was missing. More than enough to be useful to him still.

"Wrap it, quickly."

"Uncle, should I send the men?"

"No, they are all cowards. I have failed them; they are not prepared. We have to do it. They have more of our women, and we have to stop them. Please, wrap the finger."

Othniel hastily cut a piece of cloth and went to work dressing Caleb's finger to staunch the bleeding.

Seconds later, Caleb stood and pulled his blade from the Anakite's corpse. "Abnedeb will be cutting them off near the city. We can meet him down there."

More men streamed into the clearing. The alarm had been sounded all over their camp.

Caleb approached one of his senior commanders and said, "Tell the others to stay near their tents. We don't need everyone, and if the Anakites send others to raid again while we are chasing them, it will be disastrous."

The commander bowed, pivoted on his heel and began shouting orders to the men gathered around them. Caleb motioned for Othniel, and each of them led their detachments down the hillside through the thick forest.

All Caleb could think about was the state of his army. They had been capable troops up to this point, brave in the face of Canaanite arrows. But the presence of the giant Anakim had robbed them of their courage. He knew they would be shocked at their first encounter, though he had not expected the disastrous results of today.

At the bottom of the hill, they moved fast to cross the flooded wadi at a place spied out earlier, then began climbing the hill on the other side. Caleb searched for Abnedeb and his men in the clearing below the walls.

"Do you see them?" he called to Othniel.

"No, I do not."

Frustrated, Caleb increased his speed until he was within an arrow's flight of the walls. The gate of the city stood in front of him. He turned in a circle looking for his men. "Abnedeb!" he called.

"Uncle, please pull back," Othniel said as he searched the walls above them. "If they see you, they will send arrows."

Caleb ignored him and stared at the tree line, willing Abnedeb to appear. Where was the man? He had never let him down before—

Something struck the ground nearby, sending a spray of mud and water at them. Caleb whirled around and saw it was a body, thrown from the top of the wall. It did not move. He felt a heavy sensation in his gut as he knelt beside the crumpled form.

Abnedeb.

Tied to the corpse with a string was a long lock of black hair. It had been cut from a female scalp, for there was a beauty clasp fastened to it.

Caleb clenched his fists and glared up at the wall. He knew the message well. They had killed his men and had enslaved his women. Despite the rage in his heart, he fought to keep control of himself. He bent over and put his forehead in the mud to calm his spirit.

The rain increased again, as did the wind. The next wave of storms from the Great Sea had entered the hill country.

"Yahweh, what would you have me do?" he whispered. "What is your will?"

His blood coursed hot. His body ached. But he waited.

Soon, in his spirit:

They will have a man, and you will meet him in battle, and all who are present will know that I am the Lord.

Caleb held silent and prayed again, to be sure.

The voice said again:

They will have a man, and you will meet him in battle, and all who are present will know that I am the Lord.

He would not have been able to explain clearly what he had heard or how he knew what had been said. He simply . . . knew. Caleb rose and fixed his eyes on the top of the gate, where they would be watching him.

"My name is Caleb, and I am the son of Jephunneh! I am from Kenaz, adopted by the tribe of Judah!" His voice rang out against the city walls, clearly heard by the watch, even in the storm. "Send me down your man! Send me one of your sons of Anak, so that I may cut him to pieces in the name of Yahweh, God of Israel!"

No one moved on the walls, and Caleb grew angrier at their ignoring him. "I am Caleb, the son of Jephunneh! I was there when Yahweh crushed the Egyptian armies with his fist and buried them in the sea! I will slaughter you all, man, woman, and child! Send me down your man and perhaps there will be mercy for some of you!"

He panted, his chest heaving. The fire in his blood was not cooling. It was ordering him to stay. To wait. A man would come.

Rain fell hard. No other sound. No other movement. Nothing else visible. Only the dull orange of the watch fire against the sky, and the black outline of the walls.

Then came a loud clanking sound as the gears of the gate ground against each other. The men around Caleb crouched next to him, ready to receive the charge.

"If I meet my death, return to the camp and hold council. Appoint the three senior generals to command the siege of the city," Caleb said.

Othniel blanched. "I thought Yahweh told you that he had given them into your hands."

"Yahweh said that he has given us this city for our inheritance, and that all here would know that he is the Lord. That has nothing to do with whether I live or die."

"That is madness! If we lose you, we have none able to lead us."

"The will of the Lord is all that matters. He wishes to make himself known to the Anakim, just like he made himself known to the Egyptians."

"Uncle, you—"

Caleb ignored him and walked toward the gate, which now stood wide open. Through it he could see the courtyard of the city, where a mass of residents had gathered and dozens of torches burned under awnings in the marketplace, casting flickering shadows.

Othniel motioned the others forward, almost fifty of the Hebrews, their weapons tense and positioned high, waited for whatever was to come through the open gate.

To himself he noted the bravery of these men, who had ac-
quitted themselves well during the ambush and now stood ready
for the enemy in the shadow of his fortress.

People began pouring out of the gate and into the grassy
field below the walls.

"They have come to watch," Caleb said. "That is good. All
will know."

Rich and poor were present. Canaanites of all nationalities.
Othniel was surprised to see that they were not all giants like
the ones who had attacked them earlier, but regular-looking
people.

"Uncle, where are the Anakim?"

"They run the city," Caleb answered. "Others from the land
dwell here among them and serve them."

"Are they favorable to us?"

"They worship the Baals just like the Anakim. We can give
them no quarter. If we let them live, they will turn the hearts
of our people."

As though in answer, the people, realizing they appeared
to be nothing more than farmers—contrary to the rumors of
demon gods who had been sweeping through the land after
destroying Jericho—began shouting and taunting them. They
threw stones and handfuls of mud, but they were hesitant to
charge them.

Caleb closed his eyes and released the aches and pains all
over his body to Yahweh. *May they be my offering to you, God
of my people*, he prayed. *Whether I live or die, whether I am
in comfort or in pain.*

Everyone appeared to be waiting for something, and before
long it became apparent what it was.

From the back of the crowd came a giant at least three cubits taller than any other man present, much larger even than any of the Anakites who had attacked them that night. He was dressed in his armor of bronze plates and stiff leather. A bronze, full-cover helmet kept his face hidden. It was polished and shone even in the dim light, with a plume of thick horse-hair billowing from the top.

The people cheered him. Children cried out the name of their god. The giant waved at them and raised his spear.

"Who is he?" Othniel muttered.

Caleb smiled. "The Lord has given me Sheshai, the youngest of the three chiefs of Anak. But it cannot be that easy, God of Israel! I did not even breach the wall!"

Othniel looked at him as though he had lost his mind.

Sheshai gestured behind him with a huge hand, and a cluster of women were pushed forward from the crowd and thrown down on the mud in front of Caleb. Six of them had been cap-tured. They were bound together by the wrists.

"Here they are, Hebrew. Come get them," Sheshai said, his voice roaring above the clamor of the courtyard.

Caleb recognized several of the Hebrew women, including the elderly one who had served him earlier. He made himself stand as still as stone. Only his eyes moved, searching the top of the wall for their archers. The rain was falling hard, and they would have no range to strike him.

"You are Sheshai, correct?" Caleb asked in the Canaanite tongue.

The giant tilted his head. "You have heard of me?"

"I have. Your head will be mounted prominently on the gate after I have worn it on my belt, watching my warriors sack this city."

"I am honored," the giant said in a mock tone.

"And afterward I will come for the heads of your brothers and send them to the other cities I have come to conquer for my inheritance."

The giant laughed. "You must be the old man they call Caleb."

"I am."

"What is this inheritance you speak of? My kind were here long before your father's father."

"I have come to claim the land that Yahweh, the God of Heaven and Earth, has declared is mine."

"I do not know this Yahweh."

"You will soon."

Sheshai raised his weapon high, a sword as tall as Caleb himself. He barked an order, and several soldiers stepped forward and pulled at the legs of the huddled Hebrew women, who began screaming as they were separated. But their wrists were bound with cord, and once they were pulled apart, they formed a rough circle with their arms outstretched and a length of rope between them. The soldiers pressed their chests down into the mud and held blades to their necks.

Sheshai stepped on the back of one of them as he entered the circle. "We will test your god, Hebrew. If you win and kill me, you may go free with the captives. If I win and kill you, your commanders will surrender your army."

"I will kill you, and then I will destroy your city," Caleb answered.

There was a commotion, and the residents of the city pointed above them to the top of a large building on the edge of the courtyard. High above, two other giants were standing side by side next to a watch fire.

Sheshai looked up at them and waved his sword. "Brothers! The Hebrew general has offered himself to me in single combat!"

A cheer from the crowd. Sheshai held his arms up to quiet them.

"I invite you to watch as I kill him and enslave his army!"

But the Anakite chieftains above made no movement or reply. They only stood still, resembling mountains that wore cloaks.

Louder, so that everyone could hear him, Caleb said, "People of Kiriath-arba! I declare this town's new name to be Hebron, and I will put you all to the sword if you oppose us! Those who leave peacefully will be allowed to cross the Jordan out of our lands. I warn you that I will not have mercy even on your little ones if you remain."

Caleb pointed at Sheshai. "But your head will hang from my tent when I lie down to sleep this very night."

The people turned quiet, seemingly shaken by his conviction.

"They will have heard of our other sieges," Caleb said quietly. "They want no part of us without their champions."

Sheshai shouted another order, and the soldiers pinning the Hebrew women down lifted their heads up by yanking on their hair so that they faced Caleb. They put their daggers to the women's throats to keep them from moving.

Caleb locked eyes with one of them, a young wife and mother he knew from the camp. She was wincing in pain, but her gaze was hard and brave. He nodded to her. "Stay strong, my sisters," he said in the Hebrew tongue. "You will return to your men this night. You will see your children married."

Sheshai stepped into the center of the circle formed by the women and the ropes. "If your men interfere with us, mine will slit their throats," he said, gesturing at the wives.

"Are you that afraid of me?" Caleb asked, his mouth widening into a grin. "Perhaps you have heard what I have done to the rest of your kind."

Sheshai lifted his sword out in front of him at eye level. He crouched down. Caleb walked forward and stepped over the rope. As he passed the young wife he'd made eye contact with, he reached down and touched her head gently.

"May the Lord bless you with many sons and may they be full of years."

The soldiers of the city all laughed.

Blindingly fast, Caleb knelt and pivoted with his entire body's force to swing the blade, and his sword cut through the nearest soldier's neck, sending him backward with a death mask of surprise on his face.

Arrows flew through the rain from Caleb's men and struck each of the other soldiers. Only one managed to slice his blade against the neck of his captive before three shafts buried into his chest, but it was not deep enough to cause serious harm. The women, crying, jumped up and staggered toward the Hebrew soldiers, who had shifted their bows to aim at Sheshai.

The Anakite bellowed an order to the watch on the wall, but the arrows far above were driven low in the rain and thumped harmlessly fifty strides away.

Caleb rushed at Sheshai, not giving him time to realize his mistake, his weapon up to strike first, drawing out the giant's defensive posture, then at the last moment holding back to allow his men to send the arrows they had ready. The fletching made whistling sounds as they passed him, and Sheshai recoiled as a dozen arrows struck against his armor.

Caleb ran to the side and found the weak spot in his armor, at the base of the neck, and shoved his blade through it for a clean kill.

But Sheshai had recovered his balance and managed to twist aside. Caleb's strike clanged off the armor, and he pulled back to regain his own balance.

"Attack them!" Sheshai called to the gates.

An arrow deflected off Sheshai's face guard, causing him to stagger back a step. Caleb moved in with his sword up, calling out to Othniel, who closed in beside him and circled Sheshai on the other side. Othniel had a battle-axe and darted in close behind Sheshai to land a blow to his knee, which Sheshai avoided by jumping back—only to trip against Caleb's outstretched leg and crash to the earth.

By now more soldiers were rushing forward to fight the Hebrews, who maintained their perimeter around where Caleb and Othniel were struggling with Sheshai.

"Help them!" Caleb said to Othniel. "I will finish him." And as Othniel turned to hold off the attack from the gate, Caleb tried to make another cut through a gap in Sheshai's armor and landed this one, a deep gash into his flesh that made the giant yelp in pain.

To this point, he'd had Sheshai on his heels, surprised at the ferocity of his attack and his disregard of the understood rules of single combat, but now Sheshai managed to gain his feet and crouch in his defensive stance.

Neither man taunted the other; they simply attacked. Sheshai's blows were too strong for Caleb to block directly. He prayed for speed, and the warmth in his blood seemed to increase, giving him the extra step he needed to avoid Sheshai's swinging arcs with his large sword.

From nearby he heard Othniel shout, "Uncle, they are sending more Anakim outside the walls! Dozens of them!"

Caleb glanced up and saw them storming out the gates, an army of the huge men, and knew he had to order the withdrawal. "Pull back to the camp! Back to the heights!"

Caleb pressed the assault against Sheshai, but the giant

backed up and held his hands out to his men. "Stop! He is mine! He is mine!"

The Anakites running out of the city did stop, but their faces were filled with rage and confusion. They cried out to their leader. The people from the city chanted for them to attack, consumed with bloodlust.

Sheshai attacked Caleb recklessly, his anger overriding his judgment. Caleb waited for the next opening and then stabbed, making another deep cut above the breastplate near the arm.

Sheshai buckled under the blow, completely taken aback by it. Caleb felt a surge of power in his arm, a whisper in his soul: *That they may know that I am the Lord.*

He yelled, fury overtaking him, his blade finding its own way down and around the giant's neck, and then Caleb was on Sheshai's back, knocking off the helmet with his free hand and revealing a head twice as large as his own with long black hair.

Caleb pulled his hair and stabbed the blade into the neck far enough to slice the windpipe. Sheshai went rigid and gagged, grappling for Caleb, but the old man's arms were strong beyond measure, full of the power he had known since he was young. He paused so that all who were present could witness what he was about to do.

"You will know . . . that there is a God in Israel!"

Caleb rammed the blade up into Sheshai's throat as hard as he could. When it was buried to the hilt, he threw the face back into the mud with contempt.

The defeat of their champion was so complete, and so fast, that many did not know it was over. Their chanting slowly died. Children asked parents what had happened. Men stared in disbelief. The Anakites who had charged out of the city stood motionless and watched, stunned. They eyed the Hebrew archers who kept them at bay.

Caleb strode over to Othniel and held out his hand for the axe. Othniel handed it to him.

Caleb walked back to Sheshai's body, peering up at the dark shadows of the two other chieftains as he walked, and swung down several times with the axe until the head was separated. He held it up in the air.

"I have kept my vow and taken his head!" Caleb shouted, his white beard caked with so much mud and blood that it looked black and thick like a man half his age. "By the end of this week, every one of you will lie dead, and you"—he pointed at the chieftains—"will join your brother on the city gate."

Caleb turned and walked back to his men, tying the severed head to his belt with the hair.

The Hebrews kept their bows up until he had passed them, then they all withdrew into the forest. Their last glimpse of the gate was of the Anakites and the rest of the people staring after them, still unmoving.

After helping the women along the rocky part of the trail, for they had been barefoot when they were taken, Othniel drew close to Caleb as they climbed the hill.

"Well done, Uncle."

Caleb grunted. He was moving with more effort now. "We lost people tonight," he said heavily.

They passed the perimeter of the camp. Hundreds of people were running around in the night and calling out for loved ones. Wails and trilling of mourners. Caleb picked his way to the tent, where the Anakite had killed the woman.

A crowd had gathered outside the entrance. Several of them held torches; the rain had lightened enough to allow for it. They all were staring at the entrance silently. Caleb heard grunting and a few shouts.

The dead woman was lying on her back near the entrance. Her husband was smashing the corpse of the Anakite with a rock, screaming at it, cursing it.

"We know the corpses are unclean, but we cannot approach . . ." someone was saying to Caleb. He waved them off.

"Don't interrupt him because of that. Let him grieve."

Caleb felt his throat close up and choke away his voice. Tears burned in the edges of his eyes. The group parted for him as he approached the grieving husband. He knelt down next to the man and placed his hand on his back.

The husband jerked around and swung at him. Caleb ducked away from the blow but remained calm.

The man swung again and cried out, "I was hauling rocks up the hill on your orders! I was gone! She is dead because of you! I was *hauling rocks*, and this monster killed her!"

Caleb recognized him. Heliphet, the son of Japhtha, the one who had been the first back with his stone.

Heliphet threw the rock at Caleb, who avoided it but did not return his attack. Others rushed forward to protect their general. He waved them away as well.

Heliphet tore at his garments and screamed at the sky in despair. Caleb knelt near him. There was nothing he could say, no comfort he could offer the man.

Finally, Heliphet crawled over to his wife's body and put his face on her chest. He wept uncontrollably.

Caleb stood slowly, moved next to him, and knelt again. He placed his hand on Heliphet's back. This time the grieving man did not swat him away, but kept weeping. Everyone watched as the rain continued to fall.

Heliphet raised his head and looked at Caleb. Even in the darkness his eyes appeared swollen. "Forgive me, my lord," he said softly. A broken man.

"There is nothing to forgive, my son," Caleb replied. "What you say is true."

Caleb stayed with him another hour after ordering everyone else away. He let the man scream, let him weep, let him beat his chest. He convinced him not to kill himself.

It was a process he had gone through many times with so many of his men that Caleb could recognize every part of what Heliphet was going through. He would be filled with rage as well as embarrassment, violence as well as passivity.

At the end of the hour, Caleb gave him a long embrace.

"Remember who the enemy is," he said, pointing at the corpse of the Anakite. "Let it dwell in you. Not for vengeance, but for victory. Your wife will be honored with victory. We will make the burial arrangements. Be with your unit tomorrow morning."

Heliphet nodded. Caleb stood and departed.

A short distance away, Othniel emerged from the forest to fall in step next to him.

"You are not giving the man time away to grieve?" Othniel asked.

"Time away? If we *had* time, perhaps I would. But battle is what heals a man. Take him away from his brothers and the mission for too long and he will grieve poorly. Give him battle and he will grieve well, and with purpose."

Caleb did not turn to his tent but kept making his way through the crowds of his people, who were still recovering from the raid.

"Where are we going?"

"To find the watch commander. Who was it tonight?"

"Sholem."

They came to the center of the camp. A large watch fire had been built, and the cold, wet, terrified people were amassed around it and arguing with each other.

"Sholem!" Caleb called.

Everyone quieted immediately.

"Sholem!" he called again.

A few people shuffled to the side and made way for a man walking forward.

"My lord," Sholem said as he moved toward Caleb hesitantly.

Caleb walked up to him and, without pausing or slowing his movement in any way, swung his staff at Sholem's leg.

The *crack* sound was sharp in the night. Several women gasped. Sholem cried out and fell to his knees.

"You are relieved of your duties. Forever."

"Why?" Sholem gasped.

Caleb's voice was steady. "You were commander of the watch. They got through our lines easily. Many lost their lives tonight because of you."

Without another word, Caleb struck Sholem on the head savagely with the knobbed staff. Sholem crumpled forward into the mud.

"If he is still here by morning, I will execute him," Caleb said to the group, and then walked away, holding the staff in his right hand as the head of Sheshai dangled from his waist.

By the time he made it back to his tent, he felt like only a memory of himself.

"Disaster tonight," Caleb said as he peeled off his wet cloak and tunic. Someone had lit his fire again, and he stood over it, relishing the warmth.

"You killed three giants in a single battle, including one of their chiefs," Othniel said.

"There are dozens more, and that was the weakest chieftain," Caleb answered.

Caleb's breathing became labored. Each of his joints seemed to hurt in unison. The warmth in his blood was gone now. As always, when the battle was over, he felt his age again, and the frustration of it clouded his mind. He muttered silent curses to himself, but then stopped, recognizing the discouragement in the wake of battle.

"If you get any closer to those flames, Uncle, I'll have to sweep up your ashes," Othniel said gently.

"That man, Heliphet. His wife. A terrible loss."

"It could not be helped."

Caleb frowned. His bushy eyebrows hung low as he shut his eyes. When he opened them again, Othniel noticed how tired he looked. He had to know . . .

"How did you move like that tonight? So fast and fluid."

"How did you expect me to move?"

"Well . . . with all respect, like how you are moving now."

Caleb chuckled wearily. "That would have offended me if anyone else had said it."

"Please tell me, Uncle."

"Tomorrow, if we have time."

"Please. Now."

Caleb sighed. The storm shook the tent against its ropes. The wind whistled and roared.

"I do not know what it is," Caleb admitted at last, "but whenever I am engaged in battle, and I know it is the will of Yahweh for me to be in it, he gives me strength."

"What kind of strength?"

"Just . . . strength. My muscles become strong. My joints move the correct way. My mind is alert. Heat covers me, and it feels as though I could take the city alone. I feel like I am sixty years younger."

"What is this strength called?"

"I do not know. But he always seems to give me what I need, when I need it. Never more, never less. Sometimes it is not there and I just have to fight through the pain and weariness. Other times I feel like I could capture a fortress by myself. Either way, the Lord is faithful."

"Why does Yahweh allow us to be weak at times?"

"You should always find yourself in situations where you have no choice but to trust in Yahweh. The greatest victories come when you never have the most powerful chariots or most numerous armies. You should always have to depend on him utterly and completely, because he loves to demonstrate his power."

Othniel wanted to keep on questioning his uncle. But no. It had been a long day. Another one tomorrow. It was time for him to leave.

"Please get some sleep, Uncle. I am sorry I have kept you up. I will be back in the morning for the first briefing." He then left, stepping out into the night.

Caleb went over to the corner of the tent where his sleeping blankets were stacked. He wished he could drag them closer to the fire, but burning to death would get in the way of his capturing Hebron.

He spread out the blankets, slid himself under them and clutched his legs close to his body. His skin felt clammy. Never warm. Always cold.

He sat up suddenly.

"Othniel was going to let me forget. I have the first watch

tonight," he muttered to himself, then started pulling back his blankets. He winced as he put on his wet tunic. He was angry at his nephew for trying to keep him inside, but not terribly so. He understood the sentiment.

"Yahweh, my God, I need more of you now. I am tired and cold, and my heart is heavy with grief for my people who were lost today."

No flood of strength came. He waited a moment longer. Nothing.

No matter. He would dress and depart regardless. It was his duty. He could do it, he decided. It was only pain.

"Praise you, God of victory. You give and you remove. I will trust you."

After a long time, he was dressed and ready again. He ignored the welcoming, warm coals and picked up his staff and a bronze short sword from his weapons rack.

He stood at the flap and gazed out, just as he had that morning. The wind blew relentlessly, the rain steady.

He closed his eyes to brace himself.

He was on the ship, and the ship was passing into darkness. The plagues raged around him. The screaming of mothers. The sounds grew dimmer. And dimmer. Then they were gone altogether.

The Destroyer still moved in the darkness. Caleb was afraid.

He opened his eyes.

Gone now.

He drew a deep breath, then exhaled.

He walked outside and made his way to the perimeter, ready to admonish whoever was trying to take his place on the watch.

Author's Note

It's not usually considered "good form" to explain yourself as an author, but the nature of the subject matter I write about demands it.

Caleb is mentioned only a few times in the Bible. The first time we see him is when he goes on a mission with Joshua and ten other men to search the land of Canaan for strategic information that Moses would use to consider his approach.

Before that dramatic entrance on the scene, absolutely nothing is known about his life.

I have fictionalized those early years in the extreme. My purpose is not to invent an elaborate backstory because I felt the Bible was insufficient; it is to create a way for the reader to encounter the events of Exodus as the Egyptians themselves might have known them. I wanted to help the reader be there in the halls of the palace at Memphis when Moses and Aaron stood before the king, and also after they left. What terrors did the Egyptians undergo as the Lord held out his arm? What would it have been like to be in darkness so complete that you could feel it?

There is mystery surrounding Caleb's origins as a Kenazzite. That term is used to describe several potential clan and tribal areas. I have chosen to portray him as the foreigner his name implies, hoping the picture of God's grace toward a non-Hebrew would be all the more potent for it.

The Bible is always more interested in the meaning of the narrative than the details of the narrative itself. My attempt to fill in the gaps is in honor of the Word that I believe is sacred.

Perhaps by the end of this series, you will come to the same conclusion that I have: our modern focus on a comfortable retirement needs to change. May we still be planning the assault on walled cities filled with giants when we are in our eighty-fifth year.

Acknowledgments

I am grateful for so many people—people who continue to believe in what I am doing and putting their time, talents, and resources behind it. I have been blessed to be able to wage hard battle with good comrades. That's all a man can ask for in this life.

I cannot list them all, and even this list must be kept to names only, but my prayer is that everyone who has ever helped out in any manner with this vision would experience the peace and grace of the Covering and understand just how much they have meant to me.

In no specific order, for those who have had a particular hand in this project:

Jesse and Janie Ewing, Felipe and Georgina Zamora, Michael and Leah Altstiel, Nic and Sherri Ewing, Jeremy and Stephanie Banik, Adam and Lauren Haggerty, Chris and BreeAnn Duran, Margo Milianta, Adam and Kate Ritter, Jeff and Katie Doerksen, Mitch and Amy Wheeler, Andrew and Alexis Potter, David and Natalie Bruce, Ken and Elizabeth Blume, David and Judith Cunningham, Ryan and Krista Gray, Lee Rempel, Todd and Mo Hillard, Greg and Erica Schut, all the members of Five Stones First Battalion, Justin and April Becker, PK and Lindsey Carlton, Beau and Sandra Rogers, Dave and Donna Shellenberger, Ernie and Cindy Mecca, Holly and Jeff Martin, Matt and Lauren Chandler, Jane Walker, David and Shirley Walker, my parents Robert and Becki Graham.

The team at Bethany House for being brave enough to tackle this with me in the market and for patience while I worked through it. It has been an exceptionally challenging book.

Rachel McRae and the team at LifeWay for believing that there is a need for this type of content.

My loyal readers who have become more like battle buddies. Thank you for enduring every scheme and sticking by us through it all, because this is your story too.

Thanks to my arrows in the quiver for being patient with me when I am buried in projects and reminding me what motivates me: Joshua, Levi, Evan, and Audrey.

And of course, the "Spartan Queen." Thank you for your love, your grace, your dedication to excellence, your high standard set for me as a man, your willingness to let me embrace risk and challenge, and your faithfulness to call the best out of me. You have no match.

Cliff Graham is a former soldier and officer in the United States Army who now spends his time writing, speaking, and operating a growing number of media franchises. A graduate from Black Hills State University with degrees in political science and military science, he did his graduate work in theology and military ministry through Liberty Seminary and the U.S. Armed Forces Chaplain Center and School at Fort Jackson, South Carolina. Cliff currently lives in the mountains of Utah with his wife, Cassandra, and their children, and speaks at churches, conferences, and to men's groups all over the United States. To learn more, visit *www.cliffgraham.com.*